Rising Tides

KATY HAYE spends as much time as possible in either her own or someone else's imaginary worlds. She has a fearsome green tea habit, a partiality for dark chocolate brazils and a fascination with the science of storytelling.

Find out more at katyhaye.com, follow Katy on Twitter @katyhaye, or connect on Facebook /katyhayewriter.

By Katy Haye

Rising Tides

The Chronicles of Fane
The Last Gatekeeper
The Last Dreamseer

Rising Tides

Katy Haye

Copyright © 2016 Katy Haye
All rights reserved.
ISBN-13: 978-0-9935203-2-7

Cover design by J D Smith Design

All rights reserved. No part of this publication may be reproduced, stored in a retrieval system or transmitted in any form or by any means without the prior written permission of the author, nor be otherwise circulated in any form of binding or cover other than that in which it is published and without a similar condition being imposed on the purchaser.

The right of Katy Haye to be identified as Author of this work has been asserted by her in accordance with the Copyright, Designs and Patents Act, 1988.

This story is a work of fiction. All characters and events depicted in this novel are fictitious and any resemblance to actual events or persons is coincidental.

ACKNOWLEDGEMENTS

Many thanks to everyone who helped me develop Rising Tides from an idea to reality.

Thank you to Rachel Daven Skinner, editor extraordinaire for (as ever) brilliant substantive edits which prevented any of my characters falling into plot holes, and to Morgen Bailey for copy edits that stopped them gazing at each other for pages on end.

Thank you for keeping me sane to the Paisley Piranhas; always worth their weight in chocolate.

Thanks to all my RNA friends, especially the Cambridge Chapter, NWS readers and organisers, and the Critique Buddies on-line.

Thank you to Jane Dixon-Smith for creating a gorgeous cover, and to my Reader Group for helping me choose from three fabulous possibilities.

Special thanks (in no particular order) to: Anna, Ayesha, Leanne, Morgan, Sharmine, Bonny, Sue A, Catherine Donald, Stacey Woods, Lee Todd, Esther Gerdzen, Deb Philippon, Michelle Fidler, Somer Barrett, Beth Ann Miller, Connie Prosise, Laura Rose, Lori Byrd, Traci Upchurch and Daniel M.

And thank you to all my readers, without whom there'd be much less point to writing a book. Lorella, you *are* the important persons.

Chapter One

I should have gone straight home from the market, but I heard a whisper that a race was on. If I didn't go along to watch I knew what other whispers I'd hear: that Liberty Marchmont was a snooty gorm who thought she was too good to join in with the fun. That got muttered now and then, and I didn't want to hear it again, so I tucked my purchases into a pocket and clattered across the metal pontoons to where the racers would be arriving.
It wasn't that I didn't want to watch. Who wouldn't want to spend a lazy afternoon watching the boys make fools of themselves? It's just ... Oh, maybe it would be different this time.

The streets were emptier once I was away from the market. Middle of the day; everyone was busy salvaging, or working in the recycling factory or the desalination plant or at the algae fields that floated on City's edges. The boys would be in trouble when it was discovered they weren't where they were supposed to be, but that had never stopped them before.

When I turned the last corner, the wind tugged at my hair. The sea was ruffled, wavetops glinting. The floats that made the path to the recycling factory, and which would mark the finish line today, shifted on the waves. A crowd had gathered, my age and younger, people who should be my friends but who I'd never grown friendly with. It was mostly girls, sneaking away from their chores, and a few of the younger boys jealous they hadn't been allowed to join in the race.

I hung back. They made me feel ... stupid and young and I hated it. I was seventeen, for the tides' sake – old enough to make a pledge. But I didn't feel it. It was like all the other girls had been clued in to something I'd missed. I knew how to be a doctor, my father had taught me that, but I didn't know how to be a woman. With no mother, there was no one to teach me what seemed to come effortlessly to Belle and Hannah. I'd hoped it would come naturally, but that hadn't happened either, or not yet.

One of the boys gave a shout as the recycled bottle kayaks came into view. All eyes turned in that direction and I was able to step into the crowd without feeling awkward. Attention was on the three racers, and the rowdy splashing they made as they rounded the corner. It was like they didn't care about being caught, like the rules didn't apply to them.

Will Keyne finished first, crashing his kayak into the factory path floats and raising his paddle above his head with a grin of triumph. Hannah leaned over the edge of the pontoons, waving a scarf to signal the end of the race. I was slightly surprised she didn't fall in, but her balance was as perfect as the shine of her hair.

"Will! Oh, you were so fast!"

Hannah was all teeth and hair and cleavage as Will came to a stop – and *how* could she not fall in? She was more over the water than she was on the pontoons.

Binny reached the finish a second later, grabbing at the edge of the pontoons with one hand while the other held his paddle. Foo followed half a minute after. Both looked annoyed to have been beaten. Or perhaps they were just annoyed that Hannah was flashing her teeth and her cleavage at Will rather than at them.

Foo clambered out first, yanking his kayak from the

water. Everyone jumped back to give him space as his bottle kayak dripped water all over the tin pontoons. He pushed through the group, dragging it behind him, passing close to me as he stomped through. I remembered my first and only swimming race. I'd come a dismal last and not one single person had said well done – they were too busy congratulating the winners. I'd sneaked home, not sure whether I was relieved or mortified when no one who'd been there had ever mentioned the race to me again – I might as well not have been there. I could imagine how Foo felt.

I smiled at him. "Well done, that was a tough race."

He paused long enough to give me a withering look then started walking again, his shoulder jarring mine as he pushed past.

My words shrivelled to a hard lump in my throat and I fought to keep my smile steady. That was exactly what I meant. I didn't fit in, because somehow telling the truth didn't work when I did it. Maybe I needed to flash my teeth and my chest more whenever I spoke, but I knew I'd die of embarrassment if I even tried that.

Then Binny was climbing out, cat-calling to Will. "You're just lucky, Keyne!" He hadn't taken losing as poorly as Foo. The boys clustered around Binny while the girls were focused on Will.

"I would say watch and learn, but you're too far behind to see me!" Will called back, untruthfully. The only one left in the water, Will flung his paddle to one side and tipped himself to the other, rolling out of the kayak and into the water, then turning a somersault and vanishing into the depths.

Hannah leaned down to look for him but I was sure she couldn't see anything over the reflected shine of the water and the kayak and paddle he'd left behind, bobbing on the surface. Made from plastic bottles from the Time Before, it wasn't as though anything was going to sink to the seabed.

Belle stepped forward and muttered something to Hannah. Hannah turned and replied with a grin to her friend, pushing her like it was a joke. Belle staggered a few steps then returned to Hannah's side, still smiling.

When Will's head broke the surface, Hannah marked the moment with a dramatic gasp. She pressed a hand to her chest in case Will was thinking of looking anywhere else. "Oh, I thought you were never coming up!" She glanced at Belle then back to Will, who was grinning to match her as he trod water, his dark hair slicked to his head. "You should be a nautilus man," Hannah told him, "You were down there for*ever*!"

"You think I'd make a good nautilus man, huh?"

Hannah nodded so enthusiastically she ought again to have fallen into the water with him. Her boots must be lead lined to keep her safe.

Will's gaze snagged on me. "What about it, Doc? Will you conduct the operation?"

All eyes turned to me. I swallowed, trying to think of a reply that wouldn't break the mood. What could I say? We all knew Will's father would never let his precious sons go under the knife, no matter how desperate matters became. I tried to think of something witty, something that Hannah or Belle might say. Something that wouldn't get me sour looks and giggles of derision – and my brain failed me. I didn't have recourse to anything but the truth. "Do you have a licence?"

I looked around when laughter broke out – good-natured laughter, as though I'd made a joke. Even Hannah was smiling. My worry faded away as I realised I *had* made a joke. I just hadn't known it was one until afterwards.

Will placed his hands on the edge of the pontoons and surged up out of the water. "I don't know, Doc. I'll speak to my father, shall I?"

I even ventured a smile. "You do that. I'll sterilise

my instruments just in case." There was more laughter. I felt quite giddy. Will slung a dripping wet arm around Hannah's shoulders, his other around Belle's and guided them away from the water's edge. Neither seemed to mind being steered. Or soaked. He left his kayak and paddle, but that didn't matter either. Two of the younger boys jumped in, arguing over who would take what. I watched Hannah, Belle and Will walk away. Hannah's hips swayed as she walked. Will's arm was tight across her shoulders.

Hannah and I were both motherless girls. There should be some point of comparison between us, but we were nothing alike. Hannah's laughter floated back towards me. She had her skills, and I had mine, I told myself firmly. I was a trainee doctor, key to our society, vital to the future of City. What was Hannah? Pretty. Flirtatious.

And popular.

I turned for home. Where I belonged.

Chapter Two

I was humming as I pushed my front door open, but my contentment evaporated when I walked in to discover my father deep in conversation with a tatty gorm who wouldn't have made it over the threshold if I'd been there to prevent it.

"Ah, Libby, I was waiting." Pa greeted me with the gentle admonishment before the door had even shut behind me. I opened my mouth to say sorry, then closed it when I realised the youth with him was watching me. I wasn't going to apologise with an audience. I would have taken him for a messenger except that there was something about the way his feet in their very shabby shoes were planted on the floor, as though he had arrived at a desired destination after much effort and would have to be forcibly removed.

He was about my age, a little younger, his unkempt dark hair dropping over eyes that were as blue as the sky in midsummer and clouded by an expression that echoed the determination of his stance. I didn't need to be told what had brought him to the door of Dr Miracle.

We got boys knocking on our door every day. But no matter how determined they were, City had its rules. You needed a licence if you wanted to be a nautilus man – and the Magistrate didn't give those out to just anyone. I looked a question at Pa, awaiting an explanation.

He nodded as though he found nothing wrong with

the youth before us. "Yes, we have a patient. Cosimo will be undergoing the nautilus procedure as soon as you can prepare everything."

I stopped in the act of unfastening my coat and looked again. I'd hoped my first impressions were wrong, but a second examination did nothing to settle my misgivings. "You wish to become a nautilus man?" I didn't wait for a reply, throwing off my coat and his aspirations in a moment. "You're too young."

He bristled, the way a child would, and opened his mouth, but it was my father who spoke first. "Cosimo was seventeen in February."

Three months older than me? I laughed contemptuously. "Is that what he told you?" I unloaded the precious gold I'd bought at the market into a pot beside the sink, careful to ensure the boy didn't see what I was about.

My father's cold voice made me straighten. "Cosimo *will* be undergoing the procedure. Will you assist or shall I send for another helper?"

I stared. I always assisted my father during operations. Always. "Of course," I stuttered out. But I couldn't help turning back to the boy and asking, as Father should have, "You have a licence?"

"That has been taken care of," Pa answered.

I swung back, puzzled by his tone. His grey gaze didn't falter, warning me that if I persisted I would make a fool of no one but myself. I pressed my teeth hard together, although I knew at least half my ire could be set at the ill-shod feet of the stupid, presumptuous boy who had somehow persuaded my father to act contrary to his principles and against the law. I turned my back on both of them, filling the kettle with clean water and setting it on the stove. By the time I had finished coaxing the blocks of algae fibre in the fire to give a little more heat, another objection had occurred.

I turned to the boy, Cosimo. Cosimo! Even his

ridiculous name was undoubtedly false. I didn't know how he had fooled my father and I wished I hadn't stopped to watch the race. I'd have sent him on his way quickly enough. "You will need money. It's not cheap, you know." I was talking to him as though he were a child, far younger than he looked. It was unpardonable rudeness, I knew, but I didn't care. My father was treating me like an imbecile, and my irritation had to go somewhere.

"That, too, has been taken care of. You have a job to do, daughter." My father's voice was chill.

I knew I had overstepped the mark and my cheeks reddened. Pa had corrected me, and this tiresome boy was witness to my embarrassment. "Very well." I spun back to the stove, as though watching the kettle would make it boil more quickly. "Ten minutes," I promised, clattering instruments into the tray on top of the stove to mark my displeasure.

"Thank you, Libby." Pa's voice was even again. He vanished upstairs, ushering the boy before him up the metal steps, and I was left with my thoughts and my irritation until the kettle began to steam.

*

I had recovered my temper and was prepared to let the matter lie, but as I mounted the stairs with the tray of cooling, sterilised surgical instruments in one hand and a bucket filled with warm water to wash the dirt off our patient in the other, I heard their voices, murmuring together in conversation. Nothing wrong with that. My father always took great care to explain how the procedure to implant gills – so a person could breathe under water – worked. He was always at pains to put patients' minds at rest. There was nothing strange in that. What riled me straight back to wishing the boy at the bottom of the sea was the way their voices ceased the moment the door cracked open, and the way two pairs of eyes watched my entry into the tiny, brightly lamp-lit room as though I were the outsider. The boy didn't even have the manners to help with my load, just sat stupidly as I set the tray beside the table my father used for operations and carried the bucket to his side.

The patient had stripped to the waist as everyone had to do for the procedure. He was skinny, although his shoulders were already broad. Maybe he was older than he looked, but I'd have wagered everything I owned he didn't have the licence he needed for the operation. And my father had to know that as well as I did.

I held out a phial holding some of our precious soap. "You need to wash well," I told the boy. "You must be properly clean or you could contract an infection and die." My tone told him how much I would care if that eventuality came about.

His skin flushed and my heart welled with satisfaction to know my barb had struck. Then came a swell of guilt which was out of all proportion – I had only told him the truth.

"Ah've come a long way to get here," he explained.

It was the first time he'd spoken in my hearing and the shock of his voice made my eyes widen. That accent! "You're a reamer."

He didn't deny the accusation, pressing together the lips that had given him away. I turned to my father. "He's a gorming reamer, Pa." The chill inside me increased – thieves and vagabonds the lot of them. There was no way a reamer boy would be granted a licence for the procedure by City's Magistrate. How had he forced my father to agree to the operation?

"He's a patient," Pa corrected calmly.

I backed towards the door. "I'm fetching a watchman."

Cosimo stood up, fists clenching as though he'd physically force me to stay. My father reached out a hand to hold him back, looking steadily at me. "Libby, I will ask for your co-operation. And if I do not receive it, I shall command your obedience as my apprentice. Pretend you didn't hear the boy and do your job." Our gazes met and held. Pa's was calm, implacable as the sea. Mine blurred with fear. He stated, "I do this willingly. A favour for an old friend."

"We aren't friends with reamers," I countered, my gaze darting to the boy.

"Then perhaps it is time City learned to be friends with all its neighbours," Pa replied.

I watched him as the seconds passed but his expression didn't waver. He betrayed no doubt in what he planned to do. Nor any fear.

After a long time, I nodded. "I'll fetch the chloroform," I murmured.

*

When I returned, the boy had already doused his head and scrubbed with the soap, and was rubbing away the damp with our towels. His hair was a rich brown to rival even Hannah's, dark from the water but with a golden burnish where the lamp light gleamed. Also gleaming was a silver trinket on a chain around his neck. I wondered if he'd stolen it. It was a rich bauble for a scruffy reamer.

Clutching the anaesthetic, I looked down on him where he sat. "You'll have to remove that."

His hand closed immediately over the pendant. He didn't speak, but his expression told me he wouldn't comply. "It will get in the way," I snapped, tired of his opposition to everything I said.

"Ah can't lose it."

I'd already got the message that it was important to him. All I felt now was irritation. "We'll keep it safe. We're hardly likely to steal it from you." Unlike reamers, the people of City were law-abiding – usually.

"Peace, daughter. I can work around it."

No point arguing again. "Very well." I turned back

to the boy. "Are you ready for me to shave you?"

"Shave?" The blush was back, clearer now his skin was clean. I enjoyed his discomfiture, cross at the guilt that surged through me like an overdue tide a moment later.

My father explained, "You must have no hair around your ear or your throat. It would interfere with the device." He indicated the area on his own head. Then he smiled at the boy's expression. "Libby is very experienced. You're quite safe in her hands."

The boy threw a glance at me. I read very clearly that his view differed from my father's. I smiled, pleased to find he liked the situation as much as I did. "Right," he managed.

I seized the razor from the tray of instruments and turned back to him. "Hold very still."

He froze as though scared I might slit his throat if he moved. "I'll be careful," I told him. I had my pride. I wouldn't cut his throat – nor even slice his ear off, even if he deserved it. I thought touching him would be awkward, but as soon as I tilted his chin, it was just a job.

Moments later, I ran my thumb over the newly smooth surface and turned to my father for his approval, which he gave with his customary nod.

Setting the razor aside, I fetched a clean cloth for the chloroform while the boy hitched onto the operating table. "Lie back," I instructed, once more focused on the procedure rather than him. His eyes widened as many men's did when they reached that point and he grabbed my wrist as I brought the cloth closer, his gaze sliding past me to my father.

"It won't hurt." I soothed him as I would have soothed any patient. The assurance was automatic.

I felt rather than saw my father's nod behind me. "You're quite safe now, Cosimo," he promised. Disquiet ran down my spine – he spoke as though promising more than just safety during the operation. The boy lay back, clenching his eyes shut. He twitched when I placed the cloth over his nose and mouth, falling unconscious in seconds.

My father slipped the chain over his neck, dropping one eyelid in a wink of complicity that settled my agitated heart back to a normal rhythm. "No harm when he's none the wiser." He handed it to me and I slipped the chain and the thin, coin-like silver pendant into my apron pocket. Then, we started work.

I was so well practised at assisting my father during the procedure that my actions required no thought. There was plenty of capacity to think and speak while the operation progressed. "Do you plan ever to tell me why you have agreed to operate on an underage and unlicensed reamer?"

My father's movements never wavered. I wouldn't have spoken if I'd supposed they might. "Cosimo is seventeen," he stated.

Despite everything I'd thought earlier, I believed him. My father didn't lie to me. Not outright. It hadn't escaped my notice that he'd made no response to the other half of my question.

"But a gorming reamer, Pa. If anyone discovers what we've done ..."

My father's voice remained steady. "I don't expect to hear such unpleasant terms from the mouth of my daughter. She was taught better than that."

Chastened, I fell silent. But only for a moment. "Why did you agree to operate, then?" I would continue to ask questions until I got satisfactory answers. My father had taught me that too.

He was squinting into the incision he'd made. I shifted the lamp. I held the boy's wrist in one hand, evaluating his pulse with my fingertips. With the other I handed my father instruments and topped up the boy's chloroform when his pulse indicated he needed it.

I thought Pa wasn't going to answer; possibly he'd been concentrating too hard to take in my words. I was about to repeat the question when he said, "It's probably better you know as little as possible about him. He'll be gone in a day or two."

Before his voice recovered enough for his reamer accent to give him away. I opened my mouth, but Pa continued before I spoke. "His mother was an old friend of mine."

"And?"

"And I am doing for him what I hope she would do for you if the situation were reversed."

"What situation?"

"Enough, Libby. I need to concentrate."

I fell silent. But as the lamplight flickered over Pa's intent face, my mind remained busy conjuring possible explanations that could account for the boy's arrival on our doorstep and my father's willingness to break the law for his sake. Nothing that came to mind did credit to the boy.

Chapter Three

"We are promised at the Magistrate's for dinner," Pa told me as he washed his hands after the operation while I pulled a clean blanket over the boy so he might sleep in comfort. I raised my brows. "The invitation came while you were at the market."

Wasting time watching Will and Hannah flirting. "Then I'll get ready." It had been well into the afternoon before we'd started the operation. The Magistrate would be expecting us shortly. I scrubbed my hands and face, donned a clean top and brushed my hair loose, adding my mother's precious combs for decoration.

When I walked down the stairs, Pa smiled. The expression lifted his face. He looked tired and worn, and older than I remembered. When had that happened? Before or after the boy, Cosimo, had knocked on our door?

"Beautiful." He crossed the room and kissed my forehead, cradling my face in his hands. "I love you, Libby. Always know that." His eyes shone in the lamplight. My heart jolted. The idea that my beauty had brought Pa to the brink of tears was ridiculous.

"What's the matter?" My heart beat a rapid thud in my chest. That my father adored his only daughter was a given. It was never spoken aloud because it didn't need to be. "What's happened?"

"Nothing, nothing. Shall we go?" He held out his arm. I was about to slip my hand through his elbow when he spoke again. "Tonight ... I trust you will respect Cosimo's confidentiality."

I swung on Pa, furious. The expression on his face arrested the words dancing on my tongue. It wasn't a reprimand but a warning. I swallowed, a prickle of apprehension shivering down my spine. "He's brought trouble to our door. You should have let me fetch a watchman."

Father smiled his gentle smile. "Any trouble was there long before Cosimo arrived."

"Who *is* he?"

"I told you: the son of an old friend."

"And we are placing ourselves in danger for the sake of an old friendship?" Anger swelled. My father always confided in me. I didn't like being treated like a child.

"Not danger, just a little inconvenience. And if we won't suffer that for the sake of our friends we don't deserve to call ourselves friends. Come. We mustn't be late."

I bit down my questions. It wouldn't do to keep the Magistrate waiting. By the time we returned, the boy would be rousing from his anaesthetic. I might get better answers from him, particularly when he was still drowsy and disorientated. I just hoped he'd be able to talk clearly – sometimes patients couldn't speak properly for days after the procedure.

*

The autumn day had waned to a dismal, misty night while we'd undertaken Cosimo's operation. Damp clung to my face and I pulled my scarf close around me. Father held the lantern high and I held tight to his arm as we stepped across the metal pontoons towards the Magistrate's house in the centre of City. Our home was luxurious – two floors in a metal frame filled with bottles for insulation, but the Magistrate's was finer still, with glass windows and the first floor encased in bricks brought up from the sea bed homes from the Time Before by nautilus men. Personally, I thought nautilus men should have better things to do beneath the waves, like salvaging the food we'd starve without, but I couldn't deny that the outcome was handsome. And thanks to my father, we had nautilus men enough to do both.

The reminder of the good fortune my father had brought to City made me feel better. Whoever this Cosimo was, *we* couldn't be in trouble. Not my father. He was the second most important man in our world. And while I would never voice such treacherous words aloud, I was sure we could survive without the Magistrate far more easily than we could manage without Dr Miracle.

My father knocked at the door and it swung wide immediately, spilling bright lamplight onto the step and over our toes. I smiled as I stepped inside, and kept the gesture steady when Will Keyne materialised and placed a glass of something intoxicating into my hand with a grin and a bow.

"A pleasure to see you again, Doc." He gave a smile that made his blue eyes shine. Will and Hannah were one of a piece with their good looks and easy charm. I thought him shallow. I didn't think there was a great deal behind the gloss of Will's prettiness. Still, not having my regard was unlikely to wound him. He had plenty of other admirers.

"And you, Will." I managed a smile, and stretched the gesture when Josiah, the elder son, sidled into the room. "Good evening, Josiah." Serious where Will was silly, Josiah ran the recycling factory tethered a little way outside City. I suppose that gave him less to be silly about than the flirting and races that filled Will's days.

"Hello, Liberty." He nodded a polite welcome then

crossed the room to engage my father in talk, leaving me to be entertained by Will.

I took a sip of my drink and wracked my brains for chit-chat. It was no easier to relax and be myself with only Will for an audience than it had been with the bigger group earlier. And I was always awkward with the Magistrate's sons. I was bound to become the wife of one of them eventually – because who else could I marry? – but I couldn't think of the event with a great deal of enthusiasm.

I knew them well because we'd all grown up together. I'd even been close to Josiah once – fellow brainboxes united by being top of the class and disliked by all our less able peers. But we didn't have anything in common, not anymore. Will was charming but had little substance and relied on charisma where brains might be more appropriate. And Josiah was infuriatingly morose, although there had always been keen intelligence behind his silence. I knew myself well enough to know I wouldn't like a husband capable of out-thinking me any more than I'd like a stupid one. And neither brother gave any sign that they held me in esteem, although that didn't mean much these days. We weren't blood relations, a consideration that became more important as each generation tied the people of City in tighter and tighter genetic groups, and whichever one I wed I would make a good and loyal wife. That couldn't be so hard, could it?

The Magistrate strode into the room and nodded to my father before crossing the room to take my hand, turning me towards him and away from Will who had been making a joke about a market vendor. "Miss Marchmont. You bring the sun wherever you go."

"Thank you for the invitation, sir." I made a smiling reply to his slick greeting. It was easy to see where Will got his charm.

He smiled, showing his teeth. "Your presence is

always welcome, Liberty. I hope you will excuse me if conversation over dinner is a trifle dull. I have matters to discuss with your father."

"I quite understand." I watched him cross the room to clasp hands with my father while my heart jumped against my ribs. Were those matters connected to Cosimo's sudden arrival on City?

"Let me escort you to your seat, Doc," Will offered, and I let him guide me while I watched my father and the Magistrate, heads together as they sat down. Perhaps I was being foolish – they might just be discussing which of the Magistrate's sons I should make a pledge to. That idea settled a dull lump of distaste in my stomach. I was seventeen, but there was no rush to start the process that might end in marriage and unbreakable vows, surely?

I forced a smile. A minute later, as the scent of our meal drifted into the room, the gesture became genuine. Dining at the Magistrate's home was always a pleasure. His was the only house on City where meals didn't primarily consist of algae disguised in one of fifty-nine ways.

I was the only woman at the table. The Magistrate's wife was unwell and had kept to her room. I had long since guessed their marriage wasn't a happy one. I'd seen the Magistrate's wife only once in public and never at their home. And she was ill far more often than could be possible for a woman who made no call on my father's medical expertise.

We started to eat and my taste buds exploded with pleasure. Tinned fish, but served with real carrots and greens. The Magistrate professed himself proud of the fact that – with the tins the nautilus men raided from the houses drowned beneath us – City could feed itself. We were beholden to no one, he often proclaimed. That didn't explain why so much of his food was grown on New Eden, the last piece of land a day's sailing away, rather than coming from our own algae fields.

I spent the meal flanked by Will and Josiah. Josiah appeared distracted and Will was forward. To be fair to them, I was far from an ideal guest. I was distracted – trying to listen to the conversation at the far end of the table. But without rudely telling Will to shut up, I couldn't catch more than incomprehensible snatches. The one phrase I heard clearly was when my father mentioned, "… the jewel of my household." It meant they were discussing my marriage, and once I knew that, I didn't want to hear any more.

I tried to find sensible replies to Will's conversation while my mind returned home. I wondered whether Cosimo was awake yet. I wanted answers. Then I hoped he was still sleeping. Patients were usually disorientated and often in pain when they awoke. It was unkind to let him face that alone. My father had only left him because to do otherwise would alert the Magistrate to the irregularity in our household. Which brought me right back to the trouble my father had promised me we weren't in.

I was so distracted it wasn't until Will nudged my elbow that I saw what had been brought to the table for our dessert: apples. My mouth watered immediately. The first of the harvest from New Eden. I forgot my father and the Magistrate's sons and even Cosimo while I sank my teeth into the luscious fruit and did my best to hold back my groan of pleasure. Apples from New Eden never got as far as the market. It might be worth marrying one of the Magistrate's sons purely for the food.

*

When the meal ended, the Magistrate, Josiah, and my father disappeared into the Magistrate's study. Will escorted me back to the sitting room. The size and luxury of the Magistrate's home would provide further consolation for the inadequacies of the groom if I were ever to marry one or other of his sons. I wandered around the room, looking at the pictures on the walls. Each time I visited, I found a new one. Will stood by the fireplace. When I turned, I met his warm, twinkling grin and found myself smiling. Perhaps marriage to Will would be easiest. I would turn a blind eye to his flirting and he would let me guide him into the choices I thought were best. I swallowed down my distaste at such a cold choice. City was a pragmatic place, and I was a pragmatic young woman.

I held on to my smile. "I'm sorry to keep you away from the men's talk," I told Will, seizing on the only thought in my head to break the silence that seemed very thick while he was looking at me.

"How could I regret spending time with you, Doc?" He smiled a genuine, warm smile that placed a wicked glint in his eyes and he boasted, "I'm already aware of my father's plans."

I raised my brows. "And what are they?"

He waved a hand. "Order between City and New Eden; ensuring the reamers don't encroach."

The same as ever, then, and scarcely a need for secrecy.

Will stepped close and I was warmed by the heat radiating from him. "And I have plans all of my own."

Was he flirting with me? If he was, what was I supposed to do about it? I tried to match his tone and expression. "Really?"

He smiled, then shrugged. "Of course. Many of them. A wife, a family of my own. Who knows what I might then achieve?"

I concentrated on the picture in front of me to make it hard for him to see my face. Was he about to make a declaration? My breath caught. Did I want him to? I cleared my throat. "I see. And have you selected your partner for this domestic felicity?"

He coughed, his gaze sliding away from mine. My heart thrilled at the idea that he might be about to make a pledge without reference to my father or his – what on earth would I say in response? "It would not do to show my cards too early," he said, and a dull disappointment settled over me.

There was a noise outside the door. Will clutched my sleeve. His fingers were warm and strong. "Don't tell my father – he wouldn't understand."

"Of course. There's nothing to tell."

That was true. For a moment Will had been desirable. Then he'd made himself contemptible by being afraid of his father. I turned my attention back to the picture, although now I was impatient at the impossible vista it presented to me, showing trees and flowers that had not been seen since the Time Before – things I could never hope to see and didn't want to wish for.

The door opened and my father asked, "Are you ready to leave, Libby? We have trespassed on the Magistrate's hospitality for long enough."

I crossed to his side at once. "Of course, Pa."

*

We were halfway home before my father spoke again, his lantern once more an island of muzzy light over our heads. "Libby, this is important." There was a pause. Our footsteps thudded on the mist-damp sheets of metal beneath our soles. I could hear the slosh of water against the floats beneath them. I waited. Pa sighed. "Are you in love with Josiah Keyne?"

I was so dumbfounded I couldn't speak for a moment. "In *love*? Of course not!"

My father stopped so abruptly I bumped into him. "What? But the Magistrate indicated – yet again – that he believed you would be in favour of marriage to the boy."

I sighed, my breath a cloud before me. "And so I would, but love has nothing to do with that." I crossed my arms over my chest to fend off the cold and my offence. "I should hope I'm not such a lackwit as to fall in love with that dull oaf."

"Oh, Libby!" My father was laughing so hard he could barely speak. "We should have spoken of this months ago. I feared you were infatuated with the boy!"

My incredulity sent giggles through me. "Hardly! I can see Josiah Keyne's faults very clearly, Father. But a girl has to marry someone. Who else is left to me? Or would you have me wed the algae merchant?"

I could hear the laughter in my father's voice. "Davey is a good man. You could do much worse."

"And I could do much better. If I don't marry one of the Magistrate's sons – well, who else on City is my equal?"

"There are other ways a man can be your equal, Libby. For my sake, promise me you won't marry a man you despise."

"If I can *find* such a one."

Pa hugged me to him. "My dear child. You are like your mother – peerless!"

"And you are biased."

"You disagree?" he challenged.

I pulled a face. "Of course not. I *am* perfect in every way it's possible for a woman to be."

My father laughed. Then he sobered. "So there is no one else?"

"There's no one at all, Pa." When I said that my chest felt strange, but it was only a momentary sensation.

He nodded and we walked a little further. Pa sighed, all humour wiped away. "I need to go away for a short while. If there is no one here to tempt you to stay, will you come with me?"

I stared at him, my feet stumbling. "To where, Pa?" The world had flooded and shrunk. City was all there was – apart from New Eden and the Wastes. Pa couldn't mean the Wastes. "Are we going to New Eden? What for?"

The lantern light bobbed ahead as my father's pace increased. "I'll explain on the way, Libby."

My heart leapt with alarm. "What's happening, Pa? It's Cosimo, isn't it? I knew he was trouble."

"This is not Cosimo's fault." My father sounded very certain of that, but I couldn't believe him.

I pestered him for answers all the way home, but the journey was short and he'd given nothing away by the time we reached our door.

Chapter Four

The boy, Cosimo, was rousing when we arrived home, pulse high and breathing shallow as he returned to consciousness. I sat on the bed beside him.

"Sit up. Water will help."

He sat up and started coughing. They almost all did that. "Your breathing will be slower and shallower than you are used to. Allow your body to set the pace." I put an arm around his shoulders for reassurance. He shot me a glare compounded of fear and anger. All that whispering beforehand; Pa should have told him what to expect.

"Here." As the coughing ebbed, I held out a mug of water. He sipped and tried to speak, which again my father should have warned him about.

"It may take a while for your voice to return to normal." I looked over his face, but there were no answers there. "Which is a great shame, because I would dearly love to know why my father insists there was no danger in conducting your operation, yet is now packing for a journey which we must commence immediately, taking only one bag each."

The boy croaked something. I guessed his meaning. "Essentials only. There's quarter of an hour before we must leave." I dropped my arm and stood. "So I hope you're fit to walk. I don't intend to leave you in my house with no one watching over you."

Another croak, and a wave of his hand that I trusted meant he would do everything he could not to hold us up.

"Who *are* you?" I asked. He drained the cup. I waited, but he didn't even attempt to reply. Instead, he reached a questing hand to his neck, fingers twitching away when they met the gills.

However much I disliked him, he was still a patient. "Does the wound hurt?"

He shook his head.

I continued my assessment. "Does it feel hot?"

He shook his head again and attempted a word that was probably, "Throat."

"The pain's all internal?"

He nodded.

"As though you've swallowed a drawer full of knives?"

Another nod.

"That's entirely normal. It'll pass."

He frowned, but I was only telling him the truth. His hand settled at the front of his throat where, instead of something new, he found something missing. Before he protested, I reached past him to the cupboard beside the bed, where I'd left his talisman. "I told you we'd keep it safe."

He snatched the pendant from my hands and pulled the chain over his head, settling it so it wouldn't interfere with the devices implanted each side of his neck. His fingers paused against the gills. I guessed they took a while to get used to. Then he swung his legs off the bed and pushed me out of the way, peering around for his shoes and shirt.

"Oh, no." I put a hand on his chest and pushed him back down to the bed. "You go nowhere until my father has seen you. I'm not having your death on my conscience."

He shot me a scowl which didn't need words to

make its meaning clear, took a breath and made a reasonable attempt to say, "Fetch him."

"He's packing. He hasn't forgotten you." I strode from the room only to meet Pa coming in.

"I'll check our patient. Hold the light."

I followed him back inside and held the lamp while he checked on Cosimo, fingers dancing around the wounds. "They've taken well. Everything I could have hoped for."

The boy didn't look especially pleased to hear that. He stood up when my father did and said, "Go."

My father squeezed his shoulder. "We'll go together."

My gaze flew to Pa, who spoke before I could protest.

"We'll go together," he repeated, "and now." I looked at Cosimo, expecting him to protest, but he was pulling his shirt over his head, his face covered. "You're ready, Libby?" Pa continued.

"Give me five minutes." I turned my back on them both and hurried out to pack what I needed for a trip.

*

I was waiting with my bag on my back and the lantern in one hand when my father and the boy reached the bottom of the stairs a few minutes later.

Cosimo was empty-handed. Father pushed a knapsack into his arms. "You'll be so kind as to take that for me." The boy slid his arms through the straps and settled it on his back obediently. Pa fastened his coat, picked up his own bag, took the lantern and swung the door open to greet a damp night mired with fog. I glanced at the reamer. Pa should have given me the bag to carry – I could manage two. In the darkness, Cosimo would probably run off with our property.

I was conversely no happier when he matched my father's pace and made no attempt to run. Even if it meant we lost the bag I would by far have preferred him to slip away into the fog and get lost. Unfortunately, nothing was happening the way I wanted today. I could only hope matters would change. And soon.

*

"Where are we going, Father?" The fog had thickened in the half hour we'd spent at home, damp from the sea combining with smoke from the recycling factory to mire the sky. It swallowed detail and made noises louder. Our feet clattered on the metal pontoons, making it sound as though there were more than three of us. My question echoed louder than I'd meant. Demanding. Needy. Not how Dr Miracle's daughter ought to sound.

"Away from here."

As though that was an answer! "Where, Pa?"

"Tonight we'll go wherever we can. I apologise that our plans are a little flimsy."

I cast a sour look at the boy, Cosimo. "I don't blame *you*," I said to my father.

"Don't you? I rather think you should, Libby." I heard the smile in my father's voice and fell silent. I was clearly not going to get any sense from him while he was in this mood.

For a few minutes, the light of the lantern bobbed in front of us as we walked, haloed by the mist. The only sound was our tinny footsteps and the sloshing of the sea beneath. I was never in any doubt of our initial destination, and it was confirmed as we weaved through alleyways between houses and the sound of our feet was joined by the snap of ropes and the creak of barges shifting in the water. The quayside. Then that sound was joined by another; footsteps, coming towards us. I was anxious, but not alarmed. The tide was turning so there were bound to be people about, regardless of the foul night.

"Doctor Miracle! Are you there?"

Fear gripped me at the sudden call. My father stopped. "Ah." He sighed, as though this were an inconvenience, but nothing worse. "I had hoped we might have a little more time than this …"

"Who is it?" I didn't recognise the voice, but it had almost been drowned out by the thumping of my heart.

"No one of importance." Pa smiled, although the gesture looked forced. "You go on ahead while I deal with this. Cosimo will escort you to the boat."

I looked at the boy, who nodded as though he accepted all these slipshod arrangements. Perhaps this was what they'd been whispering about before the operation, while I'd been out of the room. Plans my father hadn't trusted to me but had given freely to a stranger.

"I'll go with you, Pa." Nothing would induce me to go with the boy without my father.

"No, you will go ahead as I bid you." Pa was calm, which sped up the rate of my heart.

I shook my head. The only word that would go past my suddenly thick throat was, "No."

"The tide's already turning. You hurry ahead and get everything ready." He spoke to reassure me, but I caught the glance he gave Cosimo, the shooing motion he made.

Fear surged through my veins, increasing with every beat of my heart. "I'm not leaving you."

"Go with Cosimo. I'll follow."

"No." I had the strongest conviction that if I let my father out of my sight I would never see him again. It was irrational, but the world didn't make sense. Not today. My father was Dr Miracle. How could he need to flee? What was there that could threaten him in all the world?

Pa looked over my head. "Take her." He pushed me towards Cosimo and turned to meet our pursuer, Pa's footsteps echoing rapidly as he strode away. I staggered, turning, and would have followed, but Cosimo's grip tightened around my arm with a strength that took me by surprise. "Let me go!" I twisted to look for Pa, already disappearing into the autumn fog, the lantern light swallowed by the night. If anything, the boy's grip tightened further. He pulled me onwards and I stumbled beside him. He was stronger than he looked. I twisted but I couldn't get away.

We turned in to the quayside and the sea came into sight. Cosimo was distracted, looking up to orient himself and find the boat we were destined for.

I took my chance. I stamped on his foot and heard a hiss of pain but still he didn't release me, his hands like steel around my wrists. I distinguished the word "idiot" from his damaged throat and fury leant me strength. It wasn't *his* father walking into danger. I paused, sagging, as though I'd given up. When he relaxed, I drove my elbow into his stomach and ran back to where I'd left my father while Cosimo was doubled over.

After a few paces, I slowed, aware of the clatter of my steps. I didn't think the boy would follow, but I didn't want to make it easy for him if he did. Nor did I want to announce my presence to my father – and the person he'd stopped to meet. I heard footsteps echoing against the walls, barely distinguishable from other sounds, although I couldn't be sure if they were my father's or someone else's. I followed the noise down an alleyway, the mist drifting thick around me, and caught sight of a bobbing light that had to be his lantern. I hurried as he turned a corner, letting my hand drift along the sides of the houses so I wouldn't miss the turn.

Another corner. Something tangled in my feet. I stumbled, hands out to protect me as I slammed headlong onto the pontoons. Rising, I distinguished the obstacle. My father's medical bag. I leaned against the wall, peering through the mist. He had to be close since he wouldn't have left that behind.

There was a glow ahead, not moving. As I hugged the wall, I heard a voice, and I relaxed to recognise my father's tones, echoey and thin in the mist but unmistakeable. "I'd hoped to be away from here by now, then you wouldn't have found me."

"We would have followed. You're too important to leave." Another man. His voice was distorted by the weather. I felt as though I should recognise him, but didn't. An old patient, perhaps, a recollection just beyond my memory. Whoever he was, he wasn't the captain of a boat contracted to take us away.

"What if I promise to come back?" There was a pause, as though the other man were considering that offer. Come back after what? I crept closer. I could distinguish two forms, but they were still no better than indistinct shapes. I'm ashamed to own, fear kept me where I was when I should have stepped right up to them.

"I can't let you leave. I have my orders."

"And I can't bear to stay." My father again. I could tell which figure was which. Pa stood with his back to me and no knowledge that I was there.

"You don't have a choice."

My heart bounced against my ribs. I was debating whether to step out and make myself known when my arm was grabbed once more. Cosimo. His face was close, shiny with damp. If I'd had any doubt that he was furious, it was eliminated by his expression and his ferocious grip.

"Don't be foolish. You won't change my mind waving that thing in my face."

Fear turned me cold and I stilled in Cosimo's grip, straining to hear. I didn't know what 'that thing' was, but I sensed the threat. The mist swirled and swallowed Pa. I stepped forward, but the boy's implacable grip held me back. I wanted to hiss at him to let me go, but I wanted more to hear what was being said.

"Stay where you are!" The other voice rose in anger. I looked, but saw nothing through the fog.

Cosimo's fingertips bit into my shoulder and my wrist.

Sudden footsteps echoed on the pontoons. There was the sound of a scuffle. A low cough carried through the mist. There was a thud followed by more footsteps, running away into the heart of City.

"Stay," Cosimo growled and ran forward, vanishing into the fog. His steps were nearly soundless. All I could hear was my own breathing, sharp and stuttery with fear. The mist swirled and revealed a shape. My father. No, it was Cosimo. The mist thickened once more. I stepped towards my father. No, it was both of them. Cosimo and my father as though they embraced.

"Pa?" I ran the final few steps to them.

Cosimo turned, wide-eyed, my father sagging in his arms. The boy stumbled and lowered his burden to the ground. Pa's eyes were closed. My heart forgot to beat. I dropped to my knees.

Pushing Cosimo aside, I pulled Pa into my lap. Blood spilled from a wound beneath his ribs. It oozed in time with his heartbeat, soaking the hand I pressed to stop the haemorrhaging. My hands shook. Cosimo had killed him. It wasn't an embrace I'd seen, but a murder.

Cosimo set a hand on my shoulder. I shook it off. My heart was pounding now, making up for lost time. I pressed my hand against the wound, warm blood flowing over it. I tried not to think about what that signified, my thoughts whirling.

The murderer couldn't be the boy. There hadn't been time. The other voice; *he* was the killer. 'That thing' must have been the knife.

My father groaned, capturing my attention. "Stay calm. It's all right," I promised. I sniffed. My eyes filled with water. I was lying. His blood was warm on my hands. His pulse slowed as the blood flowed out of him.

"Come." Cosimo pulled at my arm but it would have taken an army of watchmen to move me then.

"Father?" I stroked his hair from his forehead.

He blinked and focused on me. He sighed and his breath whistled over my cheek as I leaned close. "Ah, Libby. I'm sorry."

"Don't talk like that." I sniffed. Water flowed down my face. "We just need to get you home. I can sew up the wound." I sniffed again, knowing every word I spoke was a lie but unable to stop myself, unable to give up hope. "My stitching is very fine, you've said so yourself."

He shook his head jerkily. The blood flowing over my fingers was hardly moving now. "Too late. Go with Cosimo." His breath was coming in gasps, or perhaps it was my sobs that made me hear in gasps. "You're a smart girl. You'll do right. I'm sorry."

I hugged him closer, rocking us both. My fingers were sticky. "Father! Stay with me. It'll be all right."

Cosimo shook my shoulder, casting glances into the mist around us. "Go," he growled.

Leaving was out of the question. "Help me get him home."

He shook his head. "Go," he repeated, pulling me.

"Hold on," I whispered to Pa, my voice failing. I couldn't lose him. It wasn't possible.

His face tightened with effort. There was a cough and he fell silent.

"Father?" There was nothing but silence and damp, and the weight of him in my arms. I was apprenticed to a doctor, I knew what had happened. I just couldn't accept it. "Pa ... answer me, please."

"Gone. Go." Cosimo tried to pull me to my feet. Fury swelled inside me. I was on fire with it. He'd caused this, yet it was my father lying here. With my father's body heavy on my lap, I looked up at the reamer, opened my mouth and screamed as loud as I could.

Chapter Five

The noise rang, amplified by the fog and the metal pontoons, echoing against the walls when I fell silent, as though someone elsewhere matched me scream for scream. I startled even myself. The reamer's eyes shone with fury. Then another sound overtook the echoes – footsteps running towards us. Fear filled the place anger had just left.

My scream must have used up my resistance. Or perhaps Cosimo's anger lent him strength. "Now." He pulled at my arm once more and I didn't have the will to resist.

The mist swallowed my father's body. As we ducked into an alleyway, I stumbled again and reached down, grabbing Father's medical bag before Cosimo's implacable hold dragged me onwards.

Footsteps surrounded us, bouncing off the metal. Fear drenched me. Pa had been murdered. Whatever trouble the reamer had brought to our door, I was now embroiled in it. I wasn't safe with him, but I probably wasn't safe alone either. Cosimo pushed me into a doorway as the footsteps neared and stood in front, pressing me back with his body so Pa's bag in my arms and his knapsack on Cosimo's back were crushed between us. Footsteps and the bobbing glow of a lantern passed the mouth of the alleyway beside us.

I pushed at him. They'd gone. And I couldn't bear to stay cooped up so close that I had to breathe in the smell of him. He moved, but his hand closed around my wrist immediately. I wanted to pull away, but I wasn't stupid. I needed to get away from danger until I figured everything out. I'd spent my whole life on City – where was I going to go and how in the tides would I get there? The reamer might as well make himself useful by getting me out of the danger he'd put me in.

He pulled me through alleyways. The sounds of the sea grew louder. I knew we'd reached the quayside when he stopped abruptly, muttering a sound that would no doubt have been a profanity if he'd been able to speak clearly.

"What is it?" I tried to peer around him, but for a skinny gorm he took up a surprising amount of room.

I made out the word, "Guard."

Sometimes the quayside was guarded. A salvage barge must have arrived too late to be unloaded before darkness fell. I looked again and finally got a decent view. A sound of contempt escaped me. "Night guard. Retired watchman. He's hardly a threat." The old man was sitting down, back against a wall, wrapped up against the night's cold. I'd be surprised if he wasn't sleeping.

"Dangerous."

"Don't be ridiculous. Where's the boat? You do have a boat?"

I turned when I got no reply. Cosimo was sparing his voice and pointing instead. To the far end of the harbour.

"Follow me." I straightened, shook back my plait, squared my shoulders and stepped forward. The fog was thinner here, blown away by the sea breeze that couldn't penetrate far into the cramped streets. I walked confidently, as though I had every right to be there. I *did* have every right to be there, it was just that recent events had shaken my certainties. I did know I didn't want to be challenged with a reamer on my heels. My steps slowed as I neared the lantern under which the figure was slumped. I hoped the watchman *was* asleep.

I realised I was holding my breath. Cosimo was a little way behind me but I didn't look round. I shivered, wondering who else might be behind me. My father's killer?

And then I was past, my pulse and respiration returning to normal.

"Miss? Hey there, Miss!"

I spun around. I'd relaxed too soon. The guard was awake, after all.

"Miss Marchmont." He struggled to his feet. "Whatever are you doing here so late?"

"I wanted a walk." I stood straight on to him, hiding the bag on my back, but there was nothing I could do about Pa's bag at my side. Who took a bag on an idle walk? I shifted again, hoping he wouldn't look too closely at me, or think about what he saw.

"We should get you safely home." The guard patted his pockets. "Your father will be worried."

Grief robbed my voice so all I could do was stare stupidly at him. Cosimo was right. He was dangerous, without even meaning to be. The old man's fingers quested into a pocket and lamplight glinted on what he was seeking: a whistle.

I grabbed his hand as he lifted it to his mouth. "No. Please don't do that." I didn't want help summoned. I had a dreadful premonition that one sound and the quayside would be thronged with assassins who would kill me, not content with my father's death.

There was a thud. The night guard looked stupidly at me, then sat abruptly back down, head nodding onto his chest. My puzzlement ceased when Cosimo loomed out of the fog behind him, the guard's own cudgel dangling from one hand.

"You've killed him!" He might have prevented our discovery, but the guard had done nothing wrong.

The boy shook his head. I stepped forward and pressed my fingertips to the old man's throat until I found a pulse. Maybe he would have no worse than a sore head when he awoke. Cosimo grabbed my arm. I snatched up Father's medical bag and let the boy drag me onwards.

*

The boat that was our destination was tucked out of sight among much larger vessels jostling for space. It was a little different from the boats I was accustomed to seeing. Hard to see in the dark mist, but it was deep, deeper than the barges our nautilus men used to collect salvage. I tugged my hand from his. "I *said* you were a gorming reamer," I snapped, staring at the odd boat that gave proof of the fact.

The words hung in the air. My cheeks grew hot, as though I might hear my father's voice sharpened in a set-down. There was nothing, of course.

Cosimo lifted a shoulder, turned his back and muttered, "Wait," as he jumped down into the craft. He was instantly invisible and I wished I had the lantern. I peered through the fog, not sure if I was more afraid of what was behind me or in front. The reminder of who the boy was had startled me. I couldn't leave City with a reamer, the Magistrate would kill me – if I didn't end up at the bottom of the sea first.

With Pa dead, who could I trust?

"Come." I jumped when Cosimo loomed out of the mist, jerking his head to indicate I should join him.

"No." I shook my head. "No, I think I'll stay." I couldn't leave City – not alone with a reamer. I even took a step, but Cosimo was too quick. He grabbed my wrist and jerked me towards him so I had to either jump or fall. I jumped, the boat swaying as I landed so hard I fell anyway.

By the time I regained my feet, rubbing my bruised shins, he had unfastened the ropes tying the boat to the quayside and we were drifting in the water.

I reached out, but the metal pontoons of the quay had already vanished as we were pulled away by the current. I stared into the fog, hoping someone would appear. What I wanted, in my foolish heart, was for my father to loom out of the fog, running to fetch me and take me home. But there was nothing. I could try to swim, but the darkness in the fog was so absolute I wouldn't trust to find my way safely. I was trapped, with a reamer I didn't know and didn't trust.

Cosimo shuggled the knapsack my father had given him down his arms so it dropped onto the deck of the boat, landing beside the medical bag I'd rescued. I dropped my bag on the deck and stared at them. Three bags but only two people where there should have been three. I shivered and wrapped my arms around myself, wishing they were Pa's arms hugging me.

The boy pulled an oar from the bottom of the boat, thrusting it through the water on one side then striding to the other and dipping it in again.

I moved the bags and myself out of his way and sat on a convenient board that ran around the edge of the boat, judging that to be safer than standing. Hugging my father's medical bag to my chest, I looked at the water surrounding us and the few lights that were visible on City. My home, slipping out of reach.

The reamer took a disparaging glance at me, grunted something that could have been anything, and continued to push us away from City. I tried to decide what to do next. Pa was dead. My brain froze on that fact and wouldn't go any further.

We were alone on the sea. I clutched the medical bag, holding back my shivers. My father was dead. It couldn't be real, but my hand wrapped around his bag was gummy with drying blood. Shuddering, I pushed past the boy to dip my hand into the sea. The boat lurched to one side. Cosimo made another hissing, cursing noise and pushed me back, "Sit."

"I need to clean my hand." I held it up, although I wasn't sure how much he'd be able to make out in the near-darkness.

He pointed to the side of the boat where we weren't. "Balance."

When I stood and moved where he directed, the boat didn't move so much and I realised the sense of what he'd said. I dipped my hand into water so cold it numbed. The boy pulled the oar and we floated onwards. There was little sound and less sight. We might have been the only people in the world, cocooned in the dark. When my hand was chill and clean, I sat down again.

"Sorry. 'Bout your pa." It was the longest sentence the boy had spoken since his operation. I knew it must hurt him to speak, but I didn't care. I would gladly rip the devices from his neck if I thought it would bring my father back.

"You should be."

I huddled against the boat's side, clinging to Pa's bag. I willed myself not to weep, but the tears slid unbidden from my eyes. I bit the inside of my cheek, determined at least to stay silent.

*

Maybe a minute later there was a grunt. I looked up. The boy was holding out a cup of water. I took it, glad of something – anything – to do. I took a sip, my shaking hands rattling the cup against my teeth. My tears kept coming. It was embarrassing, with him looming there. I looked away.

If he'd had any manners at all he would have gone away and given me some privacy. Instead, he sat down, so close I could feel the warmth of his body.

A few seconds later, he put an arm awkwardly

around my shoulders.

    I wanted to shake him off. By the tides, I itched to slap the skinny gorm for his odious presumption. But he was warm. He smelled of the soap from his operation, overlaid with sweat, but not in a bad way, just a human one. As much as I wanted to push him away, I longed to cling to him and howl. I closed my eyes, tried not to think, and let the tears fall.

*

When I was composed enough to reach for the handkerchief tucked into my sleeve, I used the movement to nudge Cosimo away. He took the hint.

    He stowed the oar and pulled on a rope which sent a sail slithering up the mast in the centre of the vessel. The patchwork of discoloured bits of plastic sheeting fastened together snapped as it stretched and filled with air, propelling us forward. The boy didn't look at me as he worked, his back stiff. Once more that unwelcome guilt squeezed my chest and I rooted in my father's bag. When Cosimo's activity stopped, I held out two small bottles.

    A nautilus man had brought a whole sack of bounty when they'd found a hospital in the drowned buildings of the town beneath our feet. I'd picked through the bottles, most of which miraculously still had names printed onto the plastic, and complained that surely they wouldn't be any use after all this time. Pa, who had looked like a child on Christmas Day, had said he might as well try them since he had nothing better to offer. To this day they'd at least done no harm.

    "To prevent infection." I handed him the first, then the second, telling him, "And for the pain. We normally prescribe two days of rest after the procedure."

    He grunted understanding, then snatched the pills. The boat rocked gently as he jumped down a few steps in the middle, disappearing into a covered area.

    A moment later, he returned with another cup of

water. I leaned forward and touched one bottle. "One, four times a day, and take all that are in the bottle." He nodded. I touched the painkillers. "When you need them, take two at once. But no more than eight in a day."

He nodded again. I looked around the boat as he threw back his head to swallow, seeking something that would distract me from thoughts of what I'd left behind. "Is this your boat?"

He shot me a glance I couldn't interpret. "Is now."

Of course. A thief. Small wonder reamers got their reputation. But that couldn't explain all of it. No one would kill my father just because he'd helped a thief. My father *wouldn't* help a common thief. At least, I didn't think he would. Tears brimmed again and I blinked them back. Crying wouldn't help. I needed information. I blinked until I trusted my voice. "Why did you come to my father? Why did you want to undertake the nautilus procedure?"

The boy shrugged, sullen and unwilling to answer. I already knew his reply couldn't do him credit, but it was pointless to evade my questions now. It must have been something truly awful. I shivered. The sea breeze was bitter.

He moved to the front of the boat again, disappearing into the covered section. When he reappeared, he thrust something at me. It was a blanket, damp with the mist and smelly for reasons I didn't want to investigate. But it was warm when I wrapped it around me.

"Sleep," he told me, jerking a thumb towards the cabin.

I wouldn't have done anything he said just for the telling, and I knew I was too overwrought to relax. I glanced back. It was too dark to be sure of anything, but the mist was lighter. I thought I could see lights behind us, more distant than I would have thought possible in the time we'd had to travel. I took a deep breath. The air was cool but clear of fog, the half-moon bright overhead. I closed my eyes and saw in my memory the unbearable sight of my father's body, cold and alone on the pontoons of the alleyway. I couldn't leave him like that. "Take me back. Please." I had to cover my face with an edge of the blanket the boy had given me, soaking up the tears that returned with renewed energy.

"Can't go back." The boy was stubborn. I wanted to argue, but I had no breath to speak.

Perhaps he wasn't stubborn. He was more likely to be terrified. As an unlicensed nautilus man, he faced death if City caught him. "There's no need to be afraid. I know the Magistrate. I can speak to him. You won't be punished for the procedure." I was promising things that weren't within my gift, but if the boy swore allegiance there was no reason why the Magistrate wouldn't accept him. We needed nautilus men.

"Thought you were clever."

Heat rose in my face at his tone. "Cleverer than you, reamer boy," I spat back.

"Your father's murderer?"

"The Magistrate can protect us from him."

The boy shook his head. "Stupid," he growled.

Heat rose. "If you think we'll be safer with your reamer friends, then you're the stupid one."

"Not safe anywhere," he stated. I went cold, then reminded myself that he was a reamer. He wanted me frightened and feeble. I wouldn't give him the satisfaction.

"If you won't go back, where is forward?" I looked into the black distance ahead. The Wastes surrounded us entirely. It was where the reamers lived when they weren't troubling us, an area so vast I could be lost forever once they got hold of me.

There was a long silence until I realised the truth, regarding him in surprise. "You don't know, do you?"

Cold slid down my spine at his silence. He was as

lost as I was. I took a deep breath and made my decision. "Take me back to City. Leave me there and you can go wherever you want."

He ignored my offer. "Sleep. Late."

"No. Turn back."

The reamer shook his head. "Too late."

It wasn't too late. It wasn't allowed to be too late. I wouldn't let it be. I opened my mouth to argue, to order him to do as I said, but the words wouldn't come. My tears had taken my energy, as had arguing with him. It was already tomorrow, and my body was shaky with fatigue and shock. If I had been my patient, I would have diagnosed sleep – and a warm fire. That was something else I'd left behind on City and had no idea when – or if – I would find again. I stumbled in the direction Cosimo indicated, halting when the lantern light flashed on the steep steps down into the boat's cabin. I'd be trapped in the dark. What if we sank? I heard movement behind me and forced myself down the steps before the reamer could think I was afraid.

In the cold, damp-smelling cabin I wedged myself into a corner, wrapped the blanket high around my cheeks and leaned against the wooden side, hoping I'd find an edge of peace in the darkness that I could slip into.

Chapter Six

I awoke stiff and cold, but the dawn light made everything clearer.

Unfortunately, what was clearest was the danger I was in. If the reamer took me to the Wastes and handed me over to his friends, I was lost – tortured for City's secrets and dead soon after, most likely.

And then I'd never find out who had killed my father and why. I had to get back to City. On my own, if the reamer wouldn't take me.

"Morning." Clambering onto the deck, I spoke the greeting to get Cosimo's attention. If I gained his trust, maybe I could convince him to go to sleep below decks and then steal the boat while he was unconscious, but I needed to know how to operate the thing first. I'd been raised on City, surrounded by water, but I'd never been on a boat before. There'd been no need – where would I go?

The reamer, who was doing something to the boat – something I needed to understand and didn't yet – glanced towards me and grunted. Perhaps his throat was hurting him, which was no more than he deserved. I took a breath. Trust. I needed him to trust me, and I needed to stop my dislike ruling me.

"I should check the devices," I told him.

He stopped, turning. A gust of wind pushed his hair across his forehead. He looked ruddy-cheeked and indecently healthy. I probably looked like salvage: tired, grey and with any value well hidden beneath dirt.

"Why? Wouldn't you be happy if Ah caught an infection and died?"

His voice was fully recovered, accent and all. I'd preferred him when he was silent. Although not much. "My father doesn't lose patients." Then my brain caught up with my words and grief pulled my face down. That, I didn't have to fake.

"Doesn't hurt." Cosimo crossed to my side, showing more confidence than seemed decent to me. "Least, hardly at all." He stopped and tilted his chin up.

Professionalism took over. I checked the neat stitches and found them whole and healing well. "No heat?"

"No."

"And no soreness inside your throat? No scratchiness?"

"No. Nothing worse than a cold."

"And you're answering me with words instead of grunts. My father would be pleased with you." I turned quickly away so he wouldn't see the tears that brimmed to the surface.

"Did a good job. Deserves his reputation."

I nodded and stared at the waves, blinking. As the scene slid into focus, I noticed how beautiful it was. Peaceful. There was no clamour, like there always was on City. My home was a blur on the horizon. It looked so small, a threadbare raft of tin and plastic. The last civilised city in the world, it was only five miles in each direction, but it had never seemed as tiny as it did when I watched it now, hopelessly out of reach. The only other place that had survived the rising of the waves was New Eden, but I couldn't see a trace of that smudge of land. The only thing visible against the sea and the sky was the line of grey that marked the Wastes. Reamer territory. I turned to Cosimo. "Where are we going?"

He stiffened. "Ah'm taking us both to the Wastes."

Lucky me – where a short, painful life of torture to give away City's secrets beckoned. "I have to go to City. I have to know what happened to my father." I took a deep breath. "Please."

"City killed your father," he told me, not even having the grace to look at me while he pulled at the sail. "Ah'm not going back."

So I was on my own. I took another deep breath. "Are we far from the Wastes?" I couldn't tell how far away the line of grey was. I might have only hours, a day, or a week to escape.

"It'll take a while."

"And how long is that?" I tried to sound innocent to set him at ease, but I hated what I heard. I sounded like an imbecile. I cleared my throat while I calculated how better to phrase my queries.

Cosimo ignored my inane question. Instead, he made some adjustment to the sail. I couldn't see what he'd done, although the boat pulled more smoothly through the waves afterwards.

I leaned against the edge of the boat, gazing back to where City was almost gone from sight. "Why did my father make you a nautilus man?" The reamers wanted our technology – of course they did. But just because they wanted it was no reason for my father to break City's laws and share what he'd worked so hard to create.

I didn't expect an answer so was surprised when he said, "We need metal. With the gills Ah can find it."

"Why don't you just steal it from City? That's what reamers usually do." I could have bitten off my tongue when I said that. Telling the reamer a few home truths wasn't going to earn his trust.

"We aren't thieves, your Highness," he snapped.

"Of course you are. That's why a few of you are dragged in front of the Magistrate each month to receive justice," I snapped back. And cursed silently again. Why could I not appease this wretched youth however I tried?

"You call what your Magistrate does to reamers justice?"

Heat rose in me. "Thieves get what they deserve."

He didn't answer. It was possible he was too busy with the boat to hear. I remembered him and my father whispering together. Pa knew what was going on. Pa clearly approved, since he'd made Cosimo a nautilus man. But Cosimo wouldn't trust me with what he'd told Pa.

And I wasn't going to trust him if he didn't give me reason to. "The Magistrate does what he must to keep order."

"*Your* order." His face was flushed. Mine was probably the same.

All ideas of appeasing him were thrown overboard. "Yes, *our* order, because you reamers don't have any order at all."

"That's what you think."

It was more than what I thought. It was what everyone on City knew. I sat down on the ledge that ran around the edge of the boat and glared at the sea.

*

After a minute or two, my agitation dissipated. I glanced at Cosimo. He was watching the sea ahead, as though he didn't have a care in the world. Probably, he didn't. He was returning home in triumph. My future was much less certain. "What's going to happen when we get to … your people?"

There was a pause. Cosimo looked as though he couldn't decide whether to tell me or not. Anger rose. Who did he fear I might tell, in the middle of the sea as we were?

"Ah promised your father Ah'd keep you safe, whatever happened," he admitted at last.

"Are you saying I'll be safe with the reamers?" I'd said he'd be safe with me to speak up for him on City. Did he mean safe like that, or did he mean properly safe, like I'd imagined I was right up until last night? It was hard to set any store by the promise he claimed to have made. My father was dead because Cosimo had washed up at our door. And I couldn't believe the reamer truly cared whether I lived or died. Unless it was because he wasn't fully recovered and feared dying without my medical supervision.

He shook his head, and anger flared through me. Perhaps I should be pleased he didn't simply lie to me, but I wasn't. "Ah don't think anyone's safe."

A shiver ran down my spine at his tone. "Why? What's happened?"

He laughed. He didn't sound amused. "We live on a century-old rubbish heap. City is a raft of plastic. You think that's safe?"

"It's been safe enough so far."

Another laugh. "You're delusional, your Highness."

Another shiver twitched down my spine. Life was precarious. Did he think that was news to me?

"What do you know about nautilus devices?" he asked, changing the subject.

"What do you want to know?" Was he asking nicely for City's secrets so his people wouldn't need to torture me to get the information?

He made a sound of impatience. "Ah want to know what you know about nautilus devices."

My heart bounced against my ribs. I swallowed, then answered pleasantly, as though it was of no consequence. "I was my father's assistant. I'm familiar with the principles."

"Do you know how the devices work?"

I watched his face as I told him what any fool on City knew. "They convert the gases trapped in water into a form of air the human body can use." Well, perhaps any fool on City wouldn't have expressed it so clearly.

"How?"

"That's the principle," I snapped. "I'm not my father. If you wanted to know the details, you shouldn't have got him killed."

"Ah didn't get him killed," Cosimo snarled.

"Really? You arrive, and twelve hours later he's dead. There's got to be a connection."

"Your precious Magistrate killed him."

The breath in my lungs evaporated at that lie. "The Magistrate was my father's friend. But I don't expect you to understand something like friendship."

His eyes narrowed as though he wanted to hit me. I folded my arms and glared at him. I wanted him to. It would give me an unequivocal excuse to push him into the sea. I tried to think of something that would push either of us over the edge, then my stomach growled a resounding rumble.

Perhaps it was good to be brought back to reality before I put the possibility of a truce forever out of reach. "Is there anything to eat on this wretched tub?" My stomach gave another fierce gurgle, almost drowning out the words.

The boy scowled, as though I shouldn't have asked the question.

"Well? You must be hungrier than I am; it's longer since you ate." Unless he had a secret stash of food hidden somewhere on board. There was nothing in the cabin aside from the cask of fresh water. I had checked.

He rose to his feet and gave me an insolent bow. "My apologies, your Highness. Ah didn't realise my hospitality was so lacking." He jumped onto the back of the vessel, dragging my heart into my throat, until I realised he was just being showy. He shielded his eyes from the sun, scanning the waves. "Ah didn't have a chance to restock. Ah didn't know we'd be leaving so quickly."

He stomped back along the planks and leaned over the side of the boat, causing it to pitch alarmingly. I gasped and grabbed the edge of the seat before I could stop the sound of fear. My face warmed, but I didn't think the boy had heard. He was too busy peering into the depths of the sea. Then he straightened and turned to me. "You're hardly likely to starve with a nautilus man on board, are you?"

"You shouldn't dive for a week." I'd repeated my father's advice without thinking. He never lost a patient, because he was careful and because they did as he bid them.

The boy raised his brows. "You can wait that long for breakfast?"

I hardened my heart. It didn't matter if he drowned or died of an infection. At least, it only mattered if he did so before I learned how to control the boat. The only thing more terrifying than being in the power of this reamer youth was the thought of drifting hopelessly alone across the waves until I bumped into the Wastes or starved to death in the middle of the sea, alone and helpless.

Crossing to the back of the boat, he tied a length of rope to the steering stick to keep it steady.

"I'm sure I can keep us on course while you're gone." I adopted an innocent tone. I didn't suppose I could get us all the way back to City in the hour he'd spend diving, but if I could set us in the right direction, I might have been able to overpower Cosimo when he returned to the surface. If I was lucky, there would be some chloroform in my father's bag.

"Ah'd rather not take the chance."

I tried not to bristle at his poor manners. "I'm a quick learner."

A smile twitched his lips. "Then maybe there's

hope for you, your Highness." He surveyed the sea around us, turning slowly, hand raised once more to shade his eyes.

"My name's Liberty," I told him. We were stuck on the boat together until I managed to escape. There was no option but to allow him that small familiarity if I didn't want to answer to his annoying nickname.

He dropped his hand. "Oh, Ah know that, your Highness."

Irritation gnawed at me. Before I thought of an adequate put-down, he'd pulled his shirt over his head. His feet were already bare. When his hands went to his waistband, I called out for him to stop.

He looked at me with a mocking expression. "Mah, mah, your Highness. Ah had no idea you were so easily shocked."

My face flamed. "I'm not." I straightened my spine. "I'm hardly likely to be shocked by *you*. I've seen far worse sights. And far more impressive ones. I just meant – you don't need to remove your clothes. It's not as though they might weigh you down and drown you."

I turned away from his sardonic expression. If he was reading my mind, he was correct. Right that moment I would be perfectly glad if he did drown. "And you might appreciate the warmth."

"Ah'd sooner have something dry to put on when Ah get back, but your Highness's wish is of course mah command." He swept me a deep, mocking bow that made the boat rock, and my knuckles tightened on the board beneath my thighs.

Instead of undressing further, he made the boat judder again as he strode around, dropping the sail to the deck, pushing the anchor stone overboard to keep the boat from drifting while he was diving, finding a rope and fastening one end to the boat and the other around his waist.

I hitched further along the bench and peered into

the water. It was clear. I could see a long way down, shapes looming out of the grey. Despite myself, I was curious. Pa had taught me well. In his absence, I could conduct the procedure and transform someone into a nautilus man, but I would never be one myself. No women were allowed to undergo the procedure. I wondered how it felt to swim amongst the houses beneath the waves, whether you could imagine yourself in the Time Before. I looked up at Cosimo perched on the edge of the boat. A wave of something like jealousy swept through me, followed rapidly by anger. What was it about the wretched reamer that brought out the very worst in me?

"Come up if you feel any pain. And best not stay down much longer than half an hour. The chill is more of a danger than the water itself."

It was honest medical advice, but of course he took it the wrong way. "Ah'll be as quick as Ah can, your Highness. Wouldn't want you to faint of hunger."

I wouldn't give him the satisfaction.

Chapter Seven

He sat on the edge of the boat, legs dangling into the water for ages. I managed not to snap at him to get on with it, and after a minute I realised he was probably scared. First dive, it would be alarming for anyone, and Cosimo didn't have a more experienced nautilus man to guide him through, as was normally the case. My chest clenched with an odd feeling of sympathy for him.

When he still didn't move, I cleared my throat and advised him, "You need to breathe with your lungs, not your nose."

He didn't reply to that, or even acknowledge I'd spoken, and my sympathy evaporated into impatience. "Nautilus man or not, you can still drown."

"Kind of you to remind me."

"I'm trying to help!" I took a breath and stared at the heavens so the sight of him couldn't stoke my irritation further. "If you relax, your body will do everything for you. Just don't breathe in through your nose or mouth."

Finally, he pushed away from the boat and slipped into the water. I leaned over the edge to peer after him. He was just beneath the waves, close enough that he could lift his head above the water if he panicked. I watched until I saw the lift of his back that meant his lungs – and the gills – were working as they should. Then he turned a showy somersault and pushed into the depths of the water.

I watched until he'd disappeared into the gloom, then checked the rope that connected him to the boat. When I was sure he'd gone, I went to the cabin and fetched the bags that were my only remaining trace of City. I wanted an inventory of what I had with me: the contents of Pa's medical bag, and the knapsack he'd pushed into Cosimo's arms, along with the bag I'd packed myself.

My father's knapsack looked as though it had been abandoned by the boy, slung heedlessly into the cabin. More importantly, I'd saved Pa's medical bag. With that, I was Dr Miracle's daughter, and a skilled medical practitioner. Without it, I was nothing.

I stared hard at the grey horizon behind us. I couldn't see anything except water, but maybe someone was following us. I should have thought of that before. Surely I was important enough for that? They would know I was missing. Belle and Foo – even Hannah – would realise I had disappeared. The Magistrate would send help. Perhaps Will or Josiah Keyne would come after me. My heart lurched, although I wasn't sure if I was pleased or alarmed at the idea. My thoughts took a practical turn. My friends would know I was missing, but they wouldn't know I'd been taken away from City. If they found my father's body, they might think I'd been killed likewise and my body rolled into the sea, never to be found.

I swallowed. But there was a chance one of City's salvage barges would come across us by accident. That would do.

A glance at the rope the reamer had tied to himself showed it was still taut. I leaned over the side and saw no looming shape in the water. As far as I could tell, he wasn't about to reappear.

Sitting down, I hefted the knapsack into my lap, pulled the medical bag along the deck towards me and settled to explore the extent of my current worldly possessions. With the medical bag I had a profession, which was more than most females my age could boast. Perhaps the gorms Cosimo called friends wouldn't kill me if they thought I might be useful.

Let's hope I didn't have to test that idea.

I opened the bag and took a quick inventory. There was a range of medicines to treat everyday ailments. A slim bottle of chloroform and six nautilus devices, three pairs. At the bottom was a book of anatomy. When I opened it, I found a diagram of a nautilus device folded inside with neat descriptions in my father's writing of each element needed to compose the whole. I folded it carefully and replaced it within the book, then with some difficulty, tucked the book into the inside pocket of my coat. I didn't want that to fall into reamer hands. I had supposed that with my father's death had died the hopes of City. I could perform the procedure, but I couldn't make a nautilus device – my father had done that alone. But with the diagram, perhaps I could find a craftsman skilled enough to make more.

The last thing I drew from the medical bag was the box containing the tiny metalworking tools he used to construct the devices. I sighed a slow breath. Had my father known he wouldn't return to City, and been careful to take his profession with him? Had he wanted to be sure the technology wouldn't fall into the wrong hands? I placed the tools carefully back into their box. Had he believed that wrong hands were to be found on City? A breeze tugged at my hair and I shivered. His murderer might have run straight to our house, ransacking it to find what my father had hidden away. I was glad I'd stumbled upon the medical bag and brought it with us.

I wondered if Cosimo had any notion how valuable the cargo on his boat was. Anyone would give a fortune for what I held on my lap right now. The reamers would be fools not to treat me well if I really had no option but to go to them. Provided I was prepared to break City's laws and share our secrets with strangers. I touched my throat. The Magistrate would see me hanged for that, Dr Miracle's daughter or not.

Closing the medical bag, I tucked it against the side of the boat, behind my heels. Next was the knapsack, packed by my father and given to Cosimo. The hasp clicked open and I delved inside. My father's best coat. The one that hung in his wardrobe, never worn. I heaved the heavy thing to one side. Grudgingly, I thought the reamer might use it if he was cold after diving. It was a good coat, long, well made from thick wool, passed down from the Time Before but hardly patched at all. Then came an outfit of clothes. I frowned. I didn't recognise them. No one on City ever threw anything away, but if these had ever belonged to Pa I'd have thought they would have been passed on years ago to someone who could use them, because my father would certainly have no use for them. I held a shirt aloft and my frown deepened. If this had ever fit my father, it must have been years ago, being clearly made for someone with a slighter build. I dragged everything onto my lap, my heart bumping against my ribs as I tried to make sense of what I found. Trousers, a shirt, underwear that wouldn't fit my father – but would be perfect for Cosimo. I thought he had arrived on our doorstep with nothing. Why had he presented himself to us in clothes that would disgrace my ragbag if he had this respectable wardrobe with him? If it were the case that Cosimo had arrived with only the rags he stood up in, why had my father dug in his drawers for these as though it were his job to provide for the boy?

My head hurt. There were too many questions and no answers. I pushed the clothes aside and looked deeper, but there was no more in the bag. I replaced everything, pausing when I folded my father's coat to lay it over the rest. It wasn't just the thickness of the woollen fabric that made it heavy. Something was sewn into the hem.

A glance at the sea showed it peaceful, undisturbed. A nautilus man could stay beneath the waves as long as he wished. I wasn't sure whether anyone had yet found a limit. Perhaps there was no limit. Except that Cosimo was diving in rags rather than a proper suit. The cool water should drive him to the surface soon. My stomach growled and for pragmatic reasons, I hoped he wouldn't try to test his new abilities to any sort of limit.

I spread the coat over my lap, my fingers finding the hem. The stitches were neat, even, competent work. But they weren't ones I'd placed in the garment. By the time I had worked my nail into a tiny gap and forced it large enough to reveal the hem's contents, I had already guessed what I was going to find. Gold. Big, fat, golden circles, evenly melted and forged into a highly portable, highly tradable form. Twenty of them, which was enough to make a thousand nautilus devices, or to feed a person for a lifetime. They were evenly spaced around the hem so it would hang properly and give no clue as to its extra contents. With the coins in my lap and the messy hem dangling, I tried to remember what my father had said: Whatever trouble we were in, it was there long before the boy had arrived on our doorstep. My father had ... what? *Planned* this?

No. If my father had planned our escape, I wouldn't be sitting here waiting for a stranger to fetch a handful of tins from the sea for our breakfast. But my father must have known more than he had told me. He had known – or feared – that we might one day have to flee. He was Dr Miracle, saviour of City, and yet he hadn't believed himself safe.

I shivered and cast another glance over the sea towards the vanished blur that was City. No boats were dashing across the waves towards me. Now, I wasn't sure whether I wanted them to. For the first time, I wondered whether I was wise to want to return home. I had to face the fact that my father had intended our flight to be a one-way journey – to the reamers? Surely not.

Perhaps to New Eden, the other civilised place left on Earth, the last tiny piece of undrowned land. A moment's reflection showed that to be just as unlikely. If my father made the people of New Eden into nautilus men, his life would still be forfeit. Only City dwellers were permitted the procedure. If he was risking his life, it had to be for a good reason. Or a very, very bad one.

Cosimo's mother, so my father had said, was an old friend. I could hardly credit such a thing, but I had to suppose that my father had intended us to go to the reamers, with all Dr Miracle's science.

If only I understood the reason my father had decided to run. Cosimo knew. I'd bet all the gold I'd just found that he did. I needed a way to compel him to tell me.

I folded my father's coat and replaced it in the knapsack, along with half the gold. The remainder went into my pockets. I decided not to tell the boy what I'd found. The likelihood was that he'd tip me over the side for the sake of the gold, even without the nautilus devices. He was at best a criminal – at worst, I couldn't even imagine. I wished I hadn't had such a sheltered upbringing, so that I might have seen a bit more of life by the age of seventeen. Then, perhaps I wouldn't feel so at sea.

I glanced at the water lapping the boat and laughed silently at myself.

Chapter Eight

The lurch of the boat was my only warning before Cosimo clambered back on board. There was a clatter as he tipped his finds onto the deck. Half a dozen tins covered in grey slime. "Breakfast, your Highness." My hunger vanished. He leaned back over the side of the boat, washing the tins in the sea.

When he stood, chest heaving with exertion, my eyes went automatically to the devices in his neck to check that the stitches were holding. "How do you feel?"

"Tired. And cold." He stomped towards the cabin.

Much as I didn't want to help him, there was no point him freezing to death. Yet. I dug in the knapsack and walked across the deck. "Here." I stuck the clothes through the gap without entering, in case he was already undressed. "My father packed these. You might as well use them."

There was a tug on my fingers as the clothes were snatched from my grip. No word of thanks, but I knew better than to expect that.

I sat back down and shaded my eyes to look at the sea around us. The sun was higher, sparkling on the waves. The reflected light made it difficult to see. There might be other boats approaching, or we could be utterly alone.

The only sound was the slap of the waves against the boat's sides. If we were to get anywhere we'd need to refasten the sail that Cosimo had undone so the boat wouldn't travel too far while he was diving. I wondered if he would show me how it was done. If not I'd learn from watching. Pa had taught me to be observant.

"I've opened the tins. Why would he do that?" The boy stepped back onto the deck, combining two trains of thought in one conversation and trusting me to catch up.

"I've no idea why my father packed things for you. I thought you might know." I turned, taken aback by how much a decent set of clothes improved the boy. Clean from the sea, wet hair smoothed back from his brow, he looked almost ... the word handsome floated into my head, but it wasn't going to go any further than that – handsome would be overstating the matter. He looked fit to be seen.

He tucked the steering stick under his arm, sat back and dug into the tin he'd chosen. My stomach rumbled and I ventured to the cabin to see what delicacies were available.

He'd taken sweetcorn. The other open tins held pineapple, mashed peas and minced meat. I wished, as I did most times I set to cook a meal, that it was possible to know what was within the tins before we opened them. I guessed the Old Ones hadn't imagined their labels might need to be waterproof.

The pineapple would taste of nothing more than the tin it had been encased in, so I took the minced meat from the ledge inside the cabin, found a fork and returned to the deck. I sat at the back of the boat, close enough to him to watch what he did with the boat's controls without being so close he might get presumptuous ideas.

The air smelt fresher here than it ever did in City. A breeze tugged at my hair. There was no one within sight – except the boy, Cosimo – and nothing that had to be done. Perhaps there were advantages to a reamer's lifestyle, although not many.

He finished eating and dropped his tin and fork to the deck. It seemed to signal a return to normality. I swallowed my mouthful. "My father said your mother was an old friend. How did Dr Miracle get to be friends with a reamer?"

Cosimo ignored me yet again, striding to the side of the boat and heaving the anchor stone back up to the deck, muscles bunching and shifting as he did so, face growing pink with the exertion. I might have given him a hand – if he'd deigned to ask for my assistance.

He didn't, annoying me further by managing perfectly well on his own. The mast was his next destination, where he yanked the sail up to flap and fill with wind. We started forward with a perceptible jolt. Cosimo sat down at the back of the boat, slipping the restraining rope off the steering stick and adjusting our course. I watched it all and hoped I'd remember what he'd done.

"She wasn't always a reamer, you know." Another odd start to conversation, but I was growing used to them. I knew immediately that he meant his mother. "She grew up on City."

I stared. "Why on earth did she leave?" No one, with any sense, would give up a stable life on City to set up camp on the Wastes and steal for survival.

"We aren't all born into a life of privilege like you, your Highness. She ran away."

"From what?"

His jaw tightened. I didn't think he'd answer me, but he did. "From mah father."

"Why in the seas would she do that?" Run away from her husband? What a ridiculous idea. You made your life and you lived it.

"Why do women usually run from men? She was afraid. She hated him. Both."

I waited, but nothing else followed. "Aren't you curious about him?" I thought of my mother, and the void I'd never fill. And I at least had eight years of memories to sustain me.

"If she'd wanted me to know, she'd have told me. He was a liar and not to be trusted. That's all she ever said." Cosimo peered off to the side of the boat, as though there was something fascinating to be seen.

Watching him, stiff and sulky, I wondered what his life had been like before he'd arrived on our doorstep. I wasn't stupid, I knew most people didn't enjoy the privileged life that had been mine until yesterday, but it was odd to think he might have had to do without any of the certainties I enjoyed. My family was happy. My mother had died when I was young, but my father had adored her, loved her still, even years later. And I knew I had been loved by both of them. How odd, not to be sure of your place in a family, never mind a city. "Why did your mother send you to City?"

"To get the gills."

I knew that wasn't the whole of it. "And?"

"None of your gorming business."

I hadn't thought he'd give me a straight answer. "If you tell me, I might be able to help."

His voice was filled with a fury I recognised. "Ah don't want your help."

"And I never wanted yours, but look at us. Why don't we call a truce? For the duration of this voyage, anyhow?"

"You're not mah friend, your Highness. You're … the very high price Ah've had to pay for this." He waved towards his gills, turning at last to look at me.

"You didn't have to bring me with you."

"You'd be dead at the docks if Ah hadn't."

"And what would that matter to you?"

He turned away, leaving me watching his stiff back. My father had thought this boy worth helping, and he wasn't usually a bad a judge of character. I shook myself. Feeling sorry for the reamer was a bad idea until

I could be sure who was friend and who foe.

I considered how to get more information from the close-mouthed gorm. He wasn't even paying me any attention, looking out at the horizon while he chewed. Then he got showy again and stood on the lip of wood at the back of the boat, peering at the waves.

"What are you looking at?" I snapped at last. "There's nothing to see."

He jumped back onto the deck, rattling the deck. "That, your Highness, is where you're wrong."

He vanished into the cabin while I twisted to see where he'd been looking, my heart thrilling with the hope – or fear – of rescue. Nothing. Nothing but the sun glinting off the tops of the waves and dazzling me. I glanced towards the cabin but nothing would induce me to go begging to Cosimo to ask what it was he saw. Patience was important for a physician. I folded my hands in my lap, stared the other way, and waited.

*

It wasn't much later that Cosimo returned. He made a few changes to the sails. I tried not to look as though I was watching him. I pressed my teeth together so I wouldn't beg him to tell me what he'd seen.

After looking behind several times, I gave in. "I can't see anything. What do you think you saw?"

"Ah don't *think* Ah saw anything, Ah know Ah saw a boat." My heart leapt. It might have been fear, or the opposite. "It's a way off. Might be chance, or could be following us."

He was doing things to our boat, too fast for me to keep track. "Are we trying to get away?" He could be taking me further from help – or away from danger.

"Not from the boat, no."

"What then?"

"If you knew anything about anything, your Highness, you'd know the weather's changing."

Into what? I glanced up. There were more clouds in

the sky than earlier, the sun blocked behind their grey. "What does that mean?"

"Means Ah wish we hadn't just stayed still for an hour." He made it sound like that was my fault. He sat down and made another adjustment. I couldn't detect a difference, but I guessed he was trying to goad a little more speed from the vessel.

I swallowed down my annoyance. "Is there something I can do? To help?"

He didn't even take the time to consider my offer. "Unlikely."

"I'm not stupid, you know!" I shouldn't allow him to irritate me, but really, remaining calm was impossible.

"Quite the opposite, your Highness," he agreed. "You're far too clever to be of any use to me."

"You could explain how the boat works, and I could help."

"Ah don't have the time to teach you how to sail a boat in the space of half an hour."

I took a deep breath and spoke evenly. "Perhaps not. Just as I couldn't make you a doctor in the time it takes us to reach ... your people. But I could teach you to apply pressure to a wound, and how to clean and bind it so it heals healthily."

There was no answer, but I expected that. I waited and stared at the seam ahead of us where grey sea became grey Wastes. We were getting closer to the reamers with every minute, even if I couldn't yet see them. After what I'd found in Pa's bags, I wasn't sure whether I wanted to get there, or anywhere but.

If I could only control the boat so I didn't have to rely on Cosimo, I could relax. I'd have options. With Cosimo's surly back turned to me, it was unlikely to happen.

Then he heaved a sigh and twisted to face me. "Very well. Sit here." He cleared a space for me so I could sit beside the steering stick. "This is the tiller." He patted the stick. "It controls the rudder, which keeps the boat on course. Ah need you to keep it steady."

I sat down and curled my hand around the worn wood. It was warm to the touch, fitting my palm as though it welcomed me. I reflected on all the hands that must have rested here before me, then Cosimo's fingers around mine shocked me back to the present. "You only need gentle movements." I stared at his cold hand, struggling to focus on what he was saying. "Push the tiller starboard to move the ship to port, and towards port to move the ship starboard." He moved the tiller slightly to indicate the directions.

I frowned at the horizon, then at the boy. "Port? Which port? There's nothing but water here."

He muttered an oath, and I think he might have laughed at me under his breath, although such levity seemed unlikely. "Not a port like a harbour. Port means left when you're on a boat; starboard means right."

I frowned again. "Why not just say left and right?"

"Because you don't. You use the correct words, as Ah'm sure you do with your medicines. That," he pointed, "is the port side of the boat. That," he nodded to indicate the opposite, "is starboard. They remain the same whichever direction you happen to be facing on the boat itself." He grabbed the stick – the tiller. "And *don't* let your course drift because you're looking in a different direction to the one you're travelling."

He removed his hand, although I could still feel where it had covered mine, cold from the water. I focused on the sea, determined to give him nothing to complain about. Until I double-crossed him, tipped him off the boat and returned home, at least. I watched the ruffled waves – was that still my plan?

"With more experience, you'll be able to do it without thinking. For now, just keep us heading towards the sun and make sure the sails stay filled with air. You only need small corrections."

I nodded, and then practised being innocent. "What if we need to turn? More than just a tiny correction, that is."

"Ah'll deal with any large manoeuvres we need to make."

Wretched creature. It was as though he didn't trust me.

"Ah'll put up the spinnaker."

I didn't ask him what that was, simply watched. It soon became apparent that the spinnaker was another sail. The pole in the middle of the boat, sorry, the mast, looked barely strong enough to take his weight, but Cosimo scooted up it with one end of the sail – more patchwork of random materials – held between his teeth. He was probably being showy again, but it did seem a practical way to free his hands, and at the top, he held on with his knees while he fastened the sail to the top of the mast. Then he shinned down to the deck and fastened the edges of the sail – it was triangular – out to each side so it spread beyond the first sail. The boat pulled as the spinnaker filled with air and boosted us forward.

When he was done, the boy stood for another count of five, watching the sea behind us. I risked a glance, swift so I wouldn't let the boat fall off its course and give him an excuse to complain. I thought I could see something this time, a tiny speck of black on top of the waves. Since I could see it, I supposed that meant it was closer than before. It could be seeking salvage, or it might be following us. My heart jumped with hope, while a nervous shiver fled down my spine. It was odd to realise that I felt safest where I was now. Whatever his intentions regarding my future, Cosimo wasn't an immediate danger to me. The danger waited for me when we reached his people. And maybe it waited for me back home, too.

It was time I decided which alternative I was going

to fight for. "When you knocked on our door, my father was kind to you." I didn't face him, but I felt the boy watching me. "He gave you the gills, made sure you'd be safe. Will your mother extend a similar courtesy to me?"

His voice was as cold as a winter frost. "Unlikely."

I swallowed. At least I knew. Now I just needed to overpower Cosimo and race back to City.

"She's dead."

His voice was so bleak, it took me a moment to comprehend.

"She was murdered." He turned. His expression was so empty I wanted to run, except there was nowhere to run to.

"I'm sorry," I whispered.

"They're all dead. Everyone who'd stopped at that station, save me. And that was only chance."

My voice was hollow. "How many?" The reamers had stations dotted across the Wastes, but if I'd understood the stories correctly, they weren't always occupied, more like way-stations for the reamers to use in their nomadic wanderings.

"Eight of us. Two families."

I closed my eyes. "What happened?" I could hardly speak the words. My father's death was sudden and shocking and I'd assumed it to be a singular event. If it wasn't – if his death had come at the end of others – then my whole world had turned mad. My teeth wanted to chatter and I pressed them together to stop the impulse, waiting for Cosimo to reply.

"*City* happened to us. Your precious Magistrate sent his men to destroy us."

The venom in his tone raised the hairs at the back of my neck. "Why would the Magistrate seek out reamers?" I coloured. I hadn't meant that question to sound as derogatory as it did, although it was true enough. We hanged reamers who came to City to steal or hurt us, but we didn't hate them so much we'd track them down and kill them.

"We had something he wanted."

"What's that, then?"

"As though Ah'd tell you."

My flush increased. I knew he had no more reason to trust me than I did him, but his hatred still hurt. Back home, people who didn't like me at least respected me. Loathing was something new. And unwelcome. "I'm sorry for your loss," I told him quietly. He could take it any way he liked. I knew I was sincere.

He sighed, a long and gusty sound. "Yeah, Ah'm sure you are." He made an effort to throw off his mood. "He's afraid of us." It was shaky, but I heard the triumph he pushed into his tone.

"The Magistrate? Afraid of reamers?"

"He knows his time is coming to an end." He sounded like the crazy philosophers who sometimes haunted the marketplace, urging us all to repent our sins lest the waves rise once more and drown us as they'd drowned everyone in the Time Before.

"That's ridiculous."

"If that's what you choose to believe."

"It's not a question of belief. It's a question of science. It's a question of seeing what's obvious."

"Then Ah advise you to do that, your Highness."

I opened my mouth, seeking a put-down sufficient for his insolence, but the expression on his face silenced me. Waves slapped against the sides of the boat and the vessel shifted beneath me. The tiller twitched in my hand, but I kept it steady. There was nothing but sea all around us. "Where are we going, then? If your people are dead?"

He sighed, and for one cold moment I thought he was going to admit that he didn't know – that we were drifting aimlessly. Finally, he said, "That was only one station. There are others. Reamers spread ourselves over the Wastes, we keep moving. We'll find a welcome elsewhere."

He sounded very sure of himself. Perhaps that was how the reamers did things. Or perhaps it was because he had Dr Miracle's daughter to offer up to them. I shook my head. My father had trusted Cosimo. If I was going with him instead of turning back to City, I needed to do the same. My fingers cramped around the tiller and I swapped hands, stretching out the fingers to be rid of the ache. As though that small change triggered something in my mind, I looked at the boy, blinking as my thoughts cleared. "Does what the Magistrate sought from the reamers have something to do with why you need more metal?"

"Yes." That single word, spoken in a tone that told me asking more was useless.

But my father raised me to be a scientist. If I didn't ask the questions, I'd never find the answers. "What are the reamers planning?"

I didn't think he'd tell me but some caution in him seemed to have washed away. Perhaps he'd decided to trust me. He smiled, triumphant, and, frankly, a little bit crazy. "We're going to find the land of sun and roses."

Chapter Nine

"The land of sun and roses? Beyond the Wastes? That's ridiculous."

"If you say so."

My fists clenched with irritation. "The land of sun and roses is a myth. It's a fairy tale. Something we tell children to encourage them to behave: 'Be good and eat your algae and one day you'll go to the land of sun and roses.'"

"If you say so," he said again.

"You can't cross the Wastes. There isn't an end to them."

"There's an end to everything if you go far enough."

That was logical and made me even more furious. "It's not a real place!"

"So we won't find anything. You sound as though you care we might fail."

"I don't care what reamers do."

Cosimo smirked and I pressed my lips hard together so I wouldn't rise to his provocation. I looked deliberately away from him, focusing on the waves ahead.

He sat on the deck a little way off, watching the sails. I tried to concentrate on the tiller and the waves, but I couldn't settle. His stupid declaration made me jumpy. I wanted to argue with him, but there was no purpose arguing with a madman.

It would be just as worthwhile to pin him to the deck and sit on him until he saw sense. I itched to do that, except my father would be disappointed in me. Cosimo was a patient. I spied sidelong at his throat. The stitches were healing well. Once he was fully recovered, perhaps I could stop thinking of him as a patient and cease to feel obliged to behave with that consideration.

He got to his feet and sauntered around the boat, doing the tides only knew what. I tried to ignore him, truly I did, but either he'd grown or the boat had shrunk. Everywhere I looked – or tried not to – he was there.

"The land of sun and roses doesn't exist. And you'll all starve looking for a way past the Wastes, anyway."

He hid another smirk. "If you say so."

I stared at the horizon so hard my eyes burned.

After a deep breath, I forced myself to adopt a light tone. "A sad loss, but I daresay the rest of us will survive perfectly well." Let him repeat his irritating mantra to that!

He folded his arms and I smiled, knowing I'd annoyed him. "How big is the world?"

"What?" My reply escaped me before I could stop it. He was talking nonsense – not that such a thing should surprise me.

He faced me, the breeze tousling his hair. He threw his arms wide. "How big is the Earth? Do you know, or shall Ah tell you?"

"Of course I know." It took a flustered minute to bring the figure to mind from long-ago lessons. "Circumference is just under twenty-five thousand miles." My tone was snappier than I intended, irritated by the blush I couldn't help at the thought he might suppose I was ignorant.

He smiled. "So where has all the land gone?"

I stared first at him, then looked overboard. He

couldn't seriously need an answer to that one.

"Okay, your Highness, maybe that was the wrong question. Where has all the water come from?"

"The seas rose." I gestured at the waves surrounding us as I repeated the truth every child on City knew by the time they could speak. This was an odd time for the reamer to become curious about natural history.

"Yeah, yeah. The seas rose and covered the lands of the Old Ones in the Time Before." He reeled off the statement as though he'd heard it so often it had become boring. "So where did all the extra water come from?"

"It was always here." I answered too quickly, uncomfortable to realise I didn't know. It was something I'd never considered until now and I was calculating furiously. I could hardly believe my father hadn't posed the question to me.

"You're right. There isn't any 'extra' water. The water that drowns us now has always been here on Earth. But it didn't always cover the land. So it must have moved. To here, from somewhere else. So somewhere in the world it's dry. Somewhere isn't drowned. Somewhere, people live a life worth living."

I summed up his grand declarations. "So, the reamers are looking for a way past the Wastes to where a beautiful land lies waiting? No wonder the Magistrate says you're crazy."

"The Magistrate is an idiot, but Ah thought you were supposed to be clever."

I should have guessed he wouldn't be able to feign civility for long. "Cleverer than you!"

He didn't answer and I wished I hadn't allowed myself to be goaded by his jibe. I wanted to ignore him, but I couldn't stop thinking about the land of sun and roses – what if it *was* real? "You can't cross over the Wastes," I pointed out, arguing with myself as much as him. "They stretch too far."

"Maybe they do."

"Then it's impossible to find anything on the far side."

"Only because walking is too slow."

My heartbeat grew noticeable. The crazy reamers really intended to do it. "How else could you cross the Wastes?" My gaze fixed on his gills and the metal he planned to find. "You're making some sort of a machine?"

"That was the plan."

"Was?"

"Your Magistrate got in the way. Took it for himself before it was complete. Now it's up to me to see if Ah can make another one."

And I, presumably, would be compelled to do what the reamers wanted. My anger faded. Perhaps I would be doing what my father wanted. He would have loved the idea of going in search of the land of sun and roses.

"Why? Why the urgency to find what's beyond the Wastes?"

He shrugged. "The Wastes are a massive rubbish dump. From the Time Before. Did you know that?"

My turn to shrug. "I'd never thought about it."

"That figures."

His tone made me go hot – but what could I protest about? I hadn't spent any time thinking about the reamers' lives, why would I?

"Take mah word for it. We've been mining the Wastes for years, but we're running out of anything useful. We either move, or we die."

It sounded reasonable. I didn't want Cosimo to be reasonable. I wanted him to be the enemy. I needed to get back home so life could get back to normal. I swallowed. Life was never going to be normal, not without Pa.

I concentrated on the tiller and the horizon. A cold wind pushed the sails and the sky was a grey only a few shades different from the sea, making it hard to see anything. A blur of different grey arose in the distance on our right side. Starboard, rather. New Eden, smaller than City, but still more familiar than the Wastes. My last chance to return to civilisation.

Behind us, City was invisible, lost to the waves. Will, Josiah, Hannah and the others were all lost to me if I let them be. I turned back to the way we were going, to the Wastes that were a steady strand of grey against the horizon. The Magistrate said it was impossible to pass the Wastes, that there was nothing past there. But my father must have believed it could be done. And I trusted my father more than I did Mr Keyne. A sensation bubbled through me. I wasn't sure whether it was hope or fear, but the decision was made. I'd go with Cosimo and help the reamers discover a way past the Wastes and find out what lay beyond.

I opened my mouth to tell him – and shut it again. I was already on a boat heading in that direction. I didn't need to tell Cosimo I was willing to go with him since he'd already assumed I'd go – willing or not. There was no one to confide my exhilarating decision to.

I adjusted the tiller and hugged my thoughts to myself, staring at the grey sea and the grey sky and letting myself wonder what the land of sun and roses might actually be like. "I hope you knew what you were doing, Pa," I muttered, too low for the boy to hear. But I didn't really doubt. It was much better to search out the truth than to sit still in ignorance.

*

It was probably an hour later that Cosimo stood, swore and scowled at the horizon. He folded his arms, shoulders stiff, hair tousled by the wind tugging at the sails, glaring as though he could power the boat to the Wastes by willpower alone.

"How much longer before we get there?" The day was advancing more quickly than we were. I was no expert, but it didn't seem to me that we'd be able to reach somewhere that was still a barely distinguishable blur before the autumn day gave way to night.

"It's doubtful we'll get there at all."

"What?" I craned forward, trying to see whatever he could see without letting go the tiller or altering our course.

"The storm looks nasty."

"Huh?" I looked up at the clouds, the tiller wobbling as I did so. Cosimo had to have noticed, but he didn't say anything. "There's a storm?" Immediately, I didn't care whether we arrived in reamer territory or at New Eden, just that we got there before the boat was swallowed by mountainous waves and lashing rain, and we drowned. I looked in fear at the sky, and shivered at the breeze that felt stronger than it had before. Storms were bad enough endured on the relative solidity of City. I didn't want to think what it would be like on this tiny boat.

"That's right, your Highness. The weather's against us."

"What does that mean? Exactly?"

"It means things could get bumpy."

"You mean ..." I stared in horror at the grey clouds, seeing for the first time how angry they looked, puffed up and black and pushing down through the sky towards us. "Are we heading *towards* the storm?"

"More that the storm's heading towards us." Cosimo seemed calm. Reamer gorm that he was, he'd probably sailed through hundreds of them. The only thing I knew about storms was that I didn't want to go through one with nothing solid beneath my feet. What if I were to drown? I knew I ought to be comforted by the idea of being reunited with Pa and my mother, but I'd never really believed the cosy stories telling us of the paradise waiting when we died. Without those fairy tales to fend off oblivion, I was terrified, my heart thudding against my ribs.

"Can't we go around it?"

He laughed, and I was too frightened to hate him for his superiority. "Doesn't work like that." He stepped closer and made a shooing motion. "Ah'll take it from here."

I was only too pleased to let him do so. I turned my back on him and fled down into the bottom of the boat so he wouldn't see my fear.

*

It took another hour to grow fully dark, a false night of black cloud and angry wind, and I'd crept back onto the deck long before then, when the swell of the waves grew discomforting. The idea of drowning was bad enough; the notion that the boat might turn over and I would die trapped underneath without a chance to escape was far worse. The wind grew strong, but inconsistent, jerking the boat forward before leaving us to wallow to a dull stop, or pressing the sail like an invisible hand so that we dipped alarmingly to one side. I was terrified, although I fought to keep it from the boy. I'd die facing the sky if there was no way out of this, while a small voice deep inside me prayed to everything I'd never believed in for me not to die. Not today.

The rain began, chilling me to the skin within moments as my clothes stuck to me. I forced myself to fetch Pa's coat and wrapped it around my shoulders for extra warmth, taking as short a time as possible beneath the deck to collect it. Much of the time I was afraid to take a step at all. The boat was pitching so horribly to one side and then the other I thought I'd be thrown overboard. My hands hurt from gripping the side rail but it was beyond me to let go. I tried to keep my thoughts occupied. I made myself consider what I would do if the mast cracked and struck the boy on his head. For the first time, there was no trace of desire in thinking of the eventuality. I calculated everything I could, from a splinter to a crushed limb, and forced myself to revise the best treatment for each.

*

Time passed, but I had no way of knowing whether it was flying or crawling. I feared the latter. The world became nothing but the boat, chill needle-like rain and the sound of the howling wind. Cosimo had long since dropped both sails, but their absence made no difference to the unpredictable motion of the boat. The darkness swallowed everything, and the wind snatched away all sounds but itself. I didn't hear him until he was right beside me, twitching when his lips brushed my ear.

"Tie this around your waist."

"What?" I wasn't sure I'd heard right, although the sodden rope pressed into my hands indicated I'd understood perfectly.

"Tie it around your waist. Ah'll do likewise. Ah don't want to lose either of us overboard."

My fingers fumbled, clumsy with cold and inactivity. It occurred to me that if we were roped to each other, one falling overboard could just as easily mean both doing so, whoever fell first dragging the other into the angry waves. There was an ominous groaning sound from the boat. A thrill of terror turned my stomach to water and I fumbled the rope around my waist. "Are we going to survive this?" My hands were shaking and my stomach churned, but the question came out in a steady tone. My brain was growing calm, becoming detached the way it sometimes did during an operation. I was curious to know the answer rather than afraid to learn it.

"It's a long time since Ah've seen one as bad as this!" Cosimo bellowed, his voice patchy. The wind drowned him out in places. "Mah luck seems to have run out."

Luck. Was that what we were depending on? The scientist in me thought little of such superstitions, but I'd seen my father perform enough miracles to know that chance had its place. I would have to hope my luck wasn't similarly threadbare.

"I'm not a great swimmer!" I yelled in Cosimo's ear. Instead of the shameful admission it should have been, it was a simple exchange of information. There wasn't anything he could do about it now; nor did I expect him to. I simply thought he should know.

"Lucky for you Ah am."

I shivered at the mention of luck again. But Cosimo would find it hard to drown. I might not. I dragged the knots tight around my waist.

"We've sailed close to land. That's another stroke of luck."

"We have?" I had no sense of how far we had travelled, or in what direction. Cosimo nodded. At least, I think that's what he did. It was so dark now that if I looked down I couldn't have seen my feet.

"Sit in the middle. You'll be safest there."

"What are you going to do?"

"The same."

He did so and I sank to the deck close to him. He dragged a blanket over both of us. We didn't try to speak. There was no chance anything could be heard over the wind, which sounded like an angry, wounded animal. Those howls were interspersed by the groans of the boat, an obscene dialogue of pain.

Cosimo shifted so his back met mine. At first it simply pressed my damp clothes against my spine, but then the heat flowed between his body and mine. I shivered, realising how very cold I was. I wondered how long the storm would continue. I hoped the boat could outlast it.

My luck had run out, too.

The sky turned blinding silver and an echoing crack of thunder split the world apart. The boat screeched and lurched at the same time an unseen wave smashed down on us. My face was filled with saltwater. Panic swept through me as I tried and failed to find a breath. I flailed, reaching out for the boat … Cosimo … anything. The deck shifted again and all I could feel in any direction was water. The noise was deafening. My lungs burned with pain and the need for air. I was falling. Then there was nothing at all.

Chapter Ten

The first thing I knew was cold. I was shaking, shivering to replace heat the sea had stolen from me. I moved, and regretted it instantly. There was just time for me to roll onto my front before I vomited, fetching up a flow of sour water that burned my throat and left me coughing wretchedly.

My ears rang with a high-pitched buzz, but it didn't drown out the voice speaking over my head. "You're right. They are both alive. What are the chances of that?"

Another voice growled, "Doesn't mean they'll stay that way. Look at the pair of them. City spies. They'll wish the sea had killed them."

Every cell of my body ached. I forced my eyes open and even that hurt, my eyeballs scratchy in their sockets, vision blurred. I tried to wipe away a dribble of saltwater from my chin and found my fingers swollen, joints stiff. I forced my hands higher to push my hair away from my face and found a tangled mess like seaweed dumped on the quayside to dry.

I tried to focus on the men with the voices, the men who might kill us but hadn't yet. All I could make out were hairy blurs. I tried to stand up, get away from them, but one grabbed my wrist. "Don't run off, missy." My eyes started to work. He was thin, hair and beard both cropped to half an inch, his face tanned so it was hard to see what was hair and what skin. But he was smiling, and it looked like a gesture he used regularly. He looked past me to the other voice, his friend, I assumed. "No need to frighten the poor girl, Jethro."

I pulled away, as much as I could with my wrist held tight. My feet squelched in my sodden boots and I shivered as my damp clothes touched my skin. My stomach plummeted when I realised I was no longer wearing the coat – my father's coat, with all it had held. I ran my hands down my own coat, and found the extent of my loss – one pocket was ripped, and both empty. Perhaps I should be grateful. The weight of all that gold might have drowned me. At least there was still a hard lump where father's anatomy book remained in my inside pocket. I hoped it would be useable once it dried out.

I looked at the thin man. "I'm not frightened of you." My boast would have sounded better if my voice hadn't cracked halfway through. It was because of all the seawater I'd swallowed, but it sounded as though I was scared.

"You should be." I swung my head to see the other one when he spoke, the one called Jethro. My head pounded at the movement, sending nausea through me again. I held still. He was heavier built than the first man, hair and beard overgrown, and he looked like a smile would crack his weathered face. My focus stretched past him, far enough for me to see that Cosimo was on the other side of the men, hunched over on his knees, wrists bound behind his back, staring at the ground. I tried to step towards him, but the thin man wouldn't let go of my wrist.

"We're not spies. I'm from City. Isn't this New Eden?" I stared at them, puzzled. If we'd arrived at the tiny island that grew the fresh food City traded for, we should be welcomed with open arms. Nautilus man Cosimo should at any rate. I didn't expect them to care two pins for me until they knew who I was and what I was capable of.

"City. But not a spy." The heavyset man, Jethro, laughed in a way that made the hairs on the back of my neck rise.

"We're your friends." I stopped. Speaking hurt my throat and I was distressed by my impulse to plead with them. What had happened? Why did they think we were spies?

"Friends, eh? We'll find out soon enough." Jethro dragged Cosimo to his feet. "You watch the girl, Si." As though I were dangerous!

The thin man took my elbow. "Can you stand?"

"Of course." I ignored my thudding head and forced myself to my feet. I was grateful the thin man kept hold of me. I was less steady than I wanted to be. "Are you all right?" I called to Cosimo.

Instead of him answering, Jethro laughed. "You worry about yourself, missy."

Si – Simon, I supposed – squeezed my elbow. I thought the action was intended to be comforting, and I was distressed to realise that he thought I needed comforting, and that our situations were so unequal that he could provide comfort to me. I took a step, then my brain recovered enough for me to remember what I should be concerned for. My father's coat had vanished, and … I looked around, at the ground that was half sand, half scattered pebbles and weed. "My bag!" I knew it was stupid to expect it to have been washed up with us, but I couldn't help my distress. Without the medical bag, without the gold, I was nothing. I turned, looking further, dragging the thin man with me. Ahead of us, Jethro guffawed. Si smiled sadly. "You're lucky to have survived. There was no wreckage. It'll wash up elsewhere, if it washes up at all."

Lucky. We weren't dead, so of course we were lucky. Except it was hard to be grateful when a day ago I'd been Dr Miracle's daughter, and now I appeared to have become a penniless enemy spy.

We didn't have far to go. The sand with its sparse, pale vegetation soon gave way to terraced steps that led up towards New Eden proper. The sky was pink, promising a sun of which there was yet no sign, and everything around us was clear, the fog chased away by yesterday's storm.

Cosimo and his captor walked ahead of us. "Are you hurt?" I called ahead, glancing down at my squelching feet as I stumbled, then looking towards Cosimo's bowed head. He was walking well enough, but I hadn't seen his face yet. Or his throat. I wondered how long he'd been awake before I'd awoken, awake and alone with these men who believed a nautilus man and a young woman to be spies.

He gave no reply. Jethro grunted. "He's fine. For now."

I stumbled, and pushed my horrible hair out of my eyes. "There's no need to threaten us. We're valuable, you know."

Jethro laughed unkindly.

I tried again. "His operation is recent. I should examine him."

He gave another chuckle. Si squeezed my wrist. "Don't cause trouble," he muttered.

I muttered back. "He's more use to you alive than he is dead. I'm a doctor. I know what I'm doing."

Cosimo stopped suddenly and we all kicked each other's heels when the rest of us didn't.

"Shut up, Liberty! There's nothing wrong with me." He didn't look round as he spoke, then he started off again as though nothing had happened. It took me longer to start walking again. I wasn't sure what dumbfounded me more – his sudden speech after so much silence, or the fact that he had chosen this moment to address me by my name.

*

When we reached the top, the view robbed my breath. It was a scene from fairy tales, hard to believe for a girl raised in the crush of City.

It was green. So green. Plants filled the view, sectioned into fields. There were trees, tall and magnificent in their brown and green coverings. And there were houses, of course. So much space would be unimaginable without people to fill it. But the houses were small, solidly made, and scattered across the landscape rather than crushed densely onto every available inch of space.

And the smells! The salt scent of the sea was drowned out by a new, heavy, cloying smell which belonged to the rich, black soil that supported the crops. At the top of the cliff, a light, chill breeze blew away the last traces of the sea and filled my lungs with the scents of earth and vegetation, undercut with a thread of smoke that in all this expanse of space was still strong enough to make me ache at the familiarity, except that it didn't smell salty like an algae block fire, it smelled … thick, like something I could chew.

"Don't fall behind." Cosimo and his captor were ahead of us. Si was eager to provide me with more advice, delivered in the same low tone as though he didn't want to draw attention to himself. "We don't have all day."

I wanted to ask why not – what they had to do that was so pressing when they'd been able to leave the fields to guard two apparently dangerous creatures washed up on the beach by the storm.

*

Five minutes' walk along a narrow path between fields that held a crop of things I couldn't even identify, and my thighs and underarms were chafing where my still-damp clothes rubbed my skin. I glanced ahead and thought better of requesting a little consideration or an easier pace. Licking salt from my lips, I clenched my teeth and hurried onwards.

It wasn't much longer before we headed on to a still-narrower path towards the nearest of the houses. Jethro opened the door and shoved Cosimo inside. I followed with Si and a little more dignity.

Inside, the house was small and dim, same as anywhere, although it was made of stone, a luxury City barely saw. Heat radiated from a stove at one end of the room and I shivered in my clammy clothes, reminded by the heat of how cold I'd grown. Three chairs surrounded a table in the centre of the room and a water barrel stood to one side. At the back, a wooden ladder led to a sleeping loft overhead. With four of us inside, the house became uncomfortably small.

"Let's see what the tide brought in." Jethro, pushing Cosimo before him, took two steps to the side of the room, ripped the cover off the barrel and thrust Cosimo's head beneath the water inside.

I screamed, but only briefly, at the shock. "Lungs, not nose!" I called, although he probably couldn't hear me. His back was taut with tension, but from discomfort rather than resistance. With his hands bound behind his back, he couldn't hope to escape.

Jethro was watching me, a nasty expression on his face. His hand had vanished into the barrel, careless of his cargo.

"Don't touch his neck," I told him, adding a belated, "If you please." My heart thudded against my ribs, protesting the same way I was sure Cosimo's would be. "The gills need to move, or they can't work. Nautilus men can still drown." I hoped that wasn't what he intended. You would have to be mad to destroy a nautilus man, but I couldn't be sure that wasn't an accurate description of the man testing Cosimo's abilities.

The reamer shifted, but didn't try to free himself. I smiled. Jethro's expression hardened. I nodded deliberately, directing his attention to Cosimo's bound hands, both of which were now arranged in an obscene gesture. Heavyset Jethro swore and heaved him back out of the barrel.

He spun around, coughing, and glared at his captors. Hands still bound, he couldn't do anything about the water sluicing from his drenched hair into clothes that were probably barely dry like mine. Our captors looked at each other. Si smiled cautiously. "Doesn't look like a fake."

Abruptly, Cosimo shook his head violently, water flying. Jethro swore again and took a step away.

"Watch your stitches!"

Cosimo stopped, his angry gaze settling on me. I walked towards him, brought up short by Si's grip at my wrist. My turn to glare. "I told you: he's valuable. You take care of what's valuable, unless you're stupid."

I tugged my arm from his hold and examined Cosimo's neck. It was healthier than he deserved. "I can probably take the stitches out, they're nearly fully healed." I dropped my hands from his skin. "The procedure's clearly not going to kill you. However much you try."

"You know an awful lot about nautilus men." The thin man was watching me.

Cosimo butted in. "She's from City. Everyone knows about nautilus men there."

I frowned. "I'm … a doctor." The reamer's interruption had given me pause and I answered more cautiously than I might have done. If we were suddenly enemies, perhaps it was wise to keep the fact that I was Dr Miracle's daughter hidden. Cosimo scowled, but I could hardly expect to be welcomed if I didn't give the people of New Eden any reason to consider me valuable, could I?

Jethro made a sound of derision. "Doctor? Slip of a miss like you?"

I looked coldly at him. "Apprentice to a surgeon, and good at my work."

Our captors looked at each other again. The silence was suddenly heavy and I wondered if I should have hidden even that about myself.

"Perhaps we've a use for you, too, then, missy," Jethro said. He sounded happy about it. That didn't mean I'd be likewise. He motioned us both to the door.

I took a step, then paused and looked back. "Before we go, could someone get the boy a towel? Pneumonia won't do him much good. Truly, the procedure might be miraculous, but it doesn't make a man immortal."

Chapter Eleven

As we headed along the narrow paths between crops and black fields towards another of the scattered houses, I wondered what they wanted of me. Clearly, some sort of a test like the one they'd put Cosimo through. Not quite like that, I hoped. A test of my medical abilities. I wondered what medical help they needed. My father's bag was lost. All I was left with was the knowledge in my head, but a great deal of healing is achieved by the application of calm good sense combined with an understanding of how the human body functions.

I wondered what would happen when I'd proved myself and they realised we were both valuable to them. I didn't like the evidence I'd seen so far that they considered themselves to be in charge of us. I liked even less the fact that I was close to powerless. Cosimo couldn't hide what he was. Perhaps I should have focused on making myself seem harmless rather than valuable, but it was too late for that now.

Our path took us to a field full of fruit-laden trees. Several groups of people were assembled amongst the trees, picking apples. There were babies strapped to their mother's chests right up to elderly men and women. They must be the families from the village, gathered to help with the harvest. Harvest time didn't matter on City – algae was harvested daily and nautilus men dived all year round – but here things were completely different.

The smell of apples grew stronger. By the time we reached the field, my mouth was watering. Some of the harvesters stopped to watch us approach. Others continued working, passing the fruit hand to hand until it was stacked in large baskets placed close against the bottoms of the trunks. I couldn't help but stare hungrily. My stomach had recovered from its earlier sickness and realised with a vengeance how empty it was. And besides, on City apples were a rarity. My father and I ate only a few each year. Here, there were *dozens*. Some had even dropped to the ground to be disregarded by the harvesters.

When we were close enough to be heard, Jethro raised a hand and called for attention. Everyone stopped and stared at us. Some of the people up trees clambered down. Muttering began. I saw more than one gaze settle on Cosimo's gills. They didn't look friendly. My steps slowed. The thin man caught my elbow and urged me on. "No one's going to hurt you if you are what you say you are," he murmured.

I hurried forward. "I'm not afraid."

Jethro turned, gesturing towards me with a wide arm and an unpleasant smile, "… And the girl says she's a doctor."

There was more muttering at that, but it was drowned out by a shriek from a woman at the back, who pushed through her companions and grabbed my hands. "Is it true?"

I recognised her look of desperation and tried to look authoritative. "Yes, it's true. What ails you?"

"Paul, my brother's boy. Come." She dragged me after her and the others cleared a path. I was pleased that neither the thin man nor Jethro made any move to stop her. Perhaps they weren't as much in charge as they thought. It was the first cheering notion I'd had since I'd awoken on the beach.

We hurried almost at running pace, my hand tight in hers as though she feared I'd vanish if released. Some of the people from the orchard followed. I saw Si and Cosimo among them, but Jethro stayed where he was. I was pleased he didn't consider himself necessary for whatever was to follow.

One of the children had run ahead, so by the time we approached our destination, the door was already open and another female waited in the doorway.

"Ah hope you're as good as you think you are," Cosimo muttered as we came to a halt.

"You're still alive, aren't you?" I fired back, then the woman in the doorway reached out to me.

"You're a doctor?" Over-bright eyes dredged my face, seeking reassurance, hoping but not yet believing. With a glance, I diagnosed that she hadn't slept properly for several days. Clearly, the mother.

"I am," I promised. "Take me to see your son."

She led me into the house and up a flight of wooden steps. The upstairs to this house was a proper arrangement with a staircase and separate rooms, more luxurious than the previous dwelling. I followed the mother. "What happened? What ails him?"

She glanced back, her eyes skimming past me to rest for a moment, venomously, on Cosimo standing at the bottom of the stairs. Then she turned back and continued to climb. "Nautilus men happened to him."

That needed an explanation, but later. "What did they do? How is he hurt?"

"His hand is crushed." Her voice was bleak. I couldn't see her face, but I could imagine what it was costing her to speak so calmly.

"Has he seen a doctor?"

The mother made a noise that might have been a sob. I'd asked a foolish question; they wouldn't need me if there was a doctor to hand. "I mean, has anyone treated him?"

"I've done my best." Once more, her control was absolute. She reached the top of the steps and turned to me. "Paul's father was the doctor. He ... he's dead."

"I'm sorry." I dropped my gaze from her face. "I will do what I can, I promise you."

The mother stood with her hand on one of the doors that led off the small landing. "He's all I have now." She turned and I saw the desolation in her eyes. "I can't lose him."

She pushed the door open.

The room was gloomy and warm. The curtains were closed. A fire against one wall provided both illumination and heat. I took a breath, pleased not to find what I dreaded I might after a crushing injury: there was no smell of decay.

"When did it happen?" I stepped to the curtains to throw them open and then moved to the bed against the wall, where the patient lay sweaty and motionless beneath the covers.

"The day before the storm."

Paul was barely conscious, although that was probably a blessing. His skin was pale, but only where it wasn't discoloured by purple bruising and swelling around his eyes and cheekbone, more damage probably hidden by the covers. His arm, the damaged one, was outside the blankets, swathed in a bandage. I lifted it gently, but even that drew a moan of pain and his eyes opened to slits, unfocused. "I'm sorry for your pain. I'm a doctor, here to help you." I knelt to assess the wound without moving it. I hoped his mother wasn't expecting a miracle. I would do what I could, but without my father to guide me, I was already anxious Paul's injury would be beyond my abilities.

I unwrapped his bandage as gently as I could and leaned close to inspect the damage. Whoever had treated him, the mother, had tried to splint the hand, which would have been the right approach under better circumstances. But the bones were not just fractured, they were completely broken and pushed out of alignment. "What did this?" I asked. The injury affected his fingers, but not the rest of his hand. All four were mangled and swollen. "I need more light." My heart sank although I gave no sign. If a patient had arrived on my doorstep with this injury, I wouldn't even have given him painkillers without my father's say so. Now, there was no one to consult. And perhaps my life depended on the outcome.

A lamp arrived at my elbow, carried by Si, who I hadn't even noticed following us up the stairs. "We can't be sure," he said in reply to my question.

"Paul's account is unclear. He and his father were the only ones there," his mother added.

Moving the lamp to where I needed it, I inspected the skin, sniffing gingerly, pleased again to find no evidence of rot. That could only be a matter of time. I needed to remove his fingers to remove that possibility. I wished I were a better surgeon. As things stood, it would be quicker and safer to take his whole hand.

I glanced at the mother, standing impassive two steps away, and muttered to Si, "Does she know how dangerous this injury is?"

"Her husband was the doctor. She's seen things like this before."

Perhaps that accounted for her fever-bright eyes: her expectations were fighting her hopes. I palpated the skin above the boy's wrist, checking whether my initial assessment held out, and planning what I would need to do, wondering at the detached part of my mind that said yes, I really did have the audacity to attempt to save him without any direct experience of the operation I would be conducting. I had read the books. I had even assisted my father when he'd had cause to amputate a man's foot. Once.

"She knows there is a chance her son's blood will be

poisoned," he continued.

I nodded. As my assessment reached the boy's shoulder, I saw his face, lapsed back to unconsciousness. He was pale where he wasn't bruised, his hair damp with sweat, curling against his forehead. He was probably only twelve or thirteen. Too young to die in this wretched manner.

"Can you save him?" Si spoke, his voice low so Paul's mother wouldn't need to hear my reply.

My hands were shaking. I dropped them to my sides, hiding them in the folds of my borrowed skirt. I could do this. I didn't have as much experience as my father, but I couldn't do worse than letting him die slowly and painfully as his blood turned septic and poisoned him.

"I will have to remove the hand. Will she accept that?"

Si shrugged thin shoulders and stepped back.

I stood and faced the mother. "I need to operate if he is to recover. I will need to amputate his hand. Do I have your permission?"

She blinked, eyes bright in her pale face. Her voice was quiet, but steady. "Are you competent to perform such an operation?"

Si's eyes were on me too. "Yes, I am." It wasn't entirely a lie. Of course it was different to perform an operation rather than simply assist, but I had undertaken many sections of the nautilus procedure without losing a man. I had no intention of marring my and my father's perfect record.

"So you have done the operation before? How many times?" Paul's mother was full of reasonable, sensible questions. More's the pity.

I was sorry I couldn't reassure her more fully. "I have never performed an amputation myself, I have only assisted. But I have a great deal of surgical experience."

There was a long pause. I stood straight and met the mother's gaze. It wasn't the answer I would have wanted for my child, either, but we were both aware he had little choice. "There is a chance your son might die because of the operation. But if I don't operate, he will definitely die. The damage is too great for an unaided recovery."

She crossed to her son's bedside, skirts swishing, then pushed his damp hair away from his forehead, muttering words I couldn't hear and wouldn't intrude on. She faced me. Her hands were interlaced at her waist, knuckles white. "You have my permission."

Chapter Twelve

I took a deep breath, half pleased by her confidence in me, half-terrified by it. I swallowed and found my voice. "Thank you. Is water available?"

"There's a well behind the house."

As much fresh water as we needed. Not like home where we needed to collect our allowance from the desalination plant unless rain had filled the collection tank on the roof. It was a piece of fortune I couldn't have expected, but it had to overcome a great disadvantage. I didn't have my father's bag. "What did the doctor leave behind? Chloroform? Morphine?"

She shook her head. "We have very little here. I'll show you what there is." She led me to a room at the back of the house, clearly the doctor's consulting room. I was envious of the space – a room just to see patients, whereas our patients had spoken to my father while I'd cooked meals or prepared medicines around them. Then I remembered the doctor was no longer with us and my sense of injustice winked out.

The stores were sparse. It was more a herbalist's cupboard than a surgeon's. I found none of the medicines I was hoping for. But there was a decent array of knives, at least.

Paul's mother had followed me for the inspection. I listed my requirements. "I will need hot water to wash. And boiling water for the operation, soap, all these knives and any other sharp blades you can find in the house. I need a flat surface on which to operate, a needle and thread." I glanced down at myself. "If you can provide clean clothes that would fit me, I would appreciate their loan as well."

"Of course." She bustled away. I followed.

*

The crowd who had trailed after us from the orchard were in the kitchen, making preparations. My instructions had travelled impossibly before me. A kettle of water steamed atop the stove and a woman crouched before it, coaxing more heat from the fuel.

"They're all here to help," Cosimo told me. "Give them instructions, and they'll do what they can."

I nodded, eyeing the table in the centre of the room. "Shall I use that to operate on?"

An affirmative was quickly secured. "Then can someone scrub both the floor and the table? Water as hot as they can stand, and soap if possible, but the soap must be rinsed off the table with more hot water." I looked at Cosimo steadily. "Everyone must understand that cleanliness is vital for the success. It prevents infection."

I saw more heads than his nod in understanding.

"Any blades you can find should be sharpened as finely as possible, and then put in a pot of water on the stove to boil. The water must cover the blades. The handles can simply be scrubbed if they won't fit beneath the water." I glanced around the busy kitchen. It was strange not to have to do the preparation myself. I had expected that promoted to my father's role, I would be undertaking the work of both surgeon and surgeon's assistant, but that wasn't necessary here. I looked at Cosimo. "You should wash – and change clothes if you can."

He nodded.

"I have your clothes." I turned to see the mother, a

pile of neatly folded linen in her arms. "Follow me." She led me up the steps to a room that held a neatly made bed, a large wooden cupboard and a small table with a beautifully painted bowl and ewer. The air smelled of something clean and flowery. She set the clothes on the bed. "I'll fetch water," she said, and lifted the ewer and walked away.

I spoke when she was almost at the door. "My name is Liberty Marchmont. My father was the best surgeon and doctor on City. I will care for your son as though he were my brother."

Facing the door, she nodded. Then she turned, cradling the ewer. "Was?"

The event was growing distant, unreal. The ache rose, but dulled. Almost as though it was something another person had told me about; their suffering, not mine. "Yes. He was killed. I don't know who by. Or why."

She nodded. "I'm sorry. My name is Emily." She slipped from the room.

I undressed, pulling the sodden book carefully from my pocket and placing it on the windowsill to dry. I grimaced when I touched my hair. That needed a good wash, too. I'd be as quick as I could. I didn't want to give these people any chance to think we couldn't be trusted, but I had to be thorough.

"Here." When the door opened I turned, expecting water. Instead, Emily carried a tray with a dish of soup and a plate of oatcakes to me. "You must be hungry."

I was starving, but her son was a higher priority. "That can wait."

She tutted at me. "You need to eat." She smiled sadly. "I've seen Henry return from a sickroom, swaying with fatigue and insisting he was fine. I don't want your hands to tremble and harm my boy."

Put like that, I could only obey. I took the soup and the oatcakes.

*

I'd already finished by the time Emily re-entered the room and I hurried to take the heavy ewer from her, tipping the steaming water into the bowl. She'd also brought a cake of soap which gave me pause. It smelled like heaven, scented by some flower I couldn't possibly guess at. I wanted to hand it back and say it was too fine, but I was operating to save her son's life. Nothing could be too fine for that.

"Thank you." I washed and soaped my hair, then left it in a froth of suds as I cleaned the rest of me.

By the time I'd finished, Emily had returned with another ewer of water to rinse away the soap.

My skin glowed once I was dry. I wrapped the towel around my hair while I dressed. The clothes were a strange fashion, and slightly large, but they were serviceable and clean, which was all that mattered. I returned my hair to the order of a plait, covered it with a scarf, and I was ready.

*

All was prepared in the kitchen, with everything I needed set out for me. A few neighbours lingered in the room as though hoping to be further help. Cosimo stood beside the scrubbed table, and I was pleased to see someone had provided him with clean clothes and – when I moved close to him – soap and water to wash with.

Paul had been carried through and was now half-sitting, half-lying on the table before the stove. He was conscious, Emily beside him. Several neighbours stood forward. I was sure they were well-meaning, but they were actually more likely to create distractions and delay. Paul's eyes shone over-bright, but he was otherwise listless, leaning against his mother's shoulder, his damaged hand cradled in his lap. He was stripped to the waist. I could smell a different soap on his skin. In body, at least, he was ready.

"Hello, Paul." I smiled, while nerves twisted my stomach into knots. "I need to operate on your hand." I swallowed. "I am very sorry for your injury, but I must remove the damaged flesh so you can get better."

He barely had the strength to mutter a reply, and I had to take his nod for assent.

"I've told him what has to happen," Emily confirmed.

I looked away from the dull pain in his eyes. "Cosimo, you stay, and I shall need someone else."

"I will assist, of course." Emily was pale but determined.

I shook my head. "You should rest while you can. He will need you when he awakens."

She looked at me, judging whether to protest. I wouldn't accept her help. The patient's mother as assistant could prove disastrous.

"*I* will help. You go with Simon, Emily." The woman from the orchard stepped forward; the aunt. Emily paused, then nodded. I didn't know and couldn't care whether she was persuaded or defeated. Si put his arm around her and led her from the room. There was a shuffling as others in the room followed them. The aunt hurried to a cupboard and returned with a clean apron for herself and one that she held out to Cosimo. She gave a brief smile. "I'm Sarah. I have a calm head. You needn't worry I shall throw up or run screaming." She turned to her nephew and forced her smile wider. "We'll do very well, won't we, Paul?"

He nodded weakly. He was barely conscious, and I was sure oblivion would return soon enough.

"You both need to scrub your arms to the elbow," I said. Sarah nodded and moved immediately to the sink to comply.

"Ah can't stay." Cosimo was pale. His eyes darted to the door.

"I trust you more than I do them," I muttered, low

so the aunt wouldn't hear me. "I'm sorry, but if you have a weak stomach you will just have to look away and breathe through your mouth."

"Ah can't do it." His expression betrayed his desire to be anywhere but here. I could hardly blame him for wanting to run, but I couldn't let him abandon me while these people still thought I was an enemy.

"You have to stay. I can't risk this going wrong. They might kill us if it does."

"Ah know that."

"Then shut up and get a backbone." I cut off further protests by turning to my patient. "I am sorry, Paul. I will be as quick and as gentle as I can, but it will hurt. I need you to bear it as well as you can."

I glanced at the equipment set out for me. "Thread?" I questioned. "Oh, and band —" I fell silent as Cosimo pointed to a large spool of thread and a pile of bandages on a counter beside the stove. I hadn't even thought to request them earlier. "Thank you." He nodded, pale-faced. I was pleased to see he was now wearing the apron.

I checked Paul's pulse. His eyes opened long enough to look at me, then closed in relief. "I will start when you are ready." I didn't know whether it would make much difference, given what he was about to face, but I wanted him to feel as though the decision was his.

He muttered what I assumed was confirmation, and his aunt helped him wriggle down until he was lying flat on the table. I caught hold of his damaged hand so it wouldn't be jolted and wound a bandage carefully around his wrist to create a tourniquet.

I took a long look at the damage. I couldn't cut off his entire hand when the damage was only in his fingers. His thumb and the rest of his hand still functioned. My father wouldn't think much of me for taking so much good with the bad simply because I was afraid for my own safety. I breathed deeply and hoped my father's skill would guide my hands. Then I selected my knife.

Turning back, I nodded to the aunt. "Hold his good hand. Talk to him. Reassure him." I turned to a sickly-pale Cosimo and lowered my voice. "I have no anaesthetic. It's going to hurt. I need you to hold him still so I can operate. If you must be sick, be sick on the floor, not on the table and *not* on the patient."

He nodded, pale and grim-faced, and took his place at Paul's head. I motioned to indicate where his strength was likely to be needed and he set his hands on Paul's shoulders. Then I began.

Chapter Thirteen

The first incision was the worst. Paul screamed and bucked away. Cosimo and Sarah were both taken unawares and weren't quick enough to halt the movement. My knife slid across his hand until I snatched it away, my own hand shaking. I should have tied him to the wretched table.

The aunt spoke in a reassuring murmur, calm again, one hand holding Paul's good one, the other pressing firmly against his shoulder. Paul whimpered. I snatched a cloth to mop up the blood that shouldn't be there, thankful that the cut at least trailed over sick flesh.

"Ready?"

There was a pause. Paul spoke, rapid and pleading, words I couldn't quite split apart and make sense of. I didn't look at him in case my determination deserted me. "Ready?" I persisted.

His aunt's voice overrode his murmurings. "Continue," she told me through gritted teeth. Cosimo's shoulders tightened as he braced himself.

I leaned close and began my work. Paul's voice, high with fear and pain, sank into the background as I cut the skin and sliced through the flesh beneath to reach the bone. I was quick but careful; I wanted to do the best I could for him. I noticed when he slipped into unconsciousness – his muscles relaxed and my job became easier.

*

When we'd removed the man's foot, back at home, Pa had told me stories of battlefield surgeons who could remove a limb in three minutes. He had been slower than that; I was slower still. The human hand is an intricate organ, beautiful in its composition and complexity. A great many blood vessels are needed for its healthy function, and each damaged one had to be tied off.

Paul thankfully remained unconscious. His aunt spoke occasionally. Cosimo answered without involving me. I was too busy to talk.

Finally, the damaged material was all removed and I began the reverse process of sewing skin back over the remaining flesh to seal the wound. I had been able to save his thumb and the hand to the knuckle. My father, I hoped, would have been proud.

At last, I tied off the final bandage and straightened, assailed by stiffness and fatigue that had crept up on me as I worked. I glanced at the window and judged that several hours had passed. I stepped back and wiped my brow, looking at Paul rather than just his hand for the first time since I'd begun. His face was shiny with sweat, but his breathing was deep. When I touched my fingers to his pulse, it was regular.

Cosimo cleared his throat. He stared at Paul's bandaged hand. "That was the most amazing thing Ah think Ah've ever seen."

My head jerked up. I expected a mocking twist to his words, perhaps a repetition of that irritating nickname, but he seemed sincere.

"Did you think I couldn't do it?" I chided, forgetting I'd doubted myself before I'd started.

"Of course not." His colour rose, giving a lie to his words. His voice grew snappy, the tone more familiar, when he added, "Ah knew there had to be a point to you."

"And you weren't even sick." His blush deepened at my praise. "You'll make a decent assistant yet."

"Ah didn't ..." He trailed off.

"What?"

He shook his head. "Doesn't matter."

I turned to the aunt, who was consoling the unconscious Paul, stroking his hair away from his forehead. She looked up before I could speak. "Thank you. I don't think even my brother would have been able to do what you have done."

"It relies on his strength, now. He needs to sleep. The bandage must be changed every day, the wound cleaned with fresh, clean, warm water and a new bandage applied. He should keep the limb mobile as well, else it won't heal."

"But you'll stay with us." She glanced at Cosimo, then back to me. "Until you are sure he is healed, at least."

I looked at Cosimo, unsure what to say. I supposed he would want to leave to find what remained of his people as soon as possible. He didn't meet my eye so I couldn't guess his intentions. I wondered whether the people of New Eden would let him go – or me. Then his stomach broke the silence with a loud growl. Sarah laughed. "My apologies. We haven't been very hospitable, have we?"

"You had no reason to be."

"We'll make amends now." She gathered Paul into her arms and left the room to return him to his bed.

I turned to the sink and washed the blood from my hands. Several people crowded into the kitchen. I grabbed a cloth to wipe the blood from the table, grateful to Cosimo who had swept the debris of the operation into a bowl and taken it outside where it could distress no one.

As I reached for a towel to dry my hands, I saw

Cosimo outside. He was standing, head bowed, unmoving. Perhaps I'd been unkind to force him to assist during the operation. He couldn't help it if he was squeamish – it was chance, not a character failing. Perhaps I should have excused him. Now the operation was successfully over, it was easy to imagine the consequences could have been the same without his assistance.

As the neighbours bustled into the room, I slipped out of the back door. At the sound of its opening, Cosimo cast a glance round before resuming his study of the ground.

"Are you all right?"

"Yeah."

I should have expected nothing else from him. He'd die rather than acknowledge a weakness. "I meant what I said. You did a good job of helping." He made no reply. "I'm sorry you had to."

I waited. It wasn't hard to stand there, enjoying the view that was like something from a dream or a tale my father might have told me. But Cosimo's lack of manners grew tiresome, and it was too cold to stand idly. He was clearly not going to give me any sort of reply. "I think they'll be happy for us to stay awhile." I included him in Sarah's invitation, because I at least knew how to behave.

Cosimo stood straighter, staring at the far distance. I waited a while longer, then left him to himself.

*

By the time I re-entered, the table was covered with delicious-smelling dishes. Emily seized my hands, her eyes glossy. "I don't know how to thank you –" Her voice failed.

I nodded, a little embarrassed at her flood of gratitude. "I'm happy to be able to help."

"You really are, aren't you?"

Cosimo had re-entered the room. He was watching

me as though I'd grown two heads.

"Of course I am. Why wouldn't I be?" I said.

He frowned. "They aren't your friends. No one's paying you."

I would have been angry, but the operation had taken all my energy. "My father taught me better than that."

"Yeah, but he's not watching now, is he?"

That prompted a flare of pain, but it didn't last. "I don't do what's right only when I'm being watched."

"No. Ah see that now." His blue eyes were startling in his still-pale face. For a moment, I forgot he was a reamer. For the first time, I wondered whether it even mattered.

*

The meal that followed the operation lasted forever, or close to it. Time stretched around us. Every time a dish was emptied, another one appeared borne into the room by an apparently endless stream of smiling neighbours. Made entirely from fresh ingredients, every single item was tastier than anything I had ever eaten before, even at the Magistrate's house.

In danger of falling asleep through satiation, I forced myself to my feet and up the stairs to check on my patient. Emily had disappeared upstairs earlier, and because she hadn't returned I knew nothing could be seriously wrong, but I was the doctor, not her.

Paul was sleeping peacefully, his mother perched on the edge of his bed. Her hand was on the pillow above his head. I think she'd been stroking his hair until I opened the door. A flash of memory brought my mother's face to me, comforting me during some childhood illness. My father had been practical, ever the doctor. My mother was the one to provide succour.

"I wanted to check how he is," I murmured. I paused in the threshold until she smiled and waved me in.

"He's still sleeping. There's no sign of a fever."

I nodded, then walked to the bed and checked for myself. The wound was clean and dry. His forehead showed a normal temperature. It was unlikely he would be so fortunate as to escape fever entirely, but I had no way to predict what might lie ahead.

"An ideal patient, he's doing very well," I reassured Emily. I took a step away, as though I was intruding. I *was* intruding. This was her home. I glanced around the room, trim and cared for. I swallowed. It reminded me too much of the home I'd lost.

"He isn't out of danger yet."

"Not for a few days." Distracted, I agreed honestly as though I was talking with my father. Then I remembered where I was. "That is – there's no reason not to expect a happy outcome," I gabbled.

Emily smiled, and I saw more of the doctor's wife than of Paul's mother in her face. "I would sooner get more than I hope for, than less," she whispered.

"I will do everything I can."

"I know. And thank you for everything you have done so far." She turned back to her son. I shut the door quietly behind me.

Descending the stairs, I had the oddest sense of being suspended between two things. Upstairs was silent and still. My job was done and I wasn't needed there. Below, growing more obvious with each step I took was a different world, full of sound and jubilation. I paused, listening. A man was singing, rich and harmonious. I was overwhelmed by a memory of home, my parents singing together, the three of us clustered around our stove. A festive song. I hadn't even known I remembered the moment. I stilled, eyes closed, hand tight on the banister, knowing when I opened my eyes the memory would vanish. It felt like home, and I so wanted to be home. I wanted all the madness to cease so I could return to my normal life. My throat ached. The singing continued. I didn't have a normal life. Not now. I would have to make a new one.

I opened my eyes and trod slowly down the remainder of the stairs. I had been happy on City, with my father. I'd never had reason to consider whether I would be capable of being happy anywhere else.

The song finished. I paused, waiting, hoping, for another to begin. There was silence, then voices murmuring in speech. The moment was lost. This wasn't my home. I was a stranger, only welcome because I'd saved Paul, valuable because they needed a doctor. My place here was as precarious as his health. I dropped my hand and walked away, slipping out of the front door to the solitude outside.

The chill evening air bit through my clothes. My breath made a cloud of vapour. I tipped my head back and the sky was so clear I could see the stars. Thousands of them. The sight put me in mind of everything I'd left behind on City.

I wondered if anyone missed me. Will, or Hannah, or Belle. There was no reason for them to miss me – not unless they fell ill. We'd never been especially close. Now we might as well have been a million miles apart.

"You don't need to hide, you know." I jumped. Cosimo, of course. "No one thinks you're an enemy, not now."

"I know that." I looked back to the sky. "I just wanted … some peace and quiet."

"They know how to party." I heard the smile in his voice.

I should join them; relax and enjoy myself. Except that it was no easier to do that here with these people than it had been on City. I couldn't fit in just because I wanted to. A chill sneaked down the neck of my dress. I folded my hands into each other to keep warm. "You don't have to stay out here with me."

"Ah don't mind." He leaned against the wall.

Silence fell, broken by the muted sounds of merriment inside the house. I didn't want to go inside. I'd come outside to be alone, but I was oddly glad Cosimo was with me.

*

After another few minutes, he sighed and said, "Ah found her."

I turned to him, but before I could ask the question, I realised who he meant.

"Mah mother. We argued. She'd told me to go to City and find your father, ask for his help. We needed metal to make more machines, and she thought me becoming a nautilus man was the best way to get it. Ah'd told her Ah'd rather kill mahself than go there." He fell silent, his skin blanched. His throat worked before he continued. "Ah ran off to get away from her and her stupid ideas. When Ah got back she was dead. Ah found her, too late to save her. They all died, everyone who was at that station when the City men arrived."

"I wish I'd been there," I told him. I could have helped. Perhaps I could have saved her life.

He shook his head, his voice husky when he said, "No, you don't." He continued to stare at the ground. "That's why … the blood."

"I understand. I'm sorry."

He straightened and turned to the door. "Come inside. They'll welcome you."

I took a step back. "In a minute." I watched him go, saw the slice of light as the door opened and then shut behind him. Then I leaned back to stare at the stars that shone on reamer, New Eden and City folk alike, and murmured a prayer for my father. And Cosimo's mother.

Chapter Fourteen

Paul was sleeping when I checked on him in the early morning. His breathing was even, although his pulse was a little fast and his temperature was elevated. As yet, it was nothing to worry about, but there was every chance that would change. I replaced the bandage, inspected and bathed the wound. Slightly red, slightly warm. No better than was reasonable to expect, but at least no worse. By then he was awake. "How do you feel?"

"Every part of me aches." He closed his eyes and I could see his bruises in all their glorious colour, the dark rings etched under his eyes by the pain he must have suffered for the past few days. *Nautilus men did this.* To an outnumbered boy. What was happening to the world? "I'm thirsty," he added.

I fetched a glass of water and encouraged him to drink. "You must keep the hand mobile," I told him. Paul obligingly flexed and twisted what remained of his hand. "And drink as much as you wish, but only eat in moderation." It was naive of me to hope my first attempt could be a complete success, but that didn't stop me wishing for it.

He stared at the bandages. "I thought you were going to cut off my whole hand."

"The damage wasn't as bad as I thought." I couldn't tell from his expression how he felt about the loss now it was before him. No doubt it would take time for him to know how he felt.

"Can I get up?"

"No running around and getting into scrapes, but I see no harm in your coming downstairs. You should keep mobile. I'll make a sling for your hand."

Emily entered the room and helped him downstairs.

I returned to my room and dressed in my own clothes, which had been cleaned, folded and left for me, probably by one of the helpful neighbours. The ripped pocket had been neatly repaired, although that couldn't replace the contents. My father's anatomy book had survived, crinkled from the water like a wave, but the nautilus diagram within it had been rinsed clear, the ink washed into the creases, the page blank. Nautilus technology was lost.

When staying upstairs became hiding from my hosts, I went down. My footsteps were light, and my fingers as I traced the banister were numbed by the strange certainty that while I might not belong here, if I could only relax and accept where I found myself, I could make a home here. That thought faded. Without Pa I wasn't sure anywhere could be home. But I could be safe here at least, the idea of pursuing the land of sun and roses fading like the dream it could only ever truly be. If only I could forget what had happened on City. If only I could bear to live with the knowledge that I might never find out who had killed my father – and why.

*

That day was spent on medical duties. The one that followed showed me what everyday life in New Eden was like.

After breakfast, I went with Sarah to help complete the apple harvest our arrival had interrupted. I hadn't seen Cosimo, who had the misfortune to be staying at Jethro's house. He might be diving, I supposed.

It was a beautiful day, the air crisp when I breathed in, resounding with the dark scent that meant soil. It was cool, but the sky was clear, a piercing blue like Cosimo's eyes. I smiled with satisfaction when we reached the orchard, placing a hand against the rough bark of the closest tree as soon as I could, as though I needed more than one sense to assure me it was real. The apple trees had sturdy bases which divided into two and two again as they grew. They invited you to sit within them, and I longed to climb the branches. When I realised such a thing was not only permitted but required to enable all the apples to be picked, I had my foot wedged into a cleft in the trunk almost before Sarah had made the invitation.

The bark was rough beneath my fingers and scraped my skin when I slipped, but I climbed higher. It transferred some kind of greenish dust to my hands and my clothes. The apples hung, swaying as my climbing jolted the branches. Their smell drenched the air. Even the leaves smelled faintly of apples.

Sarah stood at the bottom of the tree and called something to me. I couldn't hear from where I was, with the leaves rustling, but I understood from her gesture that she meant I should throw the apples I picked down to her. I did so, leaning against one of the strong, twisting branches to keep steady as I reached out. I tugged at first, and got a cascade of leaves in my face. The knack was to twist, and the fruit as good as fell from its stem. I threw the apple to Sarah, watching as she turned gracefully, dipping to place it into the wicker basket by her knees.

We settled into a steady rhythm of activity. Elsewhere in the orchard, I heard voices raised in song, something cheerful I'd never heard before. It made the time pass more quickly, voices joining and leaving, the melody shifting easily.

The sun was high when the singing faded jaggedly.

I turned to see Cosimo and Paul running along the path towards us. Frowning, I sought a way down, cursing when my hands slipped and the bark burned my palms. I had told him gentle exercise. There was no call to go racing about the countryside.

I was hot and bothered by the time I was on solid ground. By then, everyone had gathered round. I pushed until I reached the front. "What is it? What's happened?" My eyes were on Paul. His colour was high, but when I touched his forehead he was no hotter than normal. His bandage didn't look discoloured.

"The Controller is here."

I turned to Cosimo, seeking enlightenment. "The Controller? Who is that? What is the Controller to us?" My heart bounced against my ribs. Cosimo's face, and the urgency with which they'd run here, told me this wasn't a good thing.

"He's the equivalent of your Magistrate. He's come from the main town at the other end of New Eden. To find out what we're doing here, most likely."

"So we tell him." I glanced at the faces of the villagers. I didn't like to feel scared when I didn't understand what there was to be afraid of.

Cosimo made an impatient noise. "You do remember how we were welcomed here?"

As though anyone could forget that! "Yes. And then we explained matters and now we're welcome guests." I looked around the group, waiting for someone to support me.

He made a scathing noise. "We're welcome *here*. New Eden as a whole might not be so generous."

I folded my arms. "Why not?"

"Paul's father was killed by nautilus men."

"They can hardly blame us for that."

Cosimo raised a disbelieving brow. "The same way your Magistrate would never condemn, say, any old reamer, just to make a point?"

I swallowed. "So what are we supposed to do? How do we deal with this ... this Controller?"

"For a start, you could try to be a little more conciliatory."

He was giving me a lesson in manners? I forced a smile. "Of course. I shall follow your lead."

"That would be perfect." He actually thought I was serious.

"Where is he, then?" I looked past Paul and Cosimo, as though I'd see the man striding towards us.

"Paul says we've got a few minutes until he reaches us."

"What, to run away?"

"That wouldn't be wise. We speak to him, and hope he's in a reasonable mood." I nodded dumbly. The alternative was that he might be as unreasonable as Jethro. "Ah'll do the talking if you like," Cosimo continued.

I bristled. "I'm quite capable of putting my point across."

He smiled. "Yeah. But the idea is for us not to be executed as spies, remember?"

One of the women shouted and everyone but me, Cosimo, Paul, Simon and Sarah turned back to the trees. I understood that in the manner common when faced with authority, we were all going to put every effort into behaving as normally as possible. The Controller would surely grow suspicious immediately.

Our small group hurried back to Emily's house. As we crossed the paths, I saw the Controller, a blob in the distance.

Once inside, I stood by the window to follow his progress. Distances were greater and far less crowded than at home. He was using some ingenious wheeled transport which enabled him to move faster than a man could walk. Outside the house, he dismounted and advanced to the door.

He reminded me of City's watchmen. The swaggering familiarity wasn't a comfort. I knew to expect it, but his peremptory knock still made me jump. I retreated to the table and sat opposite Emily and Sarah. Cosimo sat at the end with his back to the fire. Paul went to answer the door. Simon loitered by the stove.

"So, the stories are true." The Controller halted in the doorway and hitched his belt as he took a look at all of us. I was relieved to see he carried no weapons, but the tension radiating from Sarah and Emily stopped me from relaxing. The Magistrate didn't carry a cudgel or a sword, but he still held the power of life or death. I wanted to speak, but I had sense enough to wait until I was bidden.

The Controller's nodded at Emily. "Mrs Hayle, I was sorry to hear of the loss of your husband."

"Thank you." Emily accepted his commiserations in a quiet, dignified tone. Silence fell.

"Now, then." He took a pace forward, his attention jumping between me and Cosimo. He placed a hand on the back of a free chair. I was assailed by a dangerous urge to giggle. He looked for all the world as though he was calculating how he might take the weight off his feet without lowering himself to our level. He solved his dilemma by bracing his balled fists on the tabletop and leaning forward to glower at us. "So what's your story? How did you get here?"

I flicked a glance in Cosimo's direction. Somehow, I thought 'by boat' would be a quick route to the hangman's noose.

Behind us, Simon stirred. "They were shipwrecked. The boy's a reamer, although—"

"Shut up." The Controller didn't take his eyes from me as he snapped the command. Simon obeyed. "I want to hear what the girl has to say."

His brown eyes bored into me. I folded my hands and stared back to show I wasn't cowed. I wanted to stand up and tell him exactly who I was, wipe that superior expression from his face, but I could be politic when needed. "We were … escaping from City. We were shipwrecked, as Simon says. You have nothing to fear from us."

"Ha!" He reared back as if amused, although his eyes glittered with malice and, yes, fear. "It would take a lot more than a gorming pair like you to make us afraid! What were you escaping from?"

"I'm not sure. My father was killed. He told me to go with Cosimo."

"Killed? Who by?"

"I don't know." I faced the Controller steadily, but even as I spoke I wondered if the words were true. I might not know for certain, but I had my suspicions. My throat tightened so I couldn't say them aloud, even if I'd wanted to.

The silence that followed grew even thicker.

"I don't know what you've been told," Emily's calm voice interjected. "Liberty here is a doctor. She's already demonstrated her abilities."

"So you say, and the boy's a nautilus man, I can see that. Very useful. Very useful indeed. A sad loss to City, I would have thought." The Controller took a seat at last. "So, how grateful would City be to have you safely returned?"

I looked at Cosimo. I wouldn't give a pin for his chances, and I was far less than certain about my own. I cleared my throat. "I think we would prefer to stay here. For a time, at least."

The Controller roared with laughter. He thumped the table with a fist and I jumped. "I'm sure you would! Find out a few more of our secrets to tell them when you return, eh?"

"We aren't spies." Why were they so untrusting?

"That's for me to decide. What news do you have of City?"

I waited for him to clarify what he was seeking. All I had to offer was a list of questions that grew longer by the day. I didn't suppose they would impress him.

His frown deepened. "Aside from the obvious, why is City stealing our crops?"

I hardly knew where to start. A glance at Cosimo brought no enlightenment. The beginning. My father would always start at the beginning. "The obvious?" I queried.

The Controller seemed genuinely surprised. I'm not sure what reply I expected, but it certainly wasn't the one he gave: "The seas are rising again."

Chapter Fifteen

I stared at the Controller, waiting for laughter that didn't come. He was serious. My fingers tightened against each other as the world spun.

I swallowed down the lump in my throat. "The seas are rising?"

The Controller's eyes narrowed with interest. "You weren't aware of that?"

I shook my head dumbly. "We float. How would we know?" It was a feeble protest, not even an argument. I didn't need the Controller to point out its flaws.

"You're anchored to the seabed. Someone must have extended the chains, or you'd be ankle deep in water. Someone knows."

Maybe he realised I needed time to digest that. He turned to Cosimo. "A nautilus man. A reamer nautilus man, if the story is true. What a lucky piece of flotsam to wash up on our shore. Walk with me a while." It wasn't an invitation. The scrape of Cosimo's chair was loud on the floor as he obeyed.

After they left, silence endured until I broke it. "Is that true? Are the seas really rising again?"

Simon and Sarah shared a look as though they needed to confer before replying. "Two inches in six months." Simon abandoned his post by the stove and took a seat on Sarah's other side. She reached for his hand.

The seas were rising. I wished I had a hand to hold for comfort myself.

"I must check on Paul." Emily left the room. Paul hadn't rejoined us after letting the Controller into the house. My eyes stayed on the door a moment after it closed behind her.

Then I turned back to Sarah. "I had no idea. No one knows." I winced at my stupidity, the Controller's words echoing in my mind. "No one knows openly." It wasn't the sort of thing you'd shout about, after all. It would cause panic on City. And here, where the land was all they had – the people of New Eden had to be terrified. Except that the faces watching me were calm.

"The Controller won't harm you. Or Cosimo. We aren't barbarians." She put her free hand over mine. It was warm and I had to make a conscious effort not to pull away.

"No. But it seems we are. Thieves and murderers." Sarah opened her mouth and I couldn't bear for sympathy to spill off her tongue. "Tell me what happened to Paul and Henry. Please. Tell me what you know."

The two shared another long glance and I wanted to scream at their unity. Simon spoke softly, as though a raised voice might scare me away. "Are you sure you want to hear it?"

The room was silent. Then a log cracked and settled with a sigh of ash in the stove. A board creaked overhead and I pictured Emily at her son's bedside. I looked at Sarah, pleased she didn't look away.

I shouldn't have needed to think twice, and if we'd been speaking earlier, before the Controller came to see us, I wouldn't have done so. But there was more to it now. "I'm not sure whether I do," I said slowly. My father had wanted to shield me from what he'd known. He'd wanted to protect me. And now he was dead. "But if the world is collapsing, I need to know." I shifted, trying to get comfortable on the hard seat. My chair leg scraped overloud against the floor. "Yes, please tell me."

Sarah began the tale. "We don't need City. Not really. You understand that? We control our population carefully to ensure we can always feed ourselves. What we lack, what we trade our spare food for, is metal. If we need to make something, or when our tools wear out, we can only replace them with the metals City's nautilus men rescue from the seabed. It's been like that for years, since I was a child." She took a breath. "All that has always happened remotely. Trade is handled by the Controller in the main town at the other end of the island. No one comes here. We take what we want to trade and bring back metal in payment. Two weeks ago, for the first time ever, people came here."

"People?"

Simon touched his neck. "Nautilus men. From City," he added unnecessarily. If they were nautilus men they could come from nowhere else. Sarah and Simon shifted closer. Unease speared me. I watched them sitting shoulder to shoulder, and for a moment I doubted their wholesome domestic unity. They could be making this up as they went along, to divide me and Cosimo. I wasn't sure why they'd do that, but they weren't friends to City. They could all have been ganging up on me.

"And what did they want?" I asked. I already knew what their answer would be. I just wasn't sure whether I would believe it.

Sarah spoke again. "There was a swaggering brute who acted the leader. He said times had changed. He said the waves were rising. He said City would look after us, but it needed us to make a sacrifice. He said they couldn't spare any metal to trade, but they still needed to share in our harvest and in return they would protect us.

"We refused. A fair exchange is one thing, but anything else is theft – what does it matter to us if City only has algae and tins to eat? And the suggestion of protection was ridiculous. Protect us from what? They can't stop the seas rising." She sighed. "He grew angry. He accused us of conspiring against City, said we were plotting with the reamers and that we wanted City to fall. It was madness. None of us realised how dangerous he was." She swallowed. "They went away and we thought they'd accepted what we'd said, but they came back at night. Henry – Paul's father – tried to reason with them. Then they--" Her voice cracked and gave out. If she was acting, if she was trying to manipulate me, it was a magnificent show. I saw the shine of tears on her face and despised myself for doubting her.

Simon continued. "They attacked. One man and a boy facing six grown men. They beat them both, damaged Paul's hand as you saw and killed Henry. They took as much of the harvest as they could carry."

I remembered again the apple I'd enjoyed at the Magistrate's home. First of the harvest, I'd been overjoyed to receive one. It had never occurred to me that they could have been stolen rather than fairly traded. And yet, how did I know this new story was really the truth?

I sighed. Nothing they said convinced me either way. My thoughts turned to the other news they'd given me – the rising of the seas.

The Magistrate had concealed that, but he wouldn't reveal danger until he had a solution. If anyone else apart from the Magistrate had known what was going on, it would be my father. Second citizen of City and close friend of the Magistrate, he must have known the truth – or suspected. And he'd wanted us to leave. There, inescapably, was my answer.

New Eden had to be telling the truth. City was a monster. No wonder they hadn't trusted us. But it was a big leap to trust them. "*Are* you plotting with the reamers?"

They looked at each other once more. Selecting a response that would suit me?

"No, they're not."

I spun to see Cosimo in the doorway and wondered how long he'd been there. I looked at his neck as a reflex. "He didn't drown you, then?"

"Course not."

I waited, expecting an explanation. Cosimo simply sauntered up to the table and took a seat.

I folded my arms. "The Controller comes here full of threats and bluster, telling of the awful things City has done, he has a quick chat with you and then heads home?" *Conspiring with the reamers.* "What did he tell you? Or you tell him?"

"He set me a task."

"What task?"

"Something he thought Ah'd be good at."

Thieving. I coloured at immediately assuming the worst of him. That was a bad, City habit. It was more likely to be diving, now that a nautilus man had unexpectedly dropped into his lap.

He leaned forward. "Do you believe them, Liberty?"

The seas were rising. The Magistrate was protecting his own, and never mind if that meant harming everyone else. But if the seas were rising, the situation was just as perilous for the people of New Eden. More so since they relied on the land and didn't have nautilus men to help them survive. I didn't know what to think. With them all facing me, there wasn't space to consider everything I'd learned and find the right answer. I turned his question back on him. "Do *you* believe all this?" I just managed to stop myself adding 'nonsense' to the end of the question.

"These people are City's friends, or they were. Why

would they lie?"

"It's the truth," Sarah promised, but I ignored her.

I couldn't accept their stories. "On City, nautilus men are the saviours of humanity. Suddenly, here, they're murdering bogeymen?"

"Ah know what your Magistrate is capable of."

His family and friends dead, a whole group of reamers slain at the Magistrate's command. Confusion flooded through me, colouring everything I thought I knew. I remembered what Cosimo had said about his mother. I saw my father's body, cold and alone on City's pontoons. "I know that. I know. It's just …" I closed my eyes. I knew why I objected to the tale I was being told, but I wasn't going to admit that to these people. "I can't accept it." I opened my eyes to meet Cosimo's blue ones. I couldn't read his expression. I shouldn't expect understanding from a reamer. "I just … can't." I tried to find an objection I could safely speak aloud. "How come no one on City knows what's going on?"

"You think your Magistrate doesn't have secrets?"

I wished he would stop referring to him as 'my' Magistrate. I was increasingly sure I didn't want anything to do with the man.

Silence fell. I stared at the table. My thoughts were moving towards a conclusion I didn't want to reach. I flexed my hand as though it was still stiff with my father's blood.

"They did try to drown me when we arrived," Cosimo reminded me, finding his voice at last. "You have to be pretty angry – or scared – to do that."

I scoffed. "That's hardly conclusive. I've wanted to drown you from the minute I met you."

He almost smiled, then the gesture slid from his face. "Makes sense, Liberty."

"It does nothing of the sort." I was outnumbered and hot with injustice. I felt picked on. The truth was rushing towards me like a wave. "It's the sort of story only credible fools would be taken in by."

"It's more than that," Cosimo promised me calmly. "Something happened to Paul and his father. You saw the result of that."

"I know." My throat closed. I was afraid, truly afraid. I didn't like the feeling. My life ... my life wasn't supposed to be like this. Something had rushed out of control and I wanted my calm, orderly life back. I wanted to be at home, helping Pa. I didn't want to be here, facing this.

"And someone killed your father."

It engulfed me. I was drowning. I couldn't breathe. I closed my eyes, then covered them with my hands. I leaned forward until my elbows met the table, needing something solid to lean against.

"Liberty, I'm sorry." Sarah's voice broke through the wave. Her hand was warm on my arm. The heat was close to painful. I pulled away. Her voice twisted with anguish. "I am sorry. I didn't mean to upset you. I'm grateful to you. Truly. There aren't words for what you've done for Paul."

I took a deep, shuddering breath as the wave released me. "It was him." There. Now I'd said it aloud it was real and would never go away.

"What was him?" Sarah's voice was puzzled.

I opened my eyes and dropped my hands to the table with a dull thud. Cosimo was watching me. There was no surprise in his expression. Why would there be? He already knew. "The Magistrate killed my father."

He didn't blink.

"Oh, it wasn't his hand on the knife." I remembered the voice. The voice wasn't his. "But it was him. The nautilus men take their orders from him, after all." My father's best friend. Or so I'd thought. He'd tried to run, but the Magistrate reached him before he could escape.

I blinked. Sarah was watching me, her expression full of concern. I tried to smile. My muscles wouldn't obey. "It's all right. I believe you. But whatever is happening, the people on City aren't aware of it. I promise."

"You don't have to promise us anything. You aren't in doubt," Sarah reassured me.

Simon stood and cleared his throat. "It's late and we've given you a lot to think about. We'll leave you to rest, Liberty." Rest! As though I could sleep after this. The three of them rose to leave.

"Wait!" I called Cosimo back. "I might as well get rid of your stitches now."

He nodded and told Simon, "Ah'll follow."

Chapter Sixteen

I fetched the lamp and a small pair of sharp scissors as Cosimo sank into a seat. I drew my chair up close. The front door closed behind the others. He tilted his chin up and I inspected the wound, checking the integrity of his skin before I started. "I've never seen anyone heal so quickly," I mused. "I wonder if the salt water helps. Perhaps we should have been recommending an early dive instead of discouraging one." I wished my father were there to discuss the matter with, and closed my eyes until the longing passed.

Cosimo made a non-committal noise.

I slit the first stitch and carefully eased the thread from his warm skin. "You said the magistrate attacked your settlement for your machine. Why?"

Cosimo's breath hitched as the thread pulled free. His hands were splayed on the table in front of him, as though to brace against my actions. I left a pause so he could answer. "He knows his world might end soon."

"Because the seas are rising?" No answer to that; an answer wasn't needed. "So he also wants to find the land of sun and roses?" My tone gave my view on that impossible ambition. I returned to my work. The second stitch split and I pulled the end. "And he has the reamers' machine now?"

Cosimo waited until I'd removed the third and final stitch beneath the gill before nodding. I dropped the thread to the table and pushed the fibres together neatly.

"And he killed mah mother so she couldn't make another."

I closed my eyes while the jolt of that information faded. "Other side." I pushed his chin up and round so I could reach the stitches on the other side. His pulse beat rapidly beneath his skin. I took a breath and spoke calmly. "I'm sorry. Can't someone else make it?"

"Yeah, me. If Ah can find enough metal."

I paused a moment until my fingers steadied. "All's not quite lost, then." I focused on my work.

I got a grunt for that.

I pulled another stitch free. "Why is he bullying New Eden? Do they have a machine he wants, too?"

"Much more basic than that. They've got food. That's all he wants from here."

I still found it hard to think of the Magistrate as a petty thief. The second stitch gave. "We've got food."

"Not for long," he managed, bitterly. "The tins will be too far to reach again when the seas rise."

I nodded, as a picture of the future bloomed in my mind. Our food supply would slip out of reach, men dying to get to it while others died on the surface without it. Another twist of nature and City would be on the brink of starvation once more, as we'd been before my father designed nautilus technology.

I pulled the final stitch free and ran my thumb over his skin. It was smooth and healthy, warm to the touch, with the faintest pucker of holes where the needle had punctured the skin. Cosimo shivered. I dropped my hand. "Does it hurt?"

His tone was gruff. "No. No. Is it healed?"

"Yes." I sat straight and looked at him. "What are you going to do?"

"Do?"

It was a simple enough question. "Stay here? Go to the reamers? What did the Controller say to you? Will they even let you go?"

"This isn't City. They're hardly going to lock me up." He looked at me levelly and I realised how close we were, his face and those blazing blue eyes a moment away from me. I wanted to scoot my chair back but that might look like he made me uncomfortable.

I focused on the threads, rolling them together to give myself something to do. "That doesn't mean they'll be happy if you leave. You're valuable."

"Ah wish you'd stop saying that."

I stared. "Saying what?"

"Ah'm not *valuable*. Ah'm not a cargo of gorming tins!"

"I didn't mean—" I pushed my chair back then. "I'm sorry if I offended you." I folded my arms.

I thought he would storm out, but he stayed in his seat. There was a pause. Then he asked, "Can you perform the nautilus operation?"

I was wrong-footed by the question. "The procedure? Of course I can."

He blinked, mouth open but saying nothing. I wondered if he'd ask whether I'd performed his.

"It's academic, though. The last of the devices my father made are at the bottom of the sea. There are no more that aren't already in use."

"Oh, Ah suppose." He wouldn't look at me.

I looked sharply at him. "Do you know different? Did you save my father's bag?"

He huffed. "Ah barely saved myself."

Was he allergic to giving a straight answer to a question? "Did you save my father's bag?"

At last, an emotion. His eyes flared with anger. "No!"

"All right."

"But could you do the operation, if there were more devices?"

"Not here. On City I could. In my father's house." I

didn't say it to him, but there was every chance that back home I'd find more devices. Or at least another diagram of their construction. If I could bear to return.

"Why not here? Don't they have the right knives?"

I shook my head. "It's not that. I would need chloroform. It can't be done without anaesthetic. The shock would kill a man."

"But Paul …"

"Not the same thing at all. The devices become a part of your body. The procedure is very, very complex. Paul's operation, by comparison, was little better than butchery."

"So Ah'm the last ever nautilus man."

"I expect you are."

Again, I thought he would leave. Again, he made no move to do so. "What are you going to do, Liberty?" he asked instead. My turn for no reply. I didn't know, but I preferred to seem enigmatic rather than lost.

"Will you stay here? You can't want to return to City. Not now."

Except that I did. I hadn't been sure until Cosimo framed the idea as an impossibility. City was my home. I missed it. I even missed Hannah's pertness and Will's swaggering. More importantly, I wanted to return home and confront the Magistrate. Which would be a quick way to join my father in death. "No, I can't go back," I told Cosimo, trying to convince myself. My father had died to protect me. I had to remember that. And I had no way to get back to City now the boat had sunk. The thought was disappointing and pragmatic, but at least it settled the matter.

"So, what will you do?"

What business was it of his? "I'll wait until Paul is fully healed," I said, largely to buy myself time. Then I realised why he was so anxious. "Don't worry, I don't expect you to take me anywhere. You've fulfilled your promise. My father wouldn't expect any more from you."

Cosimo shoved his chair back. "Thank the tides for that."

The door banged behind him. I swept the threads from the table to the floor and swallowed down a sudden lump in my throat. I had no reason to be upset by a reamer's lack of manners. I had to be just tired.

*

I was awoken in the early hours by a distraught Emily, nightdress crumpled, wild hair spilling down her back.

Paul was writhing in a fever that burned my fingers when I touched his skin. This would be the true test of healing, and of Paul's strength. I damped a cloth and wiped his brow. His eyes opened and I took the opportunity of lucidity to get some water down him. "Now, try to rest," I soothed, settling him back against his pillows.

"It's wound fever, isn't it?" Emily queried at my shoulder, watching Paul anxiously.

There was no point hiding the truth. "Yes."

I saw her accept the news, saw her switch from mother to doctor's assistant. Not another word was needed as we worked together, wiping Paul's skin with damp cloths, changing his bedclothes.

*

Not long after dawn, Sarah arrived and set immediately to help. Cosimo appeared for a short while, then vanished with Simon.

Time stretched and blurred.

Some time later, Sarah turned me out of the sick room.

"We don't need a doctor for this, we know what to do. You're exhausted. Rest in case we need you later." She was gentle, and kind, but she was implacably firm. Paul's bedroom door shut behind her before I thought of a protest.

I stood at the top of the stairs, my hand curling on

the banister. If I wasn't a doctor, I wasn't anyone.

Away from the bustle of Paul's room, the house was empty and silent. I glanced at a window. Judging from the sun it was mid-morning. Everyone would be harvesting.

I understood the desire to have me rest, but I was too filled with adrenaline to sleep. I walked slowly down the stairs and slipped out of the front door. I'd go to the orchard. Perhaps I could make myself useful there. Or at least pass the time with others around me for company.

The air was clear and fresh, a slight breeze tugging at my clothes. It only took a couple of minutes to reach the orchard, but it was empty. I stared up at the leaves rustling overhead. One detached as I watched, twisting jerkily down to the ground. I was an idiot. The apples had all been harvested. No one was here.

I turned, taking in the scene. The fields were all empty, too. The wind tugged a wisp of hair free and I smoothed it behind my ear as a shiver raised the hairs on my neck. Where was everyone? I realised how little I knew about the people of New Eden. They might be fishing for seaweed, although why they'd do that when they had proper food to eat, I didn't know. They could be … Maybe they'd all gone to market at the other end of the island.

Then I saw someone. A figure made stick-small by distance came out of a building a little way past Emily's home. Another followed. They picked up something from the ground outside and made their way back into the building carrying it through thrown-wide doors that closed behind them. I couldn't see what it was, and my curiosity was piqued.

*

By the time I'd drawn close to the building, my curiosity was balanced by caution. I heard voices inside, sounds of work.

Nearly at the door, I hung back, unsure how to intrude. Hannah would doubtless throw the door open, saunter inside and charm everyone instantly, but I wasn't her. I could imagine the scene: I'd push the door open and walk inside and everyone would stare at me. I'd offer my help and the people of New Eden would continue to stare, wondering what in the seas I was about until one of them found a way to tell me kindly that I had no place there.

My hands grew sweaty and I wiped them against my skirt. But maybe I *could* help. The people of New Eden liked me, I thought. I'd wondered if I could make a home here – this was my chance to find out. I shook my plait back, straightened my shoulders and stepped forward, only to jump back as the door swung open towards me, blocking my view. Voices reached me through the barrier. "Ah'm happy to help you." That could only be one person.

"We're grateful, truly we are." I didn't recognise the second voice – one of the neighbours, no doubt. "And we'll keep it safe from City spies." The voice grew grim. "City has made its own path; now City can walk it without our help."

"Ah'd –" Whatever Cosimo replied was cut off as they turned away, the door swinging shut with a creak that drowned out their voices. I jumped back, dodging around the corner of the building so Cosimo and his friend wouldn't see me. I pressed my hands to my burning face. My first assessment had been right – I wouldn't have been welcome inside. No wonder I didn't know what they were busy with: I was City, and not to be trusted.

*

When I was sure everyone was once more inside the building, I hurried back the way I'd come, almost tripping in my haste to get away before they discovered me. Spying, no doubt that's what they'd call what I'd been doing.

"Liberty?" As I pushed the house door open, Sarah's voice greeted me.

I looked up to see her on the landing above. She regarded me with a smile that brightened her entire face. "The danger is past. Paul's temperature is normal." She hurried down the stairs towards me, seizing my hands and squeezing.

As her warm fingers soothed my skin, I found a smile. "That's wonderful." I was being silly. Of course I belonged here. I could have helped at the barn if I'd only gone inside; they wouldn't have turned me away. Maybe they'd even have welcomed me if I'd given them the chance.

"Thank you so much."

"Truly, it's a pleasure to help."

And it was. I watched Sarah vanish into the kitchen. Time was running out. I needed to make a decision. Or perhaps I just needed to accept the one circumstances were pushing on me.

Chapter Seventeen

"You need to see this." I was eating a late and solitary breakfast the following day, hanging about the house. Paul and Emily were upstairs and all the helpful neighbours were probably busy about the secret, not-for-City-eyes, project, when Cosimo slipped into the kitchen and hovered beside the table, a hand on the back of my chair as though he wanted to drag it back and hurry me along with him.

"What is it?" His restless energy made me want to set my head on the table and sleep for a week.

"Come and see." He stepped back, impatient at my shoulder while I finished my porridge and took my dish to the sink.

Was he going to show me what they were doing? Excitement flipped my stomach over. I wanted to be included, to be a part of it all. I grabbed my coat and called to Emily that I would be back in five minutes. Cosimo didn't disagree, just stood with the door open until I passed by him.

"Where are we going?" He strode on ahead. It was in the opposite direction to the building I'd found and my hopes slid away on the cool breeze. I was glad of my coat, wrapping my arms tight across my chest to ward off the cutting wind.

"Not far."

*

He came to rest where the ground fell away towards the sea. I looked down and recognised the path we'd taken from the beach we'd washed up on. Then my gaze travelled further and shock held me still, or perhaps it was fear that I'd admit to myself if not to Cosimo. On the waves, far away but clear enough that there could be no mistake, was a black blob. A flat, City barge. Heading this way.

"Way the wind's blowing, it'll be here before dark."

I nodded. I hoped Cosimo didn't realise I hadn't the breath to speak a reply. I had started to imagine I could make a life here. I hated to think I'd been fooling myself. I hated more that I'd taken myself in, even for a short while. I wrapped my arms tighter. "Raiders and thieves. How could this be happening without us even knowing it?"

"It's only you who missed it, your Highness," Cosimo murmured. "We'd love to have been unaware the Magistrate wanted to destroy us."

A sign of City was in sight and suddenly I was *your Highness* again. "What happens now?" There was something in my throat. I could hardly speak and had to swallow after just those few words.

"They'll come, and they'll shout about New Eden and the reamers being in league against City, and they'll take whatever of value they can. They might kill a few people, too." Cosimo spoke as though it didn't matter. Then I realised the coldness must have settled inside him when his mother died, numbing him like the cold that flooded through me when I thought of my father.

"But you can slip away beneath the waves." I was trying to find something positive in the situation.

He turned. "Do you really think Ah'd do that?" He scowled and turned away. "Yeah, of course you do. Ah'm a reamer."

Heat rose in me, welcome after the cold. "Of course I don't think that. Just … why die if you don't have to?"

Cosimo pushed at a pebble with his toe, then looked up. "There's something else you need to see, Liberty."

My name again. That was unexpected. "What?"

He turned away from the sea, and I knew instinctively where he was going to take me. "Come on. Ah think you'll like it."

*

The barn was quiet now. I wondered where all the busy workers had gone. "It's been a bit rushed," Cosimo threw over his shoulder as we walked. "But it covers the basics." He paused to push the heavy door open. It scraped across the beaten earth, raising a drift of dust in its wake. Inside was a single, huge room. I blinked in the sudden dark, trying to make sense of what I saw. Barrels and boxes lined the wall at one end, the start of this year's harvest, or the remains of last year's, perhaps. When I breathed in, I smelled the scent of apples. This year's harvest. All boxed up and ready to steal. I thought of the black dot heading our way and wondered if there was any possibility of another storm.

The centre of the room was simultaneously empty and full. There were a couple of large tables, bigger than the one I'd used to operate on Paul, with small items strewn across the top: tools that I recognised and other things I didn't which simply sat and glinted in the light that filtered through the shutters.

The far side of the barn was filled by a couple of hulking shapes that were clearly projects under construction. One was an elaborate arrangement of plastics and tin piping. The other was a large half-barrel made of metal. It looked a little like bathtubs the Old Ones had used for washing. It was big enough for half a dozen people to stand inside, so long as they were friendly. It was made of recycled cans; I could see the blobs on its surface where the beaten flat pieces had been riveted together.

"Do you like it?" Cosimo left me standing by the door and walked across the room until he was beside it. He tapped the half-barrel's metal surface, raising a hollow ring with his knuckles, and looked at me expectantly.

"What is it?" I followed him, watching where I placed my feet amidst the junk so I wouldn't trip.

"It's what the Magistrate sent his men to kill my mother for. We call them balloon ships."

I stared at the half-built machine as everything became clear. "This is how you're going to cross the Wastes."

He nodded. "If they can be crossed, this is how we'll do it."

I stepped closer, examining it from all sides. Motes of dust twisted in the air around me. The air smelled hot, like it did when my father made nautilus devices back home. The scent of metal heated and worked and cooled. I reached out to touch the surface of the thing, surprised to find the machine cold. It seemed as though it should be living. "Shouldn't it have wheels? How is it going to cross the Wastes?"

He shook his head. "It floats on air."

I looked at the lump of metal. "How is that possible?"

"If you heat air, it rises. Heat lots of air and it can lift a weight. The cradle carries people and cargo, while the balloon lifts the whole so it can float over the Wastes – and cross the space far more quickly than we can on foot."

I peered closer, crouching down to inspect the plastic bottles that made up the balloon. "How do you heat the air?"

"There's a closed stove. At least, there would be." He pointed to one of the tables that I'd overlooked and I transferred my attention to that. A diagram was sketched in chalk on the top of the table. I studied it to make sense while Cosimo explained, "It directs heat into the pipework, which spreads the hot air into the bottles that make up the balloon."

"It's ingenious."

Cosimo drew a line under the plan with his forefinger. "It's straightforward. The only clever part is the stove. That was mah mother's work. Heat conservation enables the machine to travel further than should be possible with the fuel used."

"How do you control where it goes?"

"This one, you can't. You have to wait for the winds to blow in the right direction."

"That sounds chancy."

His lips twitched. "Life's always chancy."

"Why are you showing me this?"

"You ought to know that there are alternatives. That no one has to stay and drown – or starve."

I nodded. "Is this how you're going to get to your people?"

He shook his head. "We're out of time for that. It's not ready for a flight yet. But at least it gives the people of New Eden some alternatives."

"Why are you giving New Eden the reamers' technology?"

He smiled. "They're welcome to it if they can use it. Ah'm not scared of competition."

"Why didn't you tell me sooner?"

"It's hardly your area of expertise." A shaft of light struck the metal and I blinked away the pain in my dazzled eyes. "And you were busy," he pointed out. It was true, but I still felt excluded.

I tapped a knuckle against the metal, the ringing sound far too cheery for the situation. "If he finds it, the Magistrate will take this, too."

"But the people of New Eden will still know what it is. They'll be able to make one for themselves."

"You're *expecting* City to steal it?"

He folded his arms. "Ah expect they'll try. Whether they manage to take it or not is up to New Eden."

My stomach hollowed out at the thought of a fight between the two. I knew why he was telling me about it now – with the boat heading this way, City finding the technology was inevitable, so keeping it secret from me no longer mattered.

"New Eden won't be able to make another if City takes this. They don't have enough metal. Or are you planning to stay?"

"Ah might do. Or you could help them."

I didn't know what he thought I could do.

"Before we started on the balloon Ah made something else." He turned his fist upwards and opened his fingers to reveal what he was holding.

I leaned closer and saw exactly what Cosimo meant. I recognised it immediately, although I couldn't believe what I was seeing.

"Thief!" I snarled. I would have grabbed it from his hand, but he was too quick for me. "You stole that from my father's bag!"

"No." He used one hand to fend me off, the other fisted around the nautilus device and held high out of my reach. "Ah made it. Calm down and Ah'll show you."

I took a step back and spread my hands to pacify him, shaking my plait back over my shoulder as I steadied my breathing. Cosimo lowered his hand and uncurled his fingers.

I reached out, expecting him to flinch back, but he let me take it. I was gentle. The last nautilus device not already in a man's neck. I turned it to the light to see properly. He was telling the truth. It wasn't my father's workmanship. It was perfect, but different.

"You made this?" I squinted from the device to him. "How in the seas?" I couldn't do it, and I knew the theory behind the devices. I'd handled dozens of pairs in my life.

"Your father showed me the plan. Before mah operation."

"You have the diagram?" There was another. Of course my father wouldn't have had just one. No wonder the boy had been so interested in whether I could perform the procedure.

"No. It's lost now."

"But—"

"Ah have a good memory."

I was so busy admiring the device, it took a while for that to sink in. "You *saw the diagram* and made this?"

He was pink with pride. For once, I couldn't complain at his arrogance. I brought the device to my lips and blew, listening for the sound as the gills turned. The steady hum was faultless. "This is astonishing."

"Ah'm glad it meets your approval, your Highness." His flush grew cross instead of pleased. I didn't know why he had to be so defensive all the time. I gave back the device. "What are you going to do?"

He pushed the tiny device back into a pocket. "It's useless, isn't it? We might have a surgeon, but without chloroform …"

"It's still valuable." Priceless. I didn't say what I was thinking, that there would certainly be some chloroform back on City. If someone was prepared to fetch it.

"Ah wasn't going to throw it away."

I focused my attention on the balloon ship so I wouldn't have to think about the decisions heading my way at the pace of that tiny boat bobbing on the waves. I peered at the plan of the stove, drinking in the details although I knew *I* wouldn't remember it from a single look. I wished my father were there to see it, grateful for the shaft of pain which twisted through me and anchored me in the moment.

"Your mother must have been a remarkable

engineer."

He reddened. "Why should she not?"

I straightened my shoulders at the tone of his voice. "I didn't think reamers had much time for education."

"We aren't stupid, your Highness. You shouldn't believe City's fairy tales."

"I don't."

"You sure?" He strode to the door.

I flicked a fingernail against the half-made balloon basket for the pleasure of the sound it made, to pass the time while my anger faded.

*

Back outside the barn, I retraced the path to the beach. Hard to believe I'd walked it in the opposite direction, bedraggled and guarded, less than a week before. It felt like a lifetime away.

When I reached the clifftop and the path down, I stopped, squinting across the sun-struck waves to see the tiny boat heading in this direction. It was more than a dot now. I could see the tiny figures crawling over the deck. The wind flicked at my hair and I scraped it out of my eyes, blinking back the stinging hurt it caused.

I wondered if the boat was coming for me. I'd been so sure I was worth rescuing; that I was valuable enough for the Magistrate to send someone after me. Now I wasn't so sure. If it came down to me or the harvest New Eden had worked so hard to grow, I didn't flatter myself that the Magistrate would prefer me to his next few meals. But I doubted he was making the journey himself. He didn't do his own dirty work – I had proof of that already.

"Homesick?"

I hadn't realised Cosimo had followed me until he spoke. I half-turned and he stepped forward to stand beside me. "Not so much," I confided.

He drew in a long breath and blew it slowly out. "The people here are prepared to fight."

Once again, they'd been discussing plans without me. Ideas I couldn't be trusted with because I was City.

"Or we could go to the reamers," Cosimo continued.

"We?"

"Ah told your father Ah'd take care of you."

I turned away. Just obligation, then. I scraped my hair from my face impatiently – what else did I expect him to feel towards me? I shook my head. "I have to go back to City." I faced him. "Is there a boat I could take? If I go out to meet them I might be able to stop them coming to New Eden. Then the machine will be safe – and the harvest."

"We could ask."

I grabbed his arm as he turned away. I didn't want him to trek back to the village and tell everyone what I intended. "There isn't time to ask. The sooner I go, the sooner that boat will turn back." I didn't want Sarah, Simon and Emily to know what I was doing. I told myself I was scared they'd stop me going and that would put them all in worse danger, but actually, I was more scared they wouldn't try to stop me. I didn't fit here, not really. I'd thought I could make a home here, but that was a dream, every bit as foolish as longing for the land of sun and roses.

Cosimo's arm was hot under my fingers. I let go, stepping away. "Don't worry. I'll look for a boat myself. No need to bother them." I started down the path to the beach.

He jogged behind me. "Ah've seen a boat. Ah'll show you."

*

When he reached the beach, Cosimo led me to one side, where the cliff jutted out into the sea and the beach vanished.

The sand turned to shingle and we crunched across the pebbles. As we drew closer, I saw the cliff had been worn away at the bottom to form a cave. Two small boats had been dragged above the tide mark and tucked out of the way of the weather. One was little more than a rowing boat. The other was smaller than Cosimo's but large enough to have a single, slim mast that jutted out towards the sky.

Cosimo didn't say a word, just bent to brace his arms against the bow of the larger boat and push it back to the waiting waves.

I stood beside him and pushed. I wanted to tell Cosimo to leave it to me, but the first shove told me that would be pointless. It was harder than it looked to move the thing; without him I'd be there until midnight.

Finally, we gave a last heave and the boat slid over the last of the lumpy pebbles to buoy into the sea, bobbing away so I had to grab at it. "Thanks." I faced Cosimo. "I'll manage from here." I scrambled in and looked around. The bottom of the boat scraped and jerked me off balance as the waves pushed it back onto the pebbles. Stupid boat – didn't it know where it was supposed to go? I needed to get the sail up, then it would start moving.

Cosimo shoved it further so the horrible scraping noise ceased.

"Thank you."

He didn't answer. He was too busy heaving himself over the side.

I jumped back as he landed on the deck, shedding water from the soaked bottoms of his trousers. "What are you doing?"

"Coming with you, of course."

I glanced towards the incoming City boat. Curiously, now we were on the same level it seemed further away, returned to a blob. "Don't be ridiculous. The Magistrate will kill you."

"Ah'm more concerned that you'll go round in circles and they'll never find you."

Because I was stupid and helpless and couldn't be trusted even to return to my lying, cheating home. I folded my arms. "I can manage."

"And two of us will manage better."

"You don't want to run the risk of being caught by watchmen."

"Ah'm not scared of your Magistrate's men."

My Magistrate – and I thought we'd got past us and them. "You should be. A reamer who stole City technology and a City girl – the Magistrate will hang you if you're left alive long enough to face him. Go back to New Eden, you stupid gorm."

"Ah've done what Ah needed to do here."

"Then go home. Go to the reamers. Build your machine and find the land of sun and roses." I glanced anxiously towards where I'd last seen the boat. "If they see you're here, they'll come after you. And nautilus men are perfectly capable of finding you beneath the waves."

He shook his head. "Fine. Ah'll go. But Ah'll follow after you later and get you away from City. Ah won't leave you with the Magistrate."

My heart jumped with hope. Then I remembered the nonsense promise he'd made to my father and all my optimism fell to the deck. His words didn't mean anything. "Oh, I don't think that would be a good idea – look what happened last time you ventured into City."

Cosimo huffed a laugh and straightened slowly, brushing his damp hands on his trousers. When he faced me, a smile twisted one side of his mouth. "Except, your Highness, this time Ah'll know what to expect, won't Ah?"

Hope and impossibility collided in my chest. Anger was the result. "Don't be stupid, he'll kill you."

"He'll have to catch me first. Ah wasn't planning to hang around for introductions."

The wind blew his brown hair into his face, hiding

his eyes. I watched as he scraped it away so he could see clearly. He actually thought he was some kind of hero who could sail in and rescue me from danger. My fingers curled into fists. I so wished he would. I didn't want to have to face the Magistrate on my own. But this wasn't some story told to pass the time on a winter's night with my father. This was real life, and a happy ending wasn't likely. All the same, the offer made my throat feel strangely thick. My fists clenched harder, nails digging into my palms. I couldn't let him risk himself. Not for me. "Look, I'm going back where I belong. You should do the same."

"You don't belong on City. Not anymore."

"Of course I do. City's my home." I made myself shrug, a shoulder lifting like I didn't have a care in the world.

He examined my face, looking for a weakness in my resolve. I glared him down, determined he wouldn't find one. "You can't mean to help the Magistrate," he said.

"I mean to help my friends. If that requires me to work with the Magistrate, then that's what I'll do."

Hurt sparked in his eyes. "You'd make a pact with the devil."

My face burned at seeing his opinion of me in those clear, blue eyes. I was in such turmoil it wasn't hard to direct my anger at him. "If I have to. Go." I shoved at his chest and he stumbled backwards. His eyes blazed anger before he turned and dived off the side of the boat without another word.

I sagged to the deck, suddenly boneless. Cosimo was safe, that was the important thing. I didn't care what a stupid reamer thought of me.

I dragged a deep breath into uncooperative lungs. How stupid, to want to cry when he'd done exactly what I wanted him to do. I *didn't* want him following me, so it was contrary to want him to *want* to follow me.

The boat lurched abruptly, tugged by a current I couldn't even see. I got to my feet and realised what an idiot I'd been – I should at least have let Cosimo raise the sail and set me off in the right direction before sending him away.

I didn't look back to see whether Cosimo had reached New Eden's beach – why would I? Instead, I set to work, trying to remember skills that were so recent they'd never had a chance to sink in to my confused brain.

Finally, when the sail billowed with wind and the boat was heading in roughly the right direction, I let myself glance back. There was nothing to see on New Eden's distant beach or the clifftop above. I hadn't thought there would be. I sat down, grasped the tiller and pointed myself towards the City boat.

Chapter Eighteen

The autumn sun faded as the boat drew closer, the light taking on an odd, glowing aspect as though the last of the day was being held for as long as possible by the dimming sky. Finally, I drew close enough to hail the sailors on the barge.

I straightened and stamped my feet, trying to encourage blood and feeling back to my limbs after hours of sitting.

"Hie there, friends!" My voice cracked on the last word but I didn't let it affect the silly smile I forced on my face.

One of the sailors stood, hands braced on hips. "Hie there!"

I swallowed down the uncomfortable thought that perhaps they were simply seeking salvage. Maybe they weren't heading deliberately to New Eden. Maybe they weren't any danger and I could have stayed. I shielded my eyes and called again. "I'm Liberty Marchmont! Can you help me?"

"With pleasure!" the sailor called back. He turned and yelled something to his fellows. Someone else joined him on deck, coiling a rope as he moved closer. "Catch this if you can." As our two boats bobbed inevitably closer, he threw the end of the rope towards me.

He nodded approval when I snatched the rope as it slapped onto my deck, before it could slither off into the sea. "Fasten it to your buoy there, we'll pull you in." I tied the rope to one of the plastic buoys hanging around the sides of the boat and the sailors heaved on the other end.

The barge drew closer until the sides of our boats bumped together. As the sailors worked to draw the crafts tight, one of their number stepped forward and held out a hand with a grin. "Do come aboard, won't you, Doc?" Leading my rescue, if you chose to see the matter like that, was Will Keyne.

*

Will's face split in a wide grin as he held out his hand to help me onto the barge. My heart gave a lurch that felt as much like regret as it did trepidation. Perhaps I was mourning the future I'd thought I would have, where all my certainties in life weren't ground to dust. I forced a calm smile and took his hand, turning my thoughts towards the decision I'd made.

Will helped me onto the City barge, checking with charming, flamboyant, irritating solicitude that I had a comfortable seat before giving the order to turn about and set off back to City.

"Praise the tides you're safe!" Will Keyne; ever the charmer. I wondered if he'd practised the words to pass the time on board. They sounded a little over-rehearsed. He gripped my hands as though assuring himself of my safety, but when he looked up, he didn't look at me but rather over my shoulder, past the boat to the shore of New Eden. Was he regretting that he would return to City empty handed? "You vanished from City. We were afraid you'd come to harm. What happened?"

I wished I'd spent more time concocting a story instead of regretting the choice I'd made. I hadn't thought I'd be quizzed – or not so soon. "I don't want to talk about it," I said, trying to sound distressed, burying my face in my hands.

"A reamer was at large on City that night. He killed

your father. Did he abduct you?"

Heat rose in me. No reamer had killed my father. I wondered if they knew Cosimo had been on City, or if it was simply a reflex to blame the reamers for every ill. Here was proof that I'd made the right decision. I had to keep City away from New Eden and away from the reamers if I could. I shook my head, "I just want to go home," I mumbled through my hands, as though too overcome to say more.

"You heard the lady – back to City!"

One of the sailors spoke out, "What about—"

"Never mind our orders," Will interrupted. "Our destination is City."

The men muttered agreement. Will turned back to me, his voice softer. "I was worried about you, Doc."

His hand settled on my shoulder and I had to make an effort not to shake him off, anger burning inside me. All Will's charm and swagger was an act, designed to befuddle his audience and enable him to get his way, just like his father. He wasn't attracted to me; he just wanted me to be attracted to him so he could manipulate me to his advantage.

"Yes, the reamer forced me to go with him," I managed through my hands.

Will dropped to sit beside me. "I'm so sorry, Liberty. Where is he now?"

Because that's what his father was really interested in. And there was one way that I could put Cosimo safely beyond their reach. "He's dead."

"Dead? How come?" I felt his eyes on me but I didn't uncover my face. I didn't want him to see me clearly – and I definitely didn't want to look at him and watch while he pretended to my face that he cared for me at all.

"He went diving too early and caught a fever," I explained, maintaining my tone that the reamer had got what he deserved.

"Diving?" I could have kicked myself when I heard his surprised tone. Will hadn't known until that moment about the operation. "So it's true, your father made him a nautilus man?"

I nodded, not trusting myself to speak.

"And he's dead now?"

Another nod.

"You saw him die?"

My, my. Will and his father were extraordinarily keen not to let a worthless reamer slip away. "He had a fever of over a hundred degrees when the storm washed him overboard. He can't possibly have survived."

Will moved away and I dared look up at him. He was staring beyond me once more, scanning the land as far as he could see. In this light, that wasn't far. He had to be calculating whether there was a possible way out I hadn't thought of, and if there was something he should challenge.

"You're sure?"

I nodded. "I know enough of medicine to be sure of that."

"Of course, of course." He looked as though he didn't know what to do now.

I continued. "Why, do you think I've been drifting in the middle of the sea through choice?"

His jaw slackened, as though he hadn't thought me capable of holding or expressing an opinion. I thought it was a surprise to him to find me so forthright. It was hard not to laugh for real. I had clearly wrong-footed smooth Will. I was better at deception than I'd supposed. I realised with a start that I wasn't at all ashamed of the fact. He recovered himself. "Of course not. I am sorry for all your travails, Doc. And happier than I can say to find you here, safe and unharmed. It will be my greatest pleasure to return you safely home."

*

The journey back to City was tedious, slow and

uncomfortable. I slept fitfully during the night, but once it was light there was nothing for me to do but wait. I was of no use and no concern to the sailors, who stepped around me while trying not to make it too obvious that I was in their way.

The spectre of City grew as the hours passed. More than that, the spectre of the Magistrate swelled to monstrous proportions. With nothing else to do, my brain rehearsed the moment of our meeting time and again, all possible words and responses, actions and reactions.

*

By the time City became a distinguishable blur of grey rising from the sea, my brain was a mush and I doubted my ability to speak a coherent word when I was actually face-to-face with the man.

I tried to sleep again to pass the time. I might have done better if I'd not been too stiff, frozen and fraught to surrender to oblivion. I dozed, and the scenarios I'd practised became nightmarish, jerking me to wakefulness with my heart racing. I wrapped my coat and a blanket more tightly around me, propped my chin on my knees, and watched as City grew larger and more oppressive as the day progressed. I wished I were on the other side of the next twenty-four hours of my life.

The journey finally ended, as awful things eventually do. We'd spent a night and a day travelling, and the sky was streaked with gold and red as we finally bumped into a space between the other vessels crowding City's quayside.

By the time the boat was secured, people had come to greet our arrival. I looked past the Harbour Master to find the Magistrate, come in person. I rose stiffly. It was the scene I'd rehearsed a thousand times in the last twelve hours. I didn't feel any more prepared now than I had when I'd begun. I didn't want to face him. I didn't want to say any of the words I had practised.

The Magistrate himself held out his hand to help me back onto land. "Miss Marchmont." He smiled. I thought I might vomit. He had ordered my father's death and he dared to smile at me as though he were my friend. My shivering increased to a pace that would worry me if I saw it in a patient.

"My deepest sympathies for the trials you have endured. You have no idea how pleased I am to see you safely returned to City." His words were as smooth as his tone, as practised as any that would have fitted perfectly into one of his public addresses. I stared at him, wondering that I had ever found anything admirable about this man. He was nothing but an actor. And now I knew what was behind the facade, I didn't even think he was a very good one.

It was that knowledge, and my sudden certainty that I could beat him, that enabled me to jam my chattering teeth together, force a smile and murmur my thanks as I set my hand unavoidably in his. "You poor child, how you must have suffered." The Magistrate frowned, as though his concern was genuine. "You will spend the night at my home, Miss Marchmont. I could not allow anything else."

I would far rather return to my own home, but I couldn't afford to arouse his suspicion. "You are kind." I stepped onto the pontoons of City and stumbled. It seemed as though the world shifted beneath my feet. I knew it was just an illusion, an error of balance due to my hours at sea, compounded by the chill in my limbs. The ground was every bit as stable as it had ever been. But that had always been the illusion. Now I had seen through it, I would never be taken in again.

Chapter Nineteen

"Welcome to my home, Miss Marchmont. Food has been prepared. You must be famished."

The Magistrate's fake concern made me suppress a shudder. "Thank you," I managed, "but all I am is tired. I would prefer simply to rest."

"Of course. I need a few minutes of your time and then you can retire. This way."

The Magistrate's study was a small room, and yet huge given the fact that all it seemed designed for was to give the Magistrate a place to sit and conduct his business, and to house his books. All four walls of the study were lined by shelves filled with volumes of all shapes and sizes. My father had books. He was considered rich for it – not many had survived the rising of the waves. Pa owned eleven volumes, all on some aspect of medicine. There had to be a hundred before me now. I had just found a further incentive to marry one of the Magistrate's sons. Not that I would do so if they had a million books.

"Miss Marchmont." The Magistrate removed his glasses and set them on the desk before him as he faced me. "Thank you for joining me. Please sit down." He glanced towards the door. "You can wait outside, Will."

I turned in time to see the door close then sat down on the edge of the seat across from the Magistrate's desk. I couldn't relax, not in this house.

He continued to watch me. I couldn't help my eyes flicking aside, jumping from one title to the next on his bookshelves, drinking them in as though this might be my last chance to be so close to such riches. I didn't want to look at him, for fear of what he might read in my face. Or me in his.

"Will tells me he met you in the middle of the sea, close to New Eden," he began. They hadn't spared any time – Will must have given his father a report while I was shedding my coat, and washing my hands and face. I waited. The Magistrate hadn't yet said anything that required an answer. "Is that right?"

"I suppose so. I'm not sure exactly where I was."

"Did you land on New Eden?"

His eyes behind his spectacles glittered. I paused before answering, the denial that sprang to my tongue freezing. I sensed a trap. And then my eyes focused on my lap – and the borrowed skirt covering it. The one Emily had pressed me to accept as a gift.

"That's right." I gave him simple agreement, deciding it was safest to say as little as I could. There was only one lie I needed to hold on to: Cosimo was dead as far as the Magistrate was concerned. But that lie fed tendrils into others. The people of New Eden could never have seen the machine he'd helped them make. *I* could never have seen it. I couldn't know anything about it. I cleared my expression and looked at the Magistrate as though I was nothing but pleased to answer his questions.

His eyes settled on my face and I prayed to the tides that he couldn't see the thoughts tumbling in disorder through my mind.

"What did the peasants of New Eden tell you, Liberty?"

I swallowed. I could pretend I didn't understand what he meant, but I was clever enough to know what a mistake that would be. I looked him straight in the eye.

"They say the seas are rising once more."

"Do they indeed?"

"They seem very sure of the matter. Two inches in six months, they said."

"I see."

His calm responses made my pulse surge. I searched his face but I couldn't find any truth there. Anger made me incautious. "They also say City is stealing their harvest."

"And did you believe them?"

I swallowed. "They said nautilus men attacked them and took their harvest without payment."

Mr Keyne steepled his fingers and watched me coldly. "That wasn't my question, Liberty."

I coloured. "I don't know whether I believe them." I lifted my chin. "Is it true? Either thing?"

His fingers tapped against each other, as though he were deciding what to tell me. "The seas are rising, yes." His lips pressed together after that. Perhaps he expected me to forget the other part of my question.

"What of the theft? Is that true, too?" I meant to face him squarely and wait for his answer, but his hard, calculating expression unnerved me and I was the one to look away.

"I will forget I heard that slur on the morals of City's nautilus men, Miss Marchmont."

The hairs on the back of my neck lifted at his tone. His lack of answer was just as telling as mine had been. The people of New Eden had been right, I was sure of it. It was both liberating and terrifying to realise I'd expected Cosimo and Jethro's low opinion of City's Magistrate to be borne out. And now it had – and I had to decide what I was going to do about it.

The Magistrate took a slow breath. "Your father was the only person I trusted with the knowledge that the seas were rising. I trusted him, and he betrayed City by turning a reamer into a nautilus man." His eyes bored into me. "Did you assist in the procedure?"

I couldn't deny it, so I nodded.

"You were happy to break City's laws? Or did you perhaps not know the patient was a reamer?"

He was offering me a way out, but I didn't trust such generosity. I held tight to as much of the truth as I could. "I knew he was a reamer. I said I would fetch a watchman and Pa forbade me."

"And you obeyed your father, as a good daughter should."

My eyes burned, remembering the last sight I had of my father, the feel of his life bleeding away over my hands. I wanted to choke the sneering superiority out of the Magistrate. With a deliberate effort, I stayed where I was. "Yes, I obeyed him."

"I see. And for thanks, the reamer murdered your father."

"No." Another evil to blame on the reamers. I wouldn't let him do that. Not this time. "Cosimo didn't murder my father." My heart thudded. The words to accuse *him* of the crime burned in my chest, then died in my throat. What would I say if he admitted to the killing? What would I do?

"No?" He drew a breath, tapping his fingertips together. "And how do you know that, Liberty?"

"Because he was forcing me to go with him to his boat when my father was killed."

"I see. So he was working with an accomplice."

I looked hard at him. His glittering eyes held mine. I wondered if he could read that I didn't believe his stories. I looked down.

Mr Keyne sucked in a deep breath. "I am sorry for your loss, Liberty. City is all the poorer without our doctor." He sighed out the last of his breath and seemed to set the whole incident aside. "Your father was fortunate to have such a good, obedient daughter. I hope you will prove trustworthy to City now that I expect you to answer to me."

"I will always do my best for the people of City, as my father taught me," I replied.

He examined my face for another minute. I was sure he heard as well as I did the evasions in what I'd just said. "Well said, Miss Marchmont."

My heart beat rapidly, expecting him to challenge me. I spoke more to distract him than because I thought I would get an honest answer. "What are we going to do about the rising seas?"

His fingers tapped together a final time, then spread apart, and his hands dropped to the desk. "The rise is slow. We have our nautilus men. We are in no danger as things stand."

I watched his bland face, wondering if he believed what he was telling me. It was impossible to read from his expression.

"You have something to say, Liberty?" he demanded.

I swallowed. "No."

"Good." His eyes glittered before he looked away. I got the message very clearly that any challenge to the Magistrate's version of how things were would not be tolerated. It seemed a mystery to me how I could have reached the age of seventeen in my father's household with regular contact with Mr Keyne and not realised how dangerous the man was.

He smiled his insincere smile. "Don't trouble yourself with thoughts of the threats we may face in the future, Liberty. That's my job. You need to focus on your own future."

I made no comment, my thoughts flitting to Cosimo, Paul and Emily, Sarah and Simon. Now I was on City, I should focus on Hannah, Belle, Foo and Binny. How could I get them to understand what was happening? The Magistrate might be telling everyone there was nothing to worry about, but I wasn't prepared to leave my safety in his hands. I had to get away from him and make sure everyone knew the danger we were in – and the alternatives we had.

My silence seemed to please him. Maybe he thought me as biddable as my father had portrayed me to be. "Knowing him as I do, I'm sure your father never told you that I asked him to make Will his apprentice." He pulled a cloth from his pocket and polished his glasses in jerky, circular movements. "Your father refused. He said you were all the apprentice he needed." He focused exclusively on the spectacles, holding them out to check he had cleaned them to his satisfaction. Only then did he look at me again. "I hope he taught you well, Liberty."

"Of course he did." My heart leapt – was he about to send me home? That was too good to be true. I sensed he was setting a trap, but not a way to evade it. It was true, after all. I was Dr Miracle's apprentice. I knew as much as he'd been able to teach me.

"That is reassuring. I had a young man at my door during your absence. He wished to undertake the nautilus procedure. Do you think such a thing will be possible?"

Of course nautilus men were the Magistrate's priority. I began to relax, which was foolish of me. "It seems doubtful, I'm afraid."

"Really?" He didn't sound surprised, or even disappointed, which gave me a presentiment of danger, but I could hardly take back my words now.

"I assisted my father during the procedure, but I am a better anaesthetist than surgeon." I paused. "If you were to insist, of course I would make the attempt in order to do my duty to City, but I wouldn't give much for the chances of my first few patients."

"I see." It was well done. It was impossible to tell whether the Magistrate was displeased by my reply. It was equally impossible to tell whether he believed I was telling the truth. "Scientific advance has always required sacrifice. We must try to ensure the sacrifice is not too great."

I was surprised at the sense of disappointment that settled like a stone in my stomach; I couldn't really have expected him to be so easily set back. I was glad there was another point of contention. "And it is a moot point. There are no more nautilus devices."

The Magistrate's brow lifted. "None?"

"I don't think so." I pushed Cosimo's creation from my memory. Cosimo was dead. "I believe my father's last devices were in his bag. It was with us on the boat when we left City, and the boat was wrecked. They are probably at the bottom of the sea now."

"You're sure the bag was not saved?"

He was staring at me so hard I was glad I was able to tell the truth. "Completely sure."

The Magistrate sighed. "Then we must make more."

"Impossible."

His gaze sharpened. "Come now, your father cannot have raised you to accept the first hurdle as the final bar in the search for a solution to any problem."

"Of course not. It's just ... there was a book, with a diagram of the devices. It was lost in the wreck, too. Without it, I could have no idea where to start."

"I see." He laced his hands together, apparently satisfied. I couldn't think why he was pleased if he believed I was telling the truth and both the last of the nautilus devices and the plan for making them was lost forever. "In that case, it is a good job that as Magistrate of City I ensure I am prepared for all eventualities."

I didn't want to ask, but I had to know. "What do you mean?"

He smiled. "You cannot suppose that I would leave City prey to the whims of a single man. When a nautilus device ... becomes available, we can take it to pieces and discover how it was made."

I watched him. So, he was waiting for someone to die. That might take a while; nautilus men were all fit and young at the time of their operation. Even the oldest hadn't yet reached forty. My mouth dried as an alternative occurred. Would he really kill a man, just to get the devices out of his neck? I shivered, gladder than ever that I'd sent Cosimo away. The Magistrate might baulk at killing a City dweller; no such consideration would hold him back if he found a reamer bearing the devices.

I needed to get away from him. I cleared my throat and spoke. "I want to continue my father's other medical work now I am back on City. I think he would want me to make myself useful."

The Magistrate smiled, but there was no warmth in the gesture. "Oh, I am quite sure we will find a use for you."

Perhaps it was unwise, but I pressed on. "I am very grateful for your hospitality, but I would like to return home in the morning."

The Magistrate ignored my request, waving a hand in dismissal. When I opened the door, Will was there. I wondered if he'd been listening at the keyhole. The Magistrate smiled again, but the gesture didn't reach his eyes. "All in good time, Liberty. Don't be in such a hurry to meet your future. Will, please escort our guest to her room."

Shutting the study door behind us, Will extended his arm for me to place my hand on his sleeve for escort, a genial smile on his face. "This way, Doc. The guest room is all prepared. If you need anything, just shout. We'll do whatever we can to make your stay comfortable."

That sounded ominously as though he expected me to be there for some time. Not if I could avoid it. I murmured something I hoped sounded polite, unwilling to lie outright. I wished I hadn't told Cosimo to forget about me and return to his people. It would be reassuring to think help was on its way. But I wasn't a child to need that sort of comfort. I didn't need Cosimo, and I certainly didn't want him to come within reach of the Magistrate.

Will led me upstairs in what seemed to be an empty house. Josiah might still be at work, but I wondered where the Magistrate's wife was. The house seemed eerily quiet, unlike the last time I'd visited.

"Here, Doc." Will swung a door wide and motioned me inside.

"Thank you." I stepped inside the room.

"If you need anything, just ring the bell. Sleep well." He inclined his head and backed out, closing the door behind him. I listened but there was no sound of a key turning before his tread sounded on the stairs. It was a small victory: I was not, openly, a prisoner.

My coat had already been set on the hook behind the door as though the household were used to my presence. I sat on the bed. The room was small but, because it was the Magistrate's home, still luxurious. The mattress beneath me was soft, there were pictures on the white walls, and the lamp set on the bedside cabinet shone with a bright, clear flame in the autumn gloom.

A suddenly slamming door broke the silence and I jumped. Footsteps pounded along the landing outside my room, heading towards the noise. Another door slammed and a cold voice said something I couldn't make out. A different voice rose in shrill laughter and then there was silence. Mrs Keyne had to be at home after all. I shivered, although there was nothing wrong with the temperature in my room. This was the Magistrate's home, after all. It was the only place on City where luxury was the norm.

I removed my dress, slipped between the sheets in

my underwear and lay staring at the door. I hadn't lied to the Magistrate about wishing to seek my bed. I was tired, even more so after my interview with him, but perhaps also as a result of that discussion, I was too alert to sleep. I turned down the lamp but didn't douse it entirely.

After a few minutes that felt like an eternity of not growing drowsy, I sat up in my bed so I could see out of the window, watching the last of the day fade across City.

I must have dozed, because when more footsteps passing my door roused me the sky was fully dark, the lamp behind me bright by comparison. The household was settling to sleep. It wouldn't be long before I was the only one awake.

I focused on the door, building up courage to venture outside my room. I thought I heard a sigh coming from the other side, although that was certainly my imagination. I paused, then pushed back the covers and crossed the room as silently as I could and knelt down to peer through the keyhole. The view was distorted, but I could clearly see the other side of the landing. Movement caught my attention. The swish of skirts as they disappeared around a corner. That was just what this awful house needed: the never-seen wife drifting around the place like a ghost. I put my dress back on and remained close to the door, listening and waiting.

*

Finally, I heard a heavy tread on the stairs. I peered through the keyhole and saw the Magistrate pass my door. There was a pause, my view obscured by his unmoving form. I dodged away, afraid that he would bend and look in at my keyhole, coming face-to-face with my eye looking out.

When I heard a board creak, I returned my eye to the hole in time to see him vanish into the last room on the right.

I forced myself to wait another half hour, giving him plenty of time to settle in his bed and fall asleep. I wanted him safely out of the way. Finally, the chimes of the hall clock echoing, I slipped from my room.

My door opened without a creak. In the moonlight that stopped the darkness being absolute, I blinked and made out the shadowy shapes of the banister and the staircase. I crept downstairs, slow and soundless. I tried the front door, but that was locked with no sign of the key. I shouldn't have expected escape to be so easy.

Instead, I crossed the hallway to the Magistrate's study, scene of his plotting with my father, and with Josiah and who knew who else. If there were answers to what the Magistrate was about and why my father had died, I would surely find them there.

The door opened silently to a room filled with shadows. There were no shutters at the window, which let moonlight stream in. At least I could see my way without stumbling and waking the entire household.

The books were tempting, but not tonight. I started my examination of the room with the Magistrate's desk, shuffling through the papers on the top. I only had time to glance through them, picking up a phrase or two in the Magistrate's scrawling writing. It all seemed to relate to the acquisition of metal: tins, tins, tins. City couldn't seem to get enough. But there was no mention of my father – or even of nautilus men and the devices that made them so special.

I shuffled the papers back into the order I thought I had found them and turned my attention to the three drawers beneath the desk. They wouldn't open. Locked, with no key in the tiny hole at the top of the drawers.

"You'll find the key beneath the lamp."

I gasped and spun around in shock at the female voice. I didn't see her until she moved. Mrs Keyne was sitting in the comfortable chair in the corner, legs tucked beneath her, obscured by the shadows and the tall back of the chair. Fear in my guts told me to flee, but she already knew I was up to no good. "Forgive me," I stuttered. "I didn't know anyone was here. I thought you were ..." that thought trailed away as I looked at the woman regarding me steadily. She appeared every bit as sane as I was.

There was a glint of teeth as she smiled. "Asleep?" she offered.

I grabbed the lifeline. "Yes."

" ...or perhaps babbling hysterically to myself in a cupboard?" She laughed at the expression on my face, her laugh a natural, amused sound. "That's my camouflage, Libby. May I call you Libby?"

"I ... yes."

"My little outbursts keep my husband away and give me a little peace. He's afraid of insanity, as though it might be catching. You've caught me out. I was catching up on my reading."

I leaned against the desk, watching the woman sitting peacefully with a book on her lap. "If you don't like him, why don't you leave him?"

Another laugh greeted that. "And go where, Libby?"

I could say, but I wouldn't confide my plans, not to someone who might, after all, be her husband's spy.

"I am too old and tired to think of running away. I left it too late." She sighed. "I was young when I pledged myself to him. Too young to be pledged and married. He was handsome and clever, and I was too dazzled by that to see that he was also a petty-minded bully."

Silence fell.

"I used to dream of escaping. I would imagine myself flying away, like a bird." She laughed. "If we can make ourselves fish, why can't we make ourselves birds?" She looked straight at me. "I let go of my dreams, Libby. Don't let go of yours."

"I won't."

Mrs Keyne nodded. "Good girl. The key is under the lamp." She turned her attention back to her book.

I reached towards the lamp set on the corner of the desk, then turned back. "Do you have a key to the front door?"

She shook her head. "My husband keeps that close. Where do you plan to go?"

"I'm not sure."

She didn't look up, but I heard the smile in her voice. "You don't trust me. I can't fault you for being cautious. I wish I had been. I'll see what I can do about that key." She waved a hand. "Don't let me disturb you."

Dismissed, I turned my attention to the lamp and fitted the key I found beneath it in the keyhole of the drawers. In the second drawer, my search came to an end. For tonight, at least. The drawer was filled with yet more papers and books, but right at the bottom was a small, thin notebook. I lifted it up and flicked through, expecting more of the Magistrate's scribbles, but the writing wasn't his. It was my father's. It wasn't what I had set out to find, but I couldn't resist it. My father's notebook wouldn't tell me who had killed him, but perhaps it would hold the clues as to why the Magistrate had sent a killer after him.

Placing the notebook carefully to one side, I started to push everything else back. My attention was caught by a glint of light on metal and I reached to the back of the drawer. My fingers closed on a round shape and I nearly let go, assuming it was a coin, dropped and forgotten. But when I lifted it into the half-light my eyes widened. A slim, silver pendant. The exact match to one I'd seen before. For a brief, sharp moment I thought it was Cosimo's – that the Magistrate had found him. That was impossible. It was another. Cosimo's was one of a pair.

Mrs Keyne's voice rose out of the darkness, harder than it had been before. "Take it. I shall be glad to be rid of it."

"Oh, I'm sorry. I didn't realise it was yours."

"It's not. It's nothing to do with me. Take it."

It was command more than invitation, so I did so. I wanted to ask why it was here, what it signified, but her tone of voice forbade me voicing any of the questions circling my mind. I shoved everything else back into the drawer, replaced the key, and darted as swiftly and silently as I could back up to my room.

Hiding the pendant in my coat pocket, I sat on the bed closest to the lamp for the best light and considered the notebook. It was slim, light and flexible, the cover a shade of blue I had never seen the sky achieve. It was much marked, old and battered. Just the movement of lifting it released the scent of the Magistrate's study. My father's handwriting greeted me when I turned back the cover. I breathed slowly to fight the unwelcome prickle at my eyes. My father's notebook wasn't him. There was no way to turn back time and undo what was done.

I was a scientist. I was my father's daughter. My emotion was unimportant when compared to the knowledge I craved. I settled so the lamp cast its light where I needed it, curled my feet beneath me, and read.

It was a diary of sorts, but describing only one element of the writer's life: my father's experiments to create nautilus devices. If I had hoped for my unquiet heart to be set to rest by what I found in the pages that delusion was soon disposed of.

Unease grew as I leafed through the pages. His handwriting changed as time passed, growing more cramped as though he was engaged in a desperate race. Perhaps that was not a bad analogy. I flicked from start to finish, my own actions growing more urgent as I saw the patterns forming. The only words that got a line to themselves were the underlined titles denoting a test subject's identifier. He started with letters, and worked his way through the alphabet. Then the subjects became numbers. They went from one to thirty-nine before they stopped and I found another word alone on a line, underlined. Success. There were only two pages left in the notebook. Success had arrived just in time.

I leafed back, paying closer attention. Subjects thirty-eight and thirty-nine were the lucky ones, names noted against their numbers to provide full detail of my father's success: Tom Dawber and Peter McKay. The accounts beneath their names were longest, and ended with the date of their first dive. Before that, accounts varied in all aspects except one: every single one ended with the word 'deceased.'

Tears started in my eyes and I dashed them away as I flipped the pages back to the beginning. It had all happened when I was a baby, but I knew the stories. We had been starving. The tins hoarded by our first generation had long gone, and we'd raided everything we could find beneath the waves that we could reach by free diving. There had been nothing left, nothing within reach. City had been on the brink of annihilation. My father had saved us. The creation of nautilus men had given us hope. We had been starving to death, turning on each other. They had given us a future. But so many! It was a wonder City had managed to bear such a loss of its sons. I hardened my heart. All those deaths were regrettable, but they were few in comparison to all the people who now lived and thrived here.

With my eyes closed and the notebook pressed between my hands, I thought of my father. He had never spoken of what he'd done, not to me. All that had been concealed. I had spent my life being proud of him. Dr Miracle. The man who turned base things into gold, the man who had saved City and kept us from starving. It had never occurred to me to wonder whether he was proud of what he had achieved. "You could have told me," I murmured into the air, as though he might hear and reply from the grave.

I wished he had been more honest with me. I could have shared the burden with him. But by the time I was grown enough to understand, perhaps my father considered this ancient history, a sad time he was only too willing to turn his back on. And perhaps some of the fault was mine. I had never allowed my father to be anything but perfect. I should have known enough to realise that, brilliant as he might have been, even my father couldn't have found such a flawless solution without first finding some imperfect ones. With a sigh, I set the book aside, resting my hand on its cover. I hadn't found my answers, just something to shake more of the certainties I'd taken for granted.

Thieves and murderers. For a moment, I doubted whether City deserved to survive. Maybe the world would be a better place if we vanished beneath the waves. But I couldn't accept that. I wanted to live and I wanted the same for everyone else: Hannah, Binny and Belle, and even swaggering Will and silent Josiah.

I sighed. I still didn't know what the Magistrate was planning – if anything. Maybe he truly didn't care about the rising seas. Maybe he wouldn't take action until we were ankle-deep in water.

I doused the lamp and returned to bed, pushing my father's notebook beneath my pillow. I needed to get out of there. And if Mrs Keyne truly could be trusted, perhaps I would.

Chapter Twenty

A squall of shrieking and door slamming jerked me awake in the morning. Mrs Keyne was renewing her disguise.

A thin, harassed-looking maid brought warm water, and I washed and dressed quickly. If nothing else, I needed to return home to fetch more clothes. I could hardly wear the same ones for days on end.

When I was presentable, I made my way downstairs. I had thought I might be the only one awake, but my hostess was already in the dining room. In proper light I saw that she was tall and thin, with midnight black hair neither of her sons had inherited. Her grey eyes darted over me to the door behind, as though expecting someone to follow. I glanced back, too, surprised that neither the Magistrate nor Will 'chanced' to arrive for breakfast at the same time as myself.

Mrs Keyne nodded in greeting but didn't speak. I supposed that might have damaged her disguise, even though we were alone.

"Good morning, madam." I gave her an elegant greeting, inclining my head respectfully.

There was a sound, a step outside the room. Mrs Keyne lurched forward and grabbed my arm as the door opened. She looked as though a breeze would blow her away, but her grip was ferocious. "Ill-fortune has brought you here. This is an evil place." Her voice was high and hysterical. I knew without looking round that the Magistrate was in the doorway and her display was for his benefit. I tried to extract my hand.

She glanced at me, her expression intense. "You must not aid him. No matter what he promises you. My husband is a liar and not to be trusted."

"All I want is to return to my father's house," I told her, since it was both true and safe for the Magistrate to overhear.

"You must not trust him!" Her voice became shrill. Her hand was so tight around my wrist it grew painful.

The door snapped closed as the Magistrate entered fully. Almost faster than I could blink, his wife was on the other side of the room, pulling a chair back to take her seat. She might not look like much, but the woman could move.

I slid my sleeve down over the key she'd secreted into my hand while warning me against her husband, twisting my arm so the metal slipped down to my elbow. I had my method of escape.

Once it was safely hidden, I turned and bade the Magistrate good morning with the manners Pa had dinned into me so completely I couldn't seem to rid myself of them. Eyes narrowed, he glanced from me to Mrs Keyne, who now seemed to care for nothing but her breakfast, pouring herself a drink from the hot pot with more concentration than the task could possibly need.

"Good morning, Miss Marchmont. I see you have met my dear Melisande."

I wanted to say I'd met his wife, if that was who he meant, but I wasn't such a fool as to antagonise him to no purpose. "Yes."

The Magistrate placed a hand on the small of my back and propelled me towards the dining table. "Eat up, Liberty. You are my guest. You must not allow past traumas to affect your current wellbeing."

I paused, but it wasn't worth saying any of the

things that entered my head. The Magistrate wouldn't listen to me. I doubted he ever heard anyone who didn't agree with him.

The Magistrate smiled, his hand suspended over the hot pot. "Well done."

I shot a glance at Melisande, seeking illumination, then returned to the Magistrate. "For what?"

His smile widened. He poured a drink for himself, then filled a cup at the place he'd propelled me to. "For not arguing. A quick learner. I approve. I'm sure your father would, too."

I took a breath. When I replied my voice was quite calm. "I wish to return home, to continue my father's work."

"You are impatient, Miss Marchmont."

I could be as implacable as him. My father would approve of that, too. "I see no point in my staying here where I am of no use when I could be doing good elsewhere."

"Oh, you must not suppose yourself useless, Miss Marchmont," he assured me with a smile.

"You are never happy unless you are tormenting those around you." His wife chose then to join the conversation.

Cup arrested halfway to his lips, the Magistrate looked astonished. "Tormenting? I do no such thing. Poor Liberty has suffered an unpleasant experience, kidnapped by reamers, and stranded with the people of New Eden. I must take the part of her father and ensure she is cared for properly."

She laughed hysterically. "Oh, you dress it up in duty, but you do exactly as you please. You always have."

There was a pause. The atmosphere grew still more unpleasant. The Magistrate smiled at his wife, his tone deceptively pleasant when he spoke. "Oh, you know that isn't true, Melisande, my dear. After all, I married you, didn't I?"

She looked at him with hatred filling her expression, her fingers tight around her drink. Then she jerked the cup towards him, throwing its contents into his face. The Magistrate looked startled, a drop of liquid sparkling on the glass of his spectacles, his clothes darkened by the damp. Then he took a stride forward and slapped her hard across the face. I gasped at the cracking sound. Melisande gave no reaction. He pulled a large handkerchief from his pocket and dabbed liquid from his clothes as she glided towards the door. The Magistrate was busy with his shirt so he didn't see the wink she gave me before slipping out. I stifled my smile, and rose to follow her.

"Sit down!" the Magistrate snapped. "Finish your breakfast. I can't allow you to let Melisande's theatrical demonstrations damage your appetite."

"I'm not hungry."

"You should be. You will gain no advantage from starving yourself."

"I'm not looking for an advantage." That was the Magistrate's constant endeavour. "I am simply not hungry."

"I imagine not. A guilty conscience often leads to a lack of appetite."

Dismay bloomed in my stomach. "Guilty conscience? What do you mean?"

"I mean rooting around in my drawers to find your father's journal. What else could you imagine I mean?" He waved a hand with another of his insincere smiles. "Oh, there's no need to look so stricken, Liberty, I am not angry – although I would have preferred it if you'd asked first."

I swallowed and found my courage. "I could hardly have asked to be shown something I didn't know existed."

The Magistrate raised a brow. "Then you leave me

intrigued as to what you were looking for in my private papers."

Did he really want an answer to that? Did I dare give him the truth?

Clearly not, since he continued without waiting. "Now you know what your father had to do to ensure City's survival, I hope you won't complain when I have to deal with matters with a firm hand. If it were a choice between the survival of City and that of the reamers, I trust you would make the right one, Miss Marchmont."

I stared at him, my heart hollowing out. All those letters and numbers in my father's notebook ... Had they been reamers, not City boys? Forced, rather than willing test subjects? No wonder they hated us.

The Magistrate strode out, leaving me with that thought, shutting the door with a click behind him.

I sagged and reached for my drink. The right choice – I hoped that was what I was making.

Chapter Twenty-One

"My father says you can go home."

Will lounged in the doorway, arms crossed, while I waited for the "but" I was sure was coming. The Magistrate couldn't just be letting me go.

"So long as I come with you to ensure order is kept."

There. I knew it. "Order? Your father is expecting a riot upon the return of City's doctor?"

Will smiled. It wasn't genuine amusement, more like an acknowledgement of my effort to be witty. My cheeks heated and I willed my skin not to embarrass me.

"No, but he probably didn't like to rub my nose in the fact that the best job he could find for me was babysitting."

My face flamed. "I'm not a baby."

His eyes raked over me and I wanted to cross my arms over my chest. "You're certainly not that, Libby." He turned away before I could voice a complaint. "Come along. It's with me, or you don't go at all."

I grabbed my coat, the precious key safe in my pocket, and we left.

*

Will walked several paces apart from me. From a casual glance, you wouldn't have known he was with me rather than just happening to be walking the same way by coincidence, but I knew he was fully aware of where I was even as he turned to wave and shout smart comments to the people we passed. His father's guard dog, he'd be on me in a minute if I tried to run away.

"Will! You're back!"

Will halted at the squealed cry. I wanted to walk on, but my steps slowed so I dragged to a halt within sight as Hannah, Belle beside her, clutched Will's arm as though his return after a couple of days away was the most exciting thing to happen for years.

He grinned. "Did you miss me?"

Hannah pushed him. "We were too busy to miss you, weren't we, Belle?" She looked to her friend for confirmation, then saw me and gasped. "Liberty!" She glanced at Will – he was rarely not her focus. "You got her back!"

"That was what I went to do, wasn't it?" he drawled, enjoying playing the hero.

Hannah took a step towards me, then stopped. She tipped her head to one side and her voice dropped. "Are you all right?" Her brow furrowed.

"Of course. Why wouldn't I be?"

Her expression changed as though I were being brave in the face of a great trial. "Kidnapped by a reamer. That must have been *horrible*."

"No worse than being kidnapped by anyone else, I'm sure."

Hannah and Belle shared a glance as though deciding how to react to my sharp response. Hannah swung back with a sniff. "I'm sorry for being worried about you." She shuddered. "I'm sure *I* wouldn't want to be held captive by a grubby reamer boy." She turned to Will, her smile widening to show more bright teeth. "At least *you're* safe."

I turned my back, ignoring the smarting sense I'd made a fool of myself again. Hurrying to my door, I pushed inside while Will paused with a last word for his audience before following.

With my fingers still on the handle I stopped, arrested, of all things, by the smell. It smelled like home and my heart filled my chest, choking me for a second. It was home, and yet, without Pa … I stepped in further and kept my back turned as Will followed me in.

He shut the door behind him and peered back out of the window as though checking whether anyone had followed – or whether Hannah and Belle were hanging around, hankering after him.

"Is something the matter?" I shrugged off my coat and turned to the stove. "You can stay and chat longer if you like."

He sniffed. "If people see me spending time with you they might think we've made a pledge."

"And that's the worst fate you could possibly imagine, I don't doubt." I spoke sharply and hoped he'd think it was wit that fuelled my tone.

Will grinned. "No insult, Libby, but I want to keep my options open."

I remembered talking to him the night my father died. "Because you have other plans?" I queried as I bent to prepare the stove.

"Yeah." I could hear the grin in his voice – could nothing knock the confidence of Will Keyne? "Something like that," he conceded.

When I rose to reach for the fire steel, he had already removed his jacket and taken a seat – my father's, the comfortable one on the other side of the stove. But no doubt I'd be too busy to sit down.

The still was my first priority so there would be alcohol to clean wounds – and to sterilise skin before making the incisions for the nautilus procedure, if that were ever possible again. I turned my mind away from the thought that it would be possible if I were ever reunited with Cosimo. I'd thrown away my chance. I couldn't expect to trip over another.

"Do you know how to make someone into a nautilus man?"

I tried not to react when Will spoke as though he'd been following my thoughts.

"I know the steps of the procedure. I was my father's assistant."

"Yes. But can you do the operation?" He watched me carefully as though looking for a falsehood. He wasn't clever enough to know if I lied to him. He was checking the answers I'd already given his father, maybe because his father had told him to, but if I was to be caught out in a lie, the Magistrate would detect it before Will ever guessed.

"Probably. Would you like me to try on you? I wouldn't even demand to see your licence."

Will laughed, although I wasn't convinced I'd made a joke. "I thought there weren't any more nautilus devices left?"

"No." I watched him. "Are you happy or sad about that?"

He laughed again. "It wasn't a serious career plan. I'll find something else to do with my life."

I wanted to ask what – he couldn't coast in his father's wake forever. Or perhaps he could.

"The seas are rising, you know. Whatever your father says." I wanted to shock him out of his cheerful complaisance, but perhaps that truth was too big for his tiny brain to accept.

"And we're all doomed," he added, eyes twinkling with amusement. "You do know people have been saying that since City was created, don't you?"

"Your father knows it's true. And he might say it's nothing to worry about, but that's not what he really thinks. Why else is he stealing from New Eden? Only desperation would turn the people of City into thieves." I thought it might help my case if I sounded like I could be sympathetic to the actions taken against New Eden.

"City is in danger, and your father knows it."

Will had no glib reply to that and the sparkle in his eyes dimmed.

"Why would he hide the truth from you, Will?" I asked softly.

"Hide what? He's not hiding anything. You're a fool if you believe a reamer." His voice was gruff. His hands in his lap balled to fists.

"Maybe I am. But you could find out for sure – couldn't you?"

His expression twisted with indecision when I thought I might have swayed him, then it was lost. "You want me to find out my father's plans to protect City so you can tell your new reamer friends." His lips twisted. "That's why I have to babysit you, you know. He thinks you might run off back to the peasants on New Eden, or try to help the reamers attack us. I told him you wouldn't be so stupid, but now I'm not so sure."

"I'm not stupid, Will. The seas are rising which means we're all in danger. We have more chance of surviving if we all work together. Fighting will get us nowhere."

He stared, incredulous. "You think we should let the reamers take us over? Let them have the benefit of everything we've worked so hard to build here?"

"What if that meant we got the benefit of everything the reamers can do?"

"Please! As though they could achieve anything worth having. We have to look out for ourselves, Libby."

Liquid dripped from the still. I straightened, hands on hips. What had *he* ever achieved in his life? "Do you ever think for yourself, Will Keyne? I know it's easier to parrot back what your father says, but his ideas are just as dangerous as any dreamed up by the reamers."

Will laughed, but he couldn't disguise the flush of his skin. I knew I'd got to him. Maybe that would start him thinking. "You're deluded, Libby. Did they sit you by the fire and tell you a nice story about the land of sun and roses on the other side of the Wastes?"

"What if it's real?"

Will let out a crack of laughter. "They really did spin you a story and you believed it! What a gullible gorm you are for such a clever girl."

"There has to be something beyond the Wastes." I hated that my face was going red, but I couldn't do anything about the heat that rose in me for being laughed at.

"Yes! There's more sea!" Will kept laughing. I opened my mouth but the door swung open, the jangling bell drowning out anything I might have said. My first patient had arrived – in time to stop Will and me falling to fisticuffs.

*

The day was turning to dusk, the few patients who had found their way to my door long gone, when the door jangled again. Josiah walked in. "Good evening, Liberty."

I nodded. "Josiah."

He looked past me to his brother. "I'll keep the good doctor company a while, Will. You must be half-mad at being cooped up all day."

I expected Will to protest, to say something about the duty expected of him. He didn't. "You're a pal, Joe."

He was out almost before Josiah had stepped fully inside.

"Can I do something for you? Do you need medicines?"

"No, no. I came, as I said, to keep you company, since our father doesn't want you to be left alone."

I bristled at the reminder that I was being guarded. I couldn't protest that, so I found something else to complain about. "You shouldn't allow Will to shirk his jobs."

Josiah smiled slowly, revealing even, pale teeth.

"But Will shirking his responsibilities is an important job in itself."

"What do you mean?"

At last, Josiah took a seat, hitching onto one of the stools beside the table where I was mixing a poultice. "If Will Keyne can be found at the market, chatting with his friends and flirting with the girls, or if he's racing his kayak around City, or swimming beside the algae fields all must be well. If Will Keyne were required to do some genuine, honest, useful work then City must be in a parlous state indeed."

I scoffed, grinding my mixture harder with the pestle. "That's ridiculous. Your father wouldn't tolerate it if he knew how Will spends most of his time."

"You think he doesn't know?" Josiah propped his elbows on the table and leaned forward to watch me work. "You think he's fool enough not to see what's happening under his nose?"

I stopped. "Why does he let him be so useless, if he knows it's happening?"

"I told you." Josiah spread his hands wide. "Will tells the people of City more clearly than any of my father's speeches could that all is well in the world. And, of course, he hears things. He speaks to people, and people speak to him. He carries that chatter back to the dinner table with no idea of the coin he's holding. He's my father's best informer and he doesn't even realise it."

I fell silent and picked up my pestle again. There were two things I'd never expected: that Will's fecklessness was put to use by the Magistrate. And that Josiah had even sharper intelligence than I'd guessed at.

The silence stretched, broken by the crackle of the fire and the drip of the still. Josiah cleared his throat. "I wished to offer you my condolences. I was very sorry to hear of the death of your father."

Taken aback, emptiness filled my chest. I breathed deeply and waited for the sensation to relent.

"He was a brilliant man," Josiah added. "We are all poorer for his loss."

I blinked until I could see clearly, nodding so he would know I'd heard, hoping he would think I was simply intent on my work. After a minute I found enough breath to speak. "Thank you, Joe. It's good to know that other people care."

"Of course I do." He cleared his throat, as though embarrassed to admit it. "I once wanted to be his apprentice," he said, looking sideways at me. "My father asked on behalf of Will instead. He said I was clever enough as I was, whereas Will could stand improvement. Your father responded that he didn't need any apprentice save yourself. I regret I was pleased that Will couldn't have what I'd been denied." He smiled, weakly. "I'm not a very good brother."

"You're a good person, Joe," I argued.

He made no reply to that. After a while, he spoke again. "Clear night tonight. I might spend an hour stargazing."

"Mmm-hmm."

He turned to me. "Did your father ever teach you anything of the stars?"

He was straining for conversation. I'd prefer silence. "No, we didn't study the stars. They were too far away to be of relevance," I added and continued pounding the ingredients in my mortar.

Josiah smiled. "Just because something is far away or out of sight, that doesn't make it irrelevant." He held up a hand as I raised my head to answer. "I don't doubt you think my hobby is a joke. Everyone does." His smile twisted. "In private, I think everyone thinks *I'm* a joke. Stars and darkness and the odd son of the Magistrate."

"No one thinks you're odd."

"No one? That's very generous of you, Liberty."

I sensed he was teasing me. "I don't know what everyone thinks, how could I? But I don't think there's anything wrong with you."

"Thank you. And I'm sure my reputation would be repaired if everyone on City knew how important my silly hobby might prove to be."

I paused in my work, arrested by the expression in his blue eyes. "How important is that?"

"Do you know that you can navigate by using the positions of the stars for guidance?"

I pushed away the pestle and mortar. "I've heard of such a thing. Astro-navigation."

"That's right. Could you do it? Could you find a way through the stars?"

"No."

"I could. And that may make me indispensable for our future."

My thoughts spun. "But the Magistrate said there's nothing to worry about." I didn't believe him, but Will had. I'd thought Josiah might have been similarly fooled.

"He hides it well, but my father is afraid of change. Even if the seas don't rise any more, one day the salvage will run out. We have to find a new home, sooner or later."

Cosimo's voice rang in my memory. *Somewhere, they live a life worth living.* "Where are you intending to go?" I asked Josiah, all thought of the poultice I'd been making forgotten.

He smiled. "As far as we need to go."

Chapter Twenty-Two

The still dripped, punctuating the dark evening's sudden silence. Could I really trust Josiah? I kept my tone light. "Past the Wastes? There's nothing there." My heart thudded. "The Magistrate says we're alone, that there's nowhere else to go."

Joe's fingers tapped the tabletop. "The Magistrate *wants* everyone to believe that. I'm willing to take the chance that he's wrong."

I swallowed. "Why tell me this?"

"Because I hope I've found an ally. Because I know you're a good person, too."

My heart marked the seconds passing. Awareness prickled up my spine. I'd never expected to have such a conversation with Josiah Keyne of all people. "An ally in what? Running away to the Wastes? I tried that, it didn't work out well. Your father might forgive me for being kidnapped. He wouldn't if I tried to leave of my own accord." I waited for his reply; waiting to discover that he was his father's puppet. My heart beat against my chest, hoping he wasn't.

"That was a ramshackle flight. We can do better if we plan." Josiah watched me levelly. For the first time I noticed how blue his eyes were. Just like Cosimo's.

The prickle grew more pronounced; a shiver running up and down my spine. "The Magistrate would consider it treason to plot against him."

"I'm not plotting against him, simply making alternative plans." He leaned forward. "Will you come with us?"

"Who's 'us'?"

Josiah's cheeks pinked. "Just me today, but there'll be others. Everyone will want to come with us when they know what's possible."

I nodded, and then I thought about what we were truly planning. To escape City, find a way across the Wastes and search out the land of sun and roses.

The unreality of it gave me pause. If Will was his father's informant, how could I be sure Joe wasn't likewise? As I watched him a sudden memory came to me from school days. We'd gone swimming. I hated it – being forced to advertise how awkward and ungainly I was for all to see. At least the stupid children in the class didn't have to let others see all their mistakes.

I'd been treading water, trying to lose myself at the back, when I'd heard a hiss. When I looked to the side, Josiah was sitting in the framework that held the floats beneath City's pontoons, feet dangling in the water but hidden from sight until he'd chosen to make himself known to me.

"Want to join me?" The words had floated to me, barely audible over the rippling waves.

I'd glanced to check the teacher wasn't looking in my direction, then ducked beneath the pontoons. Josiah lent me a hand and pulled me up beside him. "We'll be in trouble if we're found." Even then I'd been naturally cautious.

Josiah had shrugged, a slim foot dragging through the water. "I'll say I got cramp, and you're helping me."

I'd settled beside him and we'd spent the hour of the lesson exchanging maths problems. We hadn't been found out. And I'd thought myself in love with him for about six weeks, until I'd realised gratitude wasn't love and there could be no future in it.

I looked at him now. He seemed uncomfortable, glancing out of the window, his fingers drumming on the table. But he was still that same boy, the one who'd helped me.

I took a breath. "Do you really think we can do this?"

His fingers tapped impatiently. "Our great, great-grandparents built City to give us a home. I think we're clever enough to find another one if we make up our minds to do so."

I watched Joe as excitement made my heart pound. "The reamers designed a machine to cross the Wastes, but your father took it. Do you know where it is?"

His face fell. "It's in pieces in the recycling plant. It was brought there as scrap."

All that hard work, wrecked because the Magistrate couldn't bear the reamers to have a way out. I wished I had Cosimo's perfect memory, then we might be able to recreate it here. "There's another one, on New Eden, but it needs more metal to finish it."

"We have metal. The plant is stuffed with it. My father keeps the nautilus men as busy as can be."

His tone sent another shiver up my back – but it wasn't excitement this time. "Why?"

"He thinks we need to make weapons to fight New Eden."

I stared at the fire as everything fell into place. "He wants to steal their land."

"If the seas are rising, New Eden will lose ground vital for growing crops and won't have anything spare for us. The tins in the sea beneath us will retreat until they're too deep for us to reach. Someone will starve and my father's determined it won't be the people of City."

"What of the people of New Eden? Don't they deserve to live?"

Another shrug. "My father tells us that the future belongs to those who don't flinch from doing what must be done."

Including murder. I shivered. "We have to get away. Soon. Do you have a plan?"

Joe looked embarrassed. "No. I keep looking at the situation from different directions and I can't see a way through. We have to keep it secret because my father will stop us if he knows. But if we keep it secret, how do we persuade people to come with us? And if we tell people, there'll be panic." Anxiety creased his face. "I'm not cut out for subterfuge, Liberty. I don't know who to trust."

Except me. Was he remembering school days, too? Thoughts chased through my mind while the fire cracked and the still dripped.

Everyone I trusted was across the sea from here ... so that was where I had to go. "Could you get me into the recycling plant?"

His eyes shone. "I daresay."

*

I was smiling as we left, walking silently at Josiah's elbow back to the Magistrate's house. He had long legs and I had to hurry to keep up. The slosh of the waves on our left provided background noise. The streets were empty. Maybe it was that, or the accompanying silence, that made me incautious.

"Did you want to marry me?" I regretted it as soon as the words were out. I wished I could tell him not to answer, but that would be even stranger than asking the question in the first place. "I'm not ... I'm only curious – because my father mentioned the idea." I told my mouth to shut up and thankfully it took that advice. Thank the tides it was dim enough that Josiah couldn't see my flaming face.

His strides paused fractionally, then resumed. He didn't look round. I thought he'd decided to ignore the question, and was grateful, when he suddenly did turn, spinning so quickly I took an involuntary step back to avoid a collision.

"My father mentioned the idea to me, too." He looked down, picking at a button on his coat. "I mean no insult, Liberty, but marriage doesn't hold much appeal for me." He cleared his throat. "I hope you aren't disappointed, but I promise I would make you a dreadful husband."

"Of course I'm not disappointed." I laughed, a grating, high-pitched sound and told myself to shut up again. I swallowed my hysteria. "Marriage isn't for everyone, after all," I finished.

Josiah looked up, a smile playing around his lips. "Exactly."

My face burned harder. "If you don't want a wife, you shouldn't be pressured. Each to their own."

His smile increased, then he thankfully turned away. "Humans are so desperate to pair off. I can't see the appeal, myself."

He started walking again and I followed. It was either that or throwing myself into the sea, never to be seen again. I'd just made a fool of myself. That wasn't new. At least my audience was small today.

*

The next day began similar to the one before. I was jerked to wakefulness by the Magistrate's wife shrieking and doors slamming. My accelerated heart continued to pound when silence fell. I dressed and plaited my hair quickly.

Will and Melisande were nowhere to be seen when I entered the dining room a few minutes later, but Josiah and Mr Keyne were there.

Joe greeted me, then turned to his father as though my arrival had prompted him to remember. "I've asked Miss Marchmont if she will come with me to the plant this morning. We need a doctor there."

The Magistrate stared hard at Josiah. "What seems to be the problem?" He abandoned his meal, sitting back and lacing his fingers as he watched his son.

I was glad I wasn't Joe. I was sure I would be squirming beneath such glittering regard. Josiah held on to a calm that I envied. I was trying not to twitch in case the Magistrate turned to look at me.

"A few of the workers are complaining of stomach pains. It might be something significant, or just that they are getting used to a change of food."

"Or they are shamming to evade their work."

The Magistrate looked at me. "We will need to take Liberty into our confidence." I swallowed. I knew his plans, but I could hardly tell him so.

"I will explain matters to her on the way," Josiah said.

"What matters?" I realised that if I didn't already know I should be curious.

The Magistrate held up a hand to silence me. "A small thing, a backup to ensure the safety of City. Joe will tell you about it." He returned his attention to his son. "I know you'll deal appropriately with the situation, whatever the outcome." He gave the words a strange emphasis.

"Of course, father."

The hairs on the back of my neck lifted. Unless I missed the matter, Josiah had just been instructed to tell me the Magistrate's plans and ... what? Contain me in some way if I didn't fall in with what they were doing? Would they hang me, like a worthless reamer? I looked at Josiah. Could I trust him, or had I just made a massive mistake? Josiah smiled, but anyone could smile. The Magistrate did so regularly. I took a deep breath. I had to trust someone – and hope Josiah hadn't changed more than I feared.

The Magistrate turned his attention on me, jolting me out of my thoughts. "How did you find your day yesterday, Liberty? You were late back."

Was that a criticism or just a statement? I'd been

past delighted to find the Magistrate had been called away on business when we'd returned the evening before. I made a polite reply. "It was good to be useful again." I swallowed. "Although it was strange to be at home without my father."

Silence greeted that. The Magistrate cleared his throat. "It may take some time to heal from your loss."

Josiah and I jumped as a knock sounded at the dining room door. I looked at Joe uneasily, but the Magistrate didn't notice, turning to greet the watchman who walked in. He bent to the Magistrate's ear and muttered a message.

Mr Keyne nodded acknowledgement and the watchman left.

Hiding a satisfied smile that sent more shivers of unease up my spine, the Magistrate pushed his seat back. "Your trip to the recycling factory will need to be delayed, I regret to say."

My heart pounded against my ribs.

Josiah stayed calmer. "What's happened, Father?"

"I need to conduct a trial. A reamer has been found skulking about City."

Chapter Twenty-Three

The door slammed behind him. I blinked in dismay. It needn't be Cosimo. There was no reason for it to be Cosimo. There were plenty of reamers; Cosimo had said there were others. He would be safely back on the Wastes by now. But good sense didn't calm my bouncing heart.

Outside, the bell rang, summoning everyone who was free to watch justice being dispensed in the square before the Magistrate's house.

"We should go. Father will expect me to be there."

I nodded to show I'd heard.

Josiah's tone softened. "Do you think this is your reamer?"

My reamer. Cosimo wasn't mine. But Josiah's words made me realise how much I wished he could be. I shook my head automatically. "It can't be him. He's dead." I wouldn't drop my guard, just in case.

"You don't need to lie to me, Liberty," Josiah said softly.

"It can't be him," I insisted, the words a plea more than anything else.

The bell stopped, the silence loud in contrast.

"We'd better go," I muttered, through lips frozen with fear. The sooner I knew it wasn't Cosimo, the sooner I'd be able to relax – and try not to think about the fate of the poor gorm who had been found.

*

A crowd had already gathered in the square outside. Josiah stood to one side, me beside him. The rest of the crowd were a step away from us, as though Josiah received some of the deference his father demanded. Josiah glanced around, then froze. "Will?"

I turned. Will was forcing his way through the crowd towards us, heedless of the angry mutters he left behind. His clothes were damp and his hair was sodden, dripping rivulets of water into his shirt. His blue eyes glinted half-mad.

"It's true." He stopped when he was inside the crowd with us, leaning over to catch his breath. When he straightened, his expression was twisted with pain and fury. "It's true. The seas are rising." He glared at me. "You're right. The people on New Eden told you the truth."

"Whatever are you talking about?" Josiah shooed me back so he could clap an arm around his brother, turning him away from the crowd who were fortunately too busy craning for a glimpse of the Magistrate and the reamer prisoner to pay much attention to Will Keyne's latest exploits. "Will, you're soaking – have you been swimming again?"

Will shook off his concern. "The seas are rising, Joe. And our father must know it. The chains have been lengthened. I swam down to see for myself. Two new links on each of them. What do you think of that?"

I'd told him to think for himself, and he'd done exactly that. I looked at Josiah. Could we risk taking him into our confidence? Will saw the exchange and gave it his own interpretation. "You know it too, Joe!" He backed away from his brother as though he'd been kicked. "You know! Father told you, and he didn't tell me." Hurt twisted his tone. "Why would he do that?"

"Will, look, we can't discuss this now." Josiah pulled Will close, lowering his voice. Some of the crowd were starting to look our way. "Yes, it's true, the seas are rising. Our father didn't want you to worry."

Again, Will wriggled away from the arm Josiah wanted to sling around his shoulders. "I'm not a child!"

"No, of course you aren't. But ... there was no need for you to know. He didn't want the information to get out before he had a response ready. It would cause panic."

"So I'm a blabbermouth who can't be trusted." Will's handsome face twisted as he spoke the words. He didn't voice them as a question.

"No, not that either." Josiah glanced around again and raked a hand through his hair. "Look, I'll tell you everything as soon as the judgement is over. Yes, the seas are rising, but there are plans afoot which mean that won't matter."

"What plans?"

Josiah blew out a breath with another anxious glance at the crowd. "I can't explain it in the middle of a crowd. Can you just trust me for a little while?"

"Trust you? Like our father trusts me?"

"Will—" This wasn't the right place, but I was about to bring him into our confidence regardless when he took the decision from me.

"I'll never trust either of you again!" Will spat. He spun away and pushed through the crowd in the other direction, away from the square.

Josiah stepped after him, straining to keep Will in sight as he vanished into the throng. "I'd better go after him."

I caught his sleeve. "Not now."

The Magistrate was walking from his front door, holding up a hand to silence the buzz of conversation as he stepped onto the makeshift stage that had been dragged into place by a pair of watchmen now standing either side.

When there was silence, or as close as it was going to get, the Magistrate adopted a sober expression and addressed the crowd.

"Thank you for joining me today, fellow citizens. It is our solemn duty to see justice done. Once again, a reamer has come to steal away property City can ill afford to lose." He motioned to the watchman on his left. "Bring forward the prisoner."

A hush fell over the crowd. I stood half-hidden behind Josiah, watching the other side of the crowd where people were parting to allow a third watchman to push through, propelling a skinny figure in front of him.

Murmurs began as people caught a glimpse of the reamer, growing louder as more people saw him. Then he came into my sight. I closed my eyes, biting back a groan. Fear was eclipsed by anger. I'd *told* him not to come here. I'd *told* him it was a death sentence. I'd have throttled him myself if I could have reached.

I opened my eyes to find the Magistrate watching me. He'd seen – they were unmistakeable – the gills gleaming at Cosimo's throat. I'd sworn this reamer was dead, and yet here he was. My face was cold, as though all my blood had drained away. After a few seconds, the Magistrate looked aside and gestured to the third watchman to bring Cosimo onto the stage.

There was a gasp as everyone in the crowd saw the prisoner – and the gills clear in his neck.

Cosimo's hands had been tied behind his back and the watchman stayed close, as usual, in case the prisoner needed to be restrained.

Silence eventually fell as the crowd got bored of whispering the obvious to their neighbours, and waited to hear judgement. Mr Keyne threw me a malevolent glare, then regarded Cosimo as though he were a piece of rotting seaweed that had attached itself to his shoe.

"Reamer, I see there is no need to discuss your guilt. That you have stolen City's most precious thing – the technology that allows us to survive in this precarious world – is clear to all of us. I can see no reason not to apply the death penalty."

A susurration of noise went through the crowd, split between satisfaction and dismay – because he was young, probably, or perhaps because we expected nautilus men to be proof against all ills.

"No," I whispered. I gripped Josiah's sleeve, twisting it between my fingers until he winced and pulled away, patting my hand for comfort. Cosimo was pale, but he didn't say a thing in his defence – what could he say?

The Magistrate gestured to the watchmen. "We will carry out the sentence immediately." The watchman closest to Cosimo bundled him off the stage towards the hanging post, where the other watchmen were already rigging a rope.

My hands were clammy and a buzzing noise started in my head. This was an awful dream. It couldn't be happening. The noise of the crowd was like a wave, one that would drown me if I let it crash over me.

I stepped forward. "Wait! He can make nautilus devices!"

The Magistrate turned slowly, allowing enough time to ensure the crowd also craned in my direction. I coloured under their regard, my cheeks growing hot. The Magistrate raised a brow. "The reamer can make nautilus devices? Impossible."

I probably glowed I was blushing so hard, but I wouldn't let the Magistrate silence me. "I saw a device he'd made. It was perfect."

The Magistrate's voice was cold and clear so everyone could hear. "Your father, Dr Miracle, shared the secret with him?"

I knew what he was about – make my father the villain to turn City against him, and me. I stared back at him, refusing to be cowed. "Yes." The word rang out clearly over the crowd, who breathed a sigh of disappointment. Dr Miracle, their saviour, was a flawed, mortal man. But the Magistrate was even more flawed. I straightened and called clearly, "I believe he knew he was in danger and didn't want the technology to die with him."

"Enough, Miss Marchmont." He gestured impatiently to the watchman to bring Cosimo back over.

When they were close enough, the Magistrate gripped Cosimo's jaw. "Is this true, reamer?"

He'd have to let go before Cosimo would be able to reply, but then the Magistrate saw a glimpse of silver and scooped Cosimo's pendant out of his shirt. He rested the circle in his palm to examine it, then let it drop. He stared at Cosimo's face for another moment then released him. "It would be merciful to give you a chance, reamer." The Magistrate stepped back. "Make us more nautilus devices and you may atone for your sins." He turned to the crowd. "Even a reamer may be redeemed if he proves himself worthwhile to City." The Magistrate threw a final command at the watchman. "Take him into custody at the watch house. Release him to no one but myself."

A hum of dismay skimmed over the crowd. At first I thought they found something wrong with the Magistrate's judgement. I feared they were hungry for blood. Then the muttered words became clearer and I realised it was a more self-interested emotion: fear.

"We're sinking!"

As the cries reached the front of the crowd, I saw a genuine emotion on the Magistrate's face for perhaps the first time ever. He blinked in shock, silenced as the crowd stirred, everyone shifting from foot to foot, trying to get away as water juddered and brimmed over the top of pontoons that should be dry. My own heart punched a tattoo of fear against my ribs.

Josiah hissed, "Will. It has to be."

I remembered Will's desperate expression, his refusal to be comforted by his brother. We should have gone after him.

"Stay calm!"

The Magistrate might as well have told us all to fly. As the water rippled and swelled underfoot, the crowd were unable to do anything but panic.

"Save us! We'll all drown!"

The shouts spread like a fire and the aimless milling of the crowd became hectic movement, with everyone seeming unsure where they intended to go but desperate to get there. In the space of a second, terror gripped people who had been peaceful a moment before. The Magistrate continued to shout but I couldn't hear what he was saying. Everyone was screaming, not listening.

"This way!" Josiah gripped my hand and pulled me through the crowd. As we passed the stage, I reached out and grabbed Cosimo to pull him with us. The watchmen had already abandoned their prisoner, intent on saving their own skins.

We ducked down an alleyway and stopped so I could unfasten the cords trapping Cosimo's hands behind his back. "I told you to go home!" I snapped once he was free to snap back at me.

He obliged. "And Ah made a promise to keep you safe, your Highness."

I hid my smile. It felt better than I could have imagined to hear him use that stupid name. "My father wouldn't hold you to your promise, you stupid gorm. Not anymore."

"Ah didn't come for your father's sake," he growled.

I went hot, glad when Josiah spoke. "We should make for the recycling plant." He leaned close as people ran past, pushing and shoving as they all tried to fit through the narrow streets.

"Agreed." I grabbed Cosimo's hand in one of mine and Josiah's in the other so we wouldn't be separated.

The pontoons splashed with each step we made. My hands were jolted as we dodged around other people running both ways down the street, but we stayed together.

"This is crazy," I muttered. People were pushing past, heedless of everything but their need to reach their destination.

"They're desperate," Josiah said.

I watched someone overtake us. Seconds later he returned, pushing past in the opposite direction. "What does he hope to achieve?"

"Ah don't think he's calm enough to have a plan." Cosimo smiled. The crowd and the noise vanished into the background, leaving just the two of us. I'd missed his sharp comments. If I hadn't missed them quite so much, perhaps I would have told him so.

"Come on. We can't hang around." Josiah tugged on my hand and we picked up speed again, splashing through an inch of water, heading for a street further along that would cut through to the path to the plant. I was sure I could feel the whole of City moving beneath my feet, pushing us deeper beneath the waves as the majority of its citizens tried to flee. I was trying not to think how deep we would have to get before sinking was inevitable. We turned a corner and ran through almost-deserted streets.

When we swung out of the final street to the edge of the pontoons, the change on City was obvious. The bobbing floats that joined City to the factory were noticeably lower than usual, dragged into the waves by City.

"We'll have to be quick," Josiah said. He stepped straight onto the path of floats that led to the factory, confidence lending him speed.

I'd never used the path before. I'd had no reason to. It was just there. Face-to-face, I wasn't keen on trusting my safety to the slimy-looking floats and the limp, damp rope that dipped at roughly waist-height from posts bound at intervals along the way.

"It's quite safe. I do this every day!" Josiah called back.

"Come on." Cosimo dived into the sea beside the path, preferring to swim, not walk.

I glanced back. City looked peaceful from here. Everyone was panicking away from the edges. There were only us three. No sign of Will or anyone else I knew. Water rushed over the toes of my boots. We didn't have time to go and fetch anyone else.

Cosimo and Josiah were already far ahead. I reached out for the rope and stepped off the secure pontoons onto the bobbing floats. I hadn't come this far to be scared off by a not-quite-straight path.

I barely looked up from my feet the whole way, my hand gripping the rope so hard it hurt when I finally uncurled it.

Josiah was there when I stepped onto the more stable platform supporting the factory. Cosimo was treading water, looking as though he'd happily stay there all day.

I looked back. City didn't look any lower than before. The rate of sinking was slow; I hoped it would be slow enough that we could save everyone.

Then I saw we weren't alone. From around the algae fields, other figures came. Will was using his bottle kayak to reach the factory, Hannah crammed in front of him. Foo was paddling close by, a couple of other boys paddling behind him.

Further afield, other craft appeared on the waves on either side of us, full boats launching from the harbour on the other side of City.

"We're not the only ones," I said in relief.

Josiah nodded. "Good." He pushed the recycling plant door open and vanished inside. I knew I should follow him, but I was irrationally afraid to take my eyes off City in case it sank while I wasn't watching.

Cosimo boosted out of the water, onto the narrow path that ran in front of the factory.

"It doesn't seem to be sinking," I added, more to reassure myself than because I thought Cosimo would be unduly concerned. "Perhaps our nautilus men have been able to stabilise it."

He sluiced water off his hair, shaking out his wet clothes. He glanced towards City. "Of course it's not sinking." As though I was stupid to think there was any danger.

"It might," I protested. "Will damaged the floats."

"Will?" Cosimo turned to me, ruffling his hair into something that probably counted as a style among the reamers. "Who's that? What's he got to do with anything?"

"You saw the water." He couldn't have thought splashing underfoot was normal. "Joe's brother did something to the floats beneath City to make it sink. We didn't get time to ask whether it was deliberate or just an accident."

"Will didn't do anything to the floats. Ah did." He stood straight, smiling with remembrance. "Ah let water into some of them. It was intended as a distraction so Ah could get you away from City, but then Ah bumped into one of your wretched watchmen."

I gaped at him. "You could have sunk City. You could have drowned us all." I knew Cosimo hated the Magistrate, but I didn't think that hatred had transferred to all of us.

"It's not sinking." He looked at me like I was mad. "Ah let enough water into the floats to bring City level with the waves, then Ah sealed them back up. It's quite stable."

I stared at him, then realised my jaw was sagging and snapped my teeth together. "I thought we were sinking. Everyone thought we were sinking."

"Of course you did. That was the point. Distraction, remember?" He watched me and laughed. "Your face, Libby!"

I coloured, as much from hearing my pet name spoken by him as from embarrassment at my mistake. "How was I supposed to know?" I snapped.

"Ah'm sorry, Ah should—" He broke off, laughing too hard to make a reply. He took a deep breath so he could speak. "Ah thought you were supposed to be the clever one!"

He pushed my arm, nearly shoving me off the path, laughing so broadly I could see his white teeth. I sniffed and folded my arms, wrapping my hand carefully over the chill patch on my arm where he'd touched me, waiting until he calmed down. I held on as long as I could, then snorted with laughter, too. "You could have told me," I grumbled.

He laughed a bit more, then calmed down, wiping his eyes. "You're right, Ah was just a bit busy trying not to get mah neck stretched."

"Don't say that. I nearly fainted when I saw it was you."

He straightened, standing so close I felt the pressure of his shoulder against mine. "Ah've missed you, your Highness."

I ignored that piece of nonsense. Warmth pinked through me but for once I didn't pick the feeling apart. I just enjoyed it.

Chapter Twenty-Four

There wasn't much time to enjoy anything, though, because Will and Hannah arrived in their bottle kayak moments later.

"Are you okay there?" I bent down as they bumped against the recycling plant path. "I'll hold the end steady while you get off, Hannah." I held one end of the kayak while Will gripped from the middle and Hannah climbed onto the factory path. I was happy to help until she stood up. She was perfectly dry and looked like she'd just turned away from her mirror. I was splashed with water and my hair had been dragged into a mess by the breeze. I tried to smooth it down and then gave up. No one was looking at me, after all.

"Thank you, Liberty." Hannah patted me on the shoulder. I resisted the urge to push her into the water.

Binny and Foo and a couple of other boys arrived, sitting in their kayaks while they looked back at City.

Once Will joined us on the path, Hannah's control crumbled. She grabbed his arm. "I was so frightened! Are we all going to drown?"

I looked at Cosimo, just in time to see him slip through the plant door. "Apparently not," I told Hannah.

Still clinging to his arm, she frowned. "How do you know?"

I opened my mouth, paused for thought, then said,

"I spoke to a nautilus man. He says it's quite safe." That was true enough for Hannah.

"Oh." She pouted and turned to Will. "Should we go back then?"

He shrugged. "No hurry, is there?"

Hannah leaned against him, all teeth and hair. "So long as you're with me, I'm in no hurry to go anywhere."

I followed Cosimo.

*

Inside the recycling plant, I was greeted by a hum of noise. I was reminded of the desalination plant I'd visited as a child. All the children went, to understand how precious our fresh water was. There was a similar hub of purposeful bustle as the workers went about their business.

There was no sign of Josiah, but Cosimo was in the middle of the room. I walked towards him, only to be brought up short when he cried out, "Suri!"

A slim woman turned – Suri, I presumed. Her face split into a grin when she saw Cosimo. I was wondering how Cosimo could know one of the workers here when my brain caught up with what my eyes were seeing. Suri was shackled, loose, so she could move and work, but shackled all the same. "Are mah eyes deceiving me?" she asked, reaching out to grip Cosimo's shoulder. She glanced down, looking at Cosimo's unbound hands. "What are you doing here?"

The pleasure at meeting a friend fell off Cosimo's face. "Ah came to help Liberty get away from City, but it looks like there's more than just her needs help to leave."

Suri frowned, glancing around. "What's happened? Are they going to let us go?"

Cosimo's face was grim. "They won't stop us."

He turned as Josiah came back into view, bunching a fist into the front of Joe's shirt before he could react.

"You were an idiot to bring me here. Did you think Ah wouldn't notice mah fellow reamers kept prisoner here?"

Josiah held up his hands. "I'm sorry. I didn't mean to conceal it from you. There wasn't time to explain. I thought you could all leave while City is in chaos."

Cosimo's fist twisted in the fabric. "And then you can follow after us so we lead you to what the Magistrate wants? Ah'm not such a fool as that."

I touched his arm. "Don't hurt him. Please."

Cosimo looked furious. "Why not? Mah friends have been kept here as slaves."

"I know, but more violence won't make things better." I remembered all the boys whose only memorial was a line in my father's notebook. "Too many lives have been lost already."

Josiah spoke up, softly. "I thought it was better they were here than dead. My father didn't offer any other alternatives."

"Please, Cosimo."

"You can take your friends and a cargo of metal. I'll help pack the barge myself," Josiah promised.

Suri interrupted. "What's happened?" She looked from Cosimo to Josiah. "Why are we able to leave?"

"City is sinking," Josiah said, still soft, Cosimo's fist lost in his shirt.

"It isn't really," I told them. Joe's eyes swivelled to me. "It's stabilised." That was the quickest explanation.

He nodded. "Then we should go quickly, before my father thinks to check what happened to his prisoner."

"Please, Cosimo. Let him help. I trust him."

Cosimo's fingers loosened. He let go. "How many reamers are here?"

"Six." Josiah dug in his pocket for a set of keys. "I've freed two already, they're loading up a barge with as much metal as it will hold."

"Then Ah'll help with that," Cosimo said. Josiah

unlocked the cuffs around Suri's wrists.

"Ah'll show you," she said.

Cosimo turned to me. "Will you help us, Liberty?"

"Of course."

On the other side of the plant was another door that led to outside. Bobbing on the waves were half a dozen barges, moored there while salvage was loaded and unloaded. Two people were busy at one of them.

When they caught sight of Cosimo, they paused for greetings. "This is Liberty." He introduced me. I stepped forward and tried to smile, hoping they wouldn't look down on me as a City girl, then wondering why they shouldn't. "She'll be coming with us," he added. Warmth slipped through me at the certainty in his voice. Then he looked at me, blue eyes clouded. "If you want to come, that is."

I nodded. "I don't want to stay here." I looked at the crates of metal in the barge. "Are we really going to make a machine and find the land of sun and roses?"

Cosimo grinned. "If it's there, we'll find it."

Suri said something I didn't catch, a joke at Cosimo's expense, I thought, when the reamers laughed. Then the factory door behind us opened again.

Josiah spilled through, followed by another three people I supposed had to be the reamers Josiah had just freed. More greetings followed.

"Will you take me, too?" Joe asked.

There was a rumble of objection from the reamers. Cosimo folded his arms. "So you can sink us when we're halfway there?"

My heart thumped – was the old enmity fated to continue? "We can work together," I suggested. "Isn't that what we wanted? No secrets and everything shared."

The reamers didn't look sure about it. I couldn't blame them.

"We're stronger if we all work together: City, New

Eden and the reamers." Their expressions didn't change. "And Josiah can navigate. He can use the stars to pinpoint where we are. He can help on the journey."

Cosimo met my eyes. I silently pleaded with him to let Joe come. We could make the future the way we wanted it to be. Cosimo looked at the other reamers, then at the barge next to us, which hadn't been loaded with anything. "Ah guess anyone useful is welcome."

I smiled with relief. Joe nodded his appreciation. "Thank you." He gestured at the next boat. "We can load that one up, too. What do you need more – metal or plastics?"

"Metal," Cosimo answered immediately. "No – both. There's a half-built machine on New Eden; with more plastic we can finish it."

My heart swelled at the idea that we could all work together.

*

"We're ready to go," Cosimo said five minutes later, once both boats were loaded. "Before City calms down enough for the Magistrate to wonder where Ah've got to."

I got into the boat with Cosimo, Suri and another reamer. "Will you be all right?" I asked Josiah, who was preparing a barge with the other four reamers.

"Of course!" Joe called back. He looked more alert – more alive – than I'd ever seen him, as though he'd been waiting for an opportunity like this his whole life.

"You'll go straight to New Eden?" Cosimo called.

The reamers raised a hand, focused on preparing the boat to launch. "We'll see you there in a day or so!"

The plan was that they would go to New Eden and finish the machine Cosimo and the people of New Eden had started there. We'd collect the stove Cosimo said was half-made on the Wastes and then join them to make another machine.

"We'll see you soon!" Joe called, as the barge I was

on slid away from the platform.

"Say hello to everyone on New Eden!" I called while I could.

Then we unfastened the ropes tethering us to City and drifted far enough away from the recycling plant that the wind caught our sail and pulled us forward. My voice was whipped away. I crossed the deck to see what I could do to help while my heart lifted. I was in no doubt this time that leaving City was the right thing to do.

Chapter Twenty-Five

The next few hours passed slowly, in an odd lull of nothingness, the other barge bobbing within sight until late in the afternoon, when it started to pull away, following a direct line towards New Eden instead of continuing straight to the Wastes.

When it was dark, I retreated to the covered cabin at the end of the deck to sleep. The boat rocked, my breaths lengthening as I listened to the sound of the waves lapping against the boards. My eyes were closed, but in my mind I saw the stars in the sky outside, the stars Josiah said would lead us to new places. This was really happening. It wasn't just me and Cosimo – other people believed in our plan, too. For the first time in my life I allowed myself to think about the land of sun and roses as a real place instead of a fairy tale.

*

When I woke it was morning. Overnight, the Wastes had swelled so they now loomed ahead of us. I swallowed. No one had ever found an end to the Wastes in any direction, so I knew they were big. I just hadn't credited quite how big – they had seemed a more human size when observed from miles away. Now it looked as though they might have been built by giants rather than people.

"Couple more hours," Cosimo told me, facing the

wall towering out of the sea. His heels kept lifting as he watched, not keeping his balance against the swell of the waves, but more as though he wanted to run towards home. He strode off to make sure the course set by Suri and the other reamer, Adil, would take us exactly where we needed to go.

I simply watched as the Wastes grew bigger and bigger and bigger.

*

I fell silent when we slipped into the shadow of the Wastes that afternoon. New Eden was beautiful; this ... this was intimidating. I straightened when I realised I'd ducked my head. It might be awe-inspiring, but I didn't need to cower before it.

I tipped my head back to watch the wall of ... whatever it was ... loom over us. Close up, it was a very pale grey mass, compacted in layers that rose high over our heads. "Do the reamers live on top? How do we get onto it?" The sides were high and mostly smooth. There was certainly no easy path like there'd been to get up the hillside to the land on New Eden.

"We jump."

I turned, open-mouthed. The top of the Wastes was higher above us than any house on City. Then I caught the expression in his eyes. He was joking. After a pause to digest that improbability, I smiled. "Go on, then. You first."

His teeth flashed in the artificial dusk created by the shadow of the Wastes. "There are steps. If you know where to look."

*

Ten minutes later, we bumped against a landing platform fastened to the side of the Wastes, finding a place beside a boat that was already there – a shorter, deeper boat like the one Cosimo had brought to City before. The three of them hurried to tie the barge to a ring set into the grey stuff. I stared at the wide, even steps that led from sea level to the top of the Wastes. From even the smallest distance, the steps were invisible, grey against grey.

Cosimo extended his hand to help me out. "Welcome to the Wastes, Liberty."

"Thanks." I accepted his help as the barge bobbed, clutching his fingers until I was safely on the platform.

"Come on. We'll go and say hello."

To the reamers Cosimo was sure would welcome us. My stomach lurched. Since we brought a cargo of precious metal, he was right probably. I let him lead me up the steps.

The surface beside us was ... bumpy, but not jagged. Up close, I could see that the striations I'd seen earlier were because the Wastes were composed of layers.

"It's rubbish." When I turned, Cosimo nodded towards it, one foot on the step above while he turned to speak to me. "From the Time Before."

"Rubbish?"

"Yeah. Stuff they threw away. We dig into the surface and find all kinds of treasures – mostly plastic, but now and then there are other treasures: metal, even tools we can use – everything except food."

I frowned as I processed that idea. "The Old Ones made it?" There were miles and miles of it. How could they have spared so much?

"We think it just ... mashed together. Pushed by the waves."

"Why didn't they use it themselves?"

"Maybe they just didn't need it. Life was very different back then."

I looked around at the vastness of it. Different? It would have to have been.

"Come along. Let's see who's here."

I followed him to the top of the Wastes. The sun had fled behind clouds, and the wind picked up so I shivered when we were out of shelter. The top was mostly grey and featureless, but a couple of shapes rose up. "Are they houses?" I asked.

"We call them stations. House, market, meeting place, workshop. They're whatever we need them to be."

"Is, er, anyone you know here?" I didn't want to remind him of what had happened to his mother, but I wanted to know what we were likely to face.

"Probably. We don't tend to stick in one place for long, but Ah expect Ah'll know someone camped out here now." He saw my expression. "They'll be welcoming to you. We don't hate all City folk."

"I don't know why not."

He smiled. "Because you're not all awful." My face warmed. Cosimo must have seen, because he nudged me. "Just naïve and gullible when it comes to trusting your Magistrate."

I nodded. We deserved that, if nothing worse.

"Come along. Don't get maudlin, your Highness."

A resumption of my irritating nickname was just what I needed. I picked up my pace to match Cosimo's as we made our way to the closest station.

*

When we drew nearer, I saw that it was made of plastic, like most houses on City, but it had been built a different way, not bottles, but plastic coaxed flat and combined into sheets that were stretched over a hoop-like framework. There was a door at one end.

When we walked inside, it was immediately warmer, the wind cut off.

We walked three steps to another door, an internal one, which seemed superfluous until we walked through it and the warmth bloomed. The difference in heat was remarkable. I looked around for a fire but couldn't find one. I craned to look around further. The building seemed to be one structure inside another. It was that which seemed to make such a difference to the heat. It was simply – and utterly – brilliant.

Cosimo walked into the middle of the room and tipped his head back. His shoulders slumped, like he was finally able to relax. I guessed he was. Back home at last.

It was missing something homely, though. "Where is everyone?"

The door swept open and I jumped, but it was Suri and Adil, not a new face.

Cosimo looked at them, but he answered me. "Ah think … Ah reckon everyone must have fled."

Adil nodded as though confirming that assessment. "There's no one in the other station. And just the one boat, left for emergencies like always."

Suri folded her arms. "Ah don't think they were attacked, though. Nothing seems to be amiss, they're just gone."

She shared a look with Adil. "We'll stay tonight and be off in the morning."

I blinked. I'd thought they were coming with us. "Don't you want to find the land of sun and roses?" I'd assumed it was a universal ambition with the reamers.

Adil laughed. Suri shook her head. "Our home is on the Wastes. We have no desire to leave." She shared another glance with Adil. "Until we have to."

Because the Magistrate drove them away. I nodded. "Should we go to New Eden, then?" If there were no reamers, there didn't seem much to keep us here.

"Not yet." Cosimo strode to the far side of the room where shelves and drawers rose almost to the ceiling, pulling out drawers and opening cupboards, rooting through for something.

I trailed after him, in time to see him pull a hunk of metal from a drawer with a triumphant grin. "Ha!"

I thought I recognised it from the chalk drawings on a table on New Eden. "Is that a stove? For the balloon ship?"

"It's the start of one." He strode to a workbench in the middle of the room and put the lump of metal on it. "The benefit of us always being on the move is that we take things with us. We share what we've discovered." The smile slipped off his face. "It's hard to destroy something once the reamers know about it."

I was trying to find words to console him when he threw off his mood and started work, clattering about finding tools.

"What can I do?" I offered.

"Give me a hand if you like. Ah'll try to explain how it works."

I joined him. "In words simple enough for a City idiot to understand?"

He grinned. "Ah'll trust you to keep up."

Cosimo explained the basics of the stove's construction, then set me to work fetching tools and parts for him.

"How does the building work? Where's the heat coming from?" Once he'd run out of instructions for me, I leaned my elbow on the workbench to see what he was doing and let my mind wander.

Engrossed in his work, he looked up with a frown. I shook my head. "Never mind." His work was more important than explaining everyday reamer life to me.

"It's us." I hadn't realised Suri was close enough to overhear.

"What's us?"

"The heat comes from body heat. We use insulation to make sure it stays inside our homes. That's why there are two doors." She drifted away again, busy about her own work. Cosimo was nodding, caught up on the conversation.

"I thought you said there's been no one in here for days."

"The insulation's very good." His expression

hardened. "That was mah mother's skill."

I fell silent at that and spread my fingers, enjoying the return of the warmth that had leached out of them during the walk. Finally, I added, "She was very clever. This is remarkable."

"Not bad for stupid gorming reamers, you mean?"

My face was hot, and not just from the temperature. "No, that's not what I mean. This is remarkable for anyone. It's so far ahead of anything we have. Why make you our enemies? Why didn't the Magistrate want us to work together? We could be halfway to the land of sun and roses by now."

I didn't expect an answer – I didn't think there was one – but Cosimo stood with fists braced on the table, staring at the wall. I waited.

"He burned his bridges."

"What bridges?"

Cosimo spun around so he was facing me, leaned back against the table and folded his arms. "Reamers all know the story. Ah forget they don't tell you on City."

"Tell us what?"

"They were friends. Your father, mah mother and the Magistrate. They were friends, they were the cleverest people left in our world, and humanity was on the brink of destruction, starving to death."

The son of old friends. I remembered the pendant I'd found in the Magistrate's drawer, which matched the one Cosimo wore. My father had known Cosimo's mother, and the Magistrate must have been friends with both of them.

"The people of New Eden were clinging to the last patch of dry ground, while City floated on pontoons moored just off its coast, a raft made two generations before that had lasted longer than anyone expected. The reamers spent their lives on their boats, fishing anything that still moved in the seas. Everyone was trying to find a way to survive, and we were all doing our bit.

"Your father focused on recovering what the people from the Time Before had left behind, the tins we'd thought were out of reach on the seabed. He found a way to enable men to breathe beneath the waves. Mah mother's skill was insulation – she created the insulation used in the suits nautilus men use when they dive."

I watched his Adam's apple bob down and up while he gathered his next words. "The Magistrate's approach to the problem was to reduce the number of mouths that needed feeding. He drove a wedge between those who wanted to settle and those content to roam. He attacked the reamers and turned us into enemies." His fists were so tight his knuckles were shiny dots of white. "Mah mother tried to change his mind. She tried to persuade him to work with the reamers rather than against them. Then she discovered the Magistrate was providing your father with test subjects for the nautilus devices – unwilling reamers. She said she would take her talents and leave if he didn't stop." Cosimo's jaw tightened, then he continued. "He claimed it was too important to stop, so important the reamers should be glad to make the sacrifice, so she left." Cosimo took a deep, deep breath. "She always said that she tried to change his mind by staying, then by leaving, but neither worked."

And now she was dead, like my father. So much waste, terrible waste, to be laid at the feet of one man.

"The Magistrate couldn't forgive her for leaving what he thought was the 'right' side, and enmity between City and the reamers was sealed."

I put my hand on his stiff arm. "I'm sorry."

"Not your fault."

"Maybe not, but ... I don't know why it's constantly a surprise to discover what he's capable of."

His lips twisted. "It's because you're a good person, Libby."

My pet name, again. There was no reason why the

word spoken by Cosimo made a tingle shiver through me. No reason at all. "Not naïve and gullible, then?"

The twist lifted further. "It's a fine line."

"Food's ready!" Adil called from the far end of the room.

Cosimo dropped the tool he was holding to clatter onto the bench. "Good. Light's fading. That's enough for the day."

Before I followed, I paused at the workbench to examine what he left behind. I wasn't an expert, but the stove looked ready for use. I touched the cool metal. A shiver ran through me. Such a simple thing, but it could carry us far from here, out across the ocean to the land of sun and roses. The impossible made real. I wished Pa were here to see it.

Chapter Twenty-Six

Adil had made seaweed soup. It tasted better than I'd feared. We sat together to eat while dusk descended and by the time we'd finished, it was too dark to do any more.

Cosimo said we'd made good progress preparing what was needed to find the land of sun and roses, and Adil and Suri were ready to leave in the morning to find other reamers and let them know what had happened on City. Adil and Cosimo bedded down on one side of the room, while Suri gave me blankets and showed me a place to sleep beside her on the other side.

*

I was the first to wake in the morning, sitting up with a stretch, and kicking my blanket away. Suri was snoring softly close by, head resting on her arm. I stood up, only to find I wasn't the first awake.

Cosimo was busy at the workbench, the stove before him. He looked up when he heard me. "You're early."

"No, they're late," I countered, pointing at Suri and Adil.

"They probably have some rest to catch up on," he whispered back, smiling.

"What can I do?"

Cosimo paused. "Ah could use some more metal. Ah want to make a start on another stove while Ah'm here."

"I'll go and fetch some."

He nodded. "Not too much; half a dozen sheets. Leave the rest – we'll take it to New Eden."

I nodded. The cargo was to be split; Suri and Adil taking some with them and us taking the rest to New Eden; amicable sharing that seemed to be beyond the Magistrate's comprehension. Perhaps it would mark a new way for us all to behave.

Outside, the sky was striped pink and blue, the sun creeping over the horizon. I hurried across the flat Wastes, then down the steps. It felt busy, the boats moored against the platform jostling like impatient children as the waves pushed at them. A prickle of unease lifted the hairs on my arms, but there was nothing to be scared of. I scanned the sea to check there was no pursuit, then stepped onto the first barge, pushing the cover from the crate in the middle of the deck. I grabbed half a dozen flattened sheets of tin and turned back towards the platform.

"Argh!" I shrieked at coming face-to-face with the Magistrate, striding across the deck towards me. The niggle at the back of my mind bloomed into understanding too late to be of use: three boats, where there had been two yesterday. Danger hadn't been heading towards me – it was already here.

"Don't come any closer." My demand might have been more convincing if I'd had something to defend myself with, rather than having my hands full of sheets of lightweight metal.

The Magistrate watched me through narrowed eyes. "You face a conundrum, Liberty. If you drive me away, you'll never discover who killed your father."

I stayed where I was, although I looked past him to the platform beyond, wishing our places exchanged. He was lying; he'd never tell me. But perhaps he would. "Who was it, then?"

Another narrowed stare, then, "Tom Dawber."

The name in my father's notebook. I couldn't bring a face to mind.

The Magistrate smiled unpleasantly. "I told him to stop your father leaving at any price. How any but a fool could have interpreted that order to mean I wanted your father dead, I fail to see." He sighed, as though seeking sympathy for his troubles. "I should have done the job myself, as I've been forced to do now."

"You were too much of a coward for that!" I spat.

"Is that what you think?" He took another step towards me. The deck creaked. I backed away. "It wasn't cowardice that brought me here today."

I looked around for something I could use as a weapon to keep him away while my foot reached back another step. "There are too many of us. We know what you've done. You can't kill us all."

His eyes glittered. "I don't expect to kill you all. One or two more deaths will send a strong enough message – do you wish to be one of them?" He continued to advance. My back met the cabin at the end of the boat and I could go no further. He'd been dangerous before. Now he was desperate, his power slipping away.

"No more deaths," I said. I flung the metal I was holding towards the Magistrate. I'd hoped to distract him enough to dodge past and reach the platform, but he grabbed my clothes, swinging me round and seizing my wrists, wrenching my arms behind me.

"Did you really think you could outsmart me?" he sneered, pulling me against him so I gasped at the pain in my shoulders. "I wouldn't let your father leave. Did you think I'd allow you to do so?"

Tears burned, but anger kept them at bay. I kicked out behind me, aiming for a knee or a shin, struggling for freedom, but the Magistrate yanked my arms higher until I feared a move would snap bones.

Once I was still, he spoke again. "Do you know what you must do in order to survive, Liberty?"

I swallowed down the pain. Walk all over everyone, it seemed.

He leaned close to my ear, hissing, "What. Ever. It. Takes."

"What do you want?" I managed.

"I want everything back the way it was, with me in charge. We will attempt fanciful flights to the land of sun and roses when *I* say we will." He shifted, gripping both my wrists with one of his hands. I tugged, trying to slither one hand or the other out of his grip, but stopped when his freed hand brought a knife to my throat. "I won't offer the insult of thinking you an idiot, Liberty. I'm sure you already know why I followed you here."

And I did: he wanted the machines. He wanted the reamers' technology, so he could control it. He wanted Cosimo.

"You can't destroy the technology. Too many people know about it. Josiah knows."

He laughed. "I will bring him to heel quickly enough. You have another job to do for me. The reamer came back to City for you. Will he seek you out now?"

I had to keep Cosimo away from him. "I shouldn't think so. He's busy."

"Busy? How unfortunate. Perhaps I should kill you and find him rather than waiting for him to come looking for you."

I swallowed, biting back the pleading answer that wanted to blurt from my lips. He had to know the reamers he'd imprisoned to do his work had escaped. I prayed he would assume they had all come here. He wouldn't want to face them. Cosimo was safe so long as he didn't follow after me. So I had to get away from the Magistrate myself. I tried to squint down and see the knife, but it was too close. His other hand pulled my wrists so high I stood on tiptoe and still my shoulders burned. The Magistrate kicked a coiled rope up from the deck and caught an end, thrusting the knife into his belt.

I struggled, but my shoulder gave a sharp crack and pain shot through me. "You can't fight me, Liberty. I will always win. The people in charge always do. We stack the cards in our favour, surely you know that by now?" He flicked the end of the rope around my wrists and tied it rapidly. "There." He tugged on the rope to check his handiwork. My arms pulled painfully towards him. I blinked back the tears of pain that pricked at my eyes, trying to burn them away with anger.

"You won't win. We will." I remembered Cosimo's words and I was nearly smiling when I told him, "Your time is at an end."

"Not yet, Liberty, not yet." He sounded unworried, tugging at my arms as he looked around the barge. "Now, how best to keep you contained?" I tried not to look at the mast – I didn't want to give him any ideas – but the Magistrate had found something else. He stepped away, eyes on me while he spooled the rope between us. I twisted my hands fruitlessly. I couldn't untie the knots because I couldn't see them – and I could only run as far as the rope would allow and I knew it wouldn't even let me reach the top of the steps, so there was no point to that either.

"This will keep you still." The Magistrate crouched down beside the anchor stone at the side of the deck, the hefty weight used to keep a barge in place on the waves while its nautilus men dived for salvage. He looped the rope through the chain that tied the anchor to the boat. Now I could move only if I could drag the stone behind me. But I could be patient. Either Keyne would get bored waiting for Cosimo to come, and he'd try to use me as some sort of a hostage against Cosimo and the other reamers, or —

"Libby? Did you find the metal?" Cosimo's voice drifted down from the top of the Wastes.

I twisted. "Cos—"

The Magistrate grabbed me, clasping a hand over my mouth, the knife returning to my throat.

"What did—?" Cosimo came into sight. His footsteps faltered at the top of the steps, then he stilled.

"Please, join us, reamer," the Magistrate drawled. "Don't try anything foolish. Not if you wish Liberty here to keep her bright blood within her pretty body."

"Don't—" My voice was strangled, but it wasn't the Magistrate's actions which prevented me from completing my sentence. I wanted to tell Cosimo to run away. I wanted to tell him to save himself because my life didn't matter as long as someone survived. I couldn't say the words. At the point of losing it, my life mattered a great deal to me.

I willed Cosimo not to come within reach of the Magistrate, hoping for a miracle to save us both.

Cosimo spoke. "What do you want?"

"I want this nonsense to stop, of course. You will both return with me to City and do as I tell you."

Cosimo slowed, pausing on a step halfway up. His eyes shifted from me to the Magistrate. "Ah don't think we will, thanks all the same."

"I'm offering you the chance to live."

Cosimo laughed. Then he folded his arms. "You didn't offer me that on City yesterday."

The Magistrate shifted. "Matters were different then."

Cosimo stepped down another two steps. I closed my eyes momentarily and prayed he'd stop. He spoke coolly. "Oh, you bet they were."

"You're angry. I can understand that."

Another step. "You killed mah mother. Do you think Ah'll just forget that?"

"I'm sorry about your mother. I didn't want her dead. I had to stop her making the machine."

Cosimo jerked a thumb back up the steps. "And

what about the other reamers you imprisoned?"

The Magistrate shrugged and I felt the knife move against my skin. "I needed workers. I could have hanged them instead."

"Are we supposed to be grateful?"

"Not at all. I know you're angry. I understand you better than you think, Cosimo."

"Ah doubt that." He continued down the steps. *Stay away, stay away, stay away* circled through my thoughts, as though I could shout loud enough inside my head for him to hear. I tried to call, but a desperate gargle was all that came out.

"Let Liberty go," he said, stopping at last at the bottom of the steps.

"Come on board and we'll discuss that," Mr Keyne countered.

Stay away, stay away, stay away.

He reached the barge. "Very well. Ah will." He made to step on board, then vanished. After a sharp, painful heartbeat, I realised he must have slipped, fallen between the platform and the barge.

The Magistrate muttered an oath, then abandoned me to stride the two steps to the edge of the barge and crane over to see where Cosimo had fallen. I hoped he wouldn't surface. He was a nautilus man, after all; he could go anywhere.

There was a splash as Cosimo surged up from the sea, the Magistrate jumping back in alarm. Cosimo caught the older man's ankle and tugged, sending him sprawling back onto the deck, his knife thrown wide to clatter on the deck. Before he gained his feet, Cosimo was on the barge and on top of him, grabbing hold of the Magistrate as he tried to scrabble away.

"The knife, Cosimo!" I cried out in alarm. The Magistrate's fingers were reaching for the weapon. Cosimo lunged forward and reached it first, his fingers closing around it, bringing it immediately to the

Magistrate's throat.

"Ah should kill you," Cosimo hissed.

The Magistrate blinked, searching for a way to escape before he returned his attention to the reamer. His eyes bulged. "You wouldn't kill your own father."

"What?" Cosimo's fingers flexed around the knife, confused. I looked from one to the other. The truth fell through me when I noticed the perfect match of their eyes, the blue shared by all three of the Magistrate's sons.

It was the chance Keyne needed. He swung a fist and caught Cosimo's temple. He rocked to the side, the knife flying from his grasp. The Magistrate shoved him off and scrambled for the weapon.

He gathered it up, holding it at arm's reach to keep Cosimo at bay as he got to his feet. I shifted as far away as the rope would allow as Keyne edged without looking back towards me.

"You can't be—" Cosimo gasped.

"I wish I weren't," he spat. "I loved your mother, fool that I was. And she betrayed me."

Cosimo's face twisted with pain.

I looked from one to the other, the similarities obvious now I looked for them. I shook my head. Cosimo was the same age as Will. The Magistrate must have been already married. In my view that made the betrayal his, not Cosimo's mother's.

Cosimo was shaking his head, too. "There's nothing Ah can do about that. But Ah'm never going to help you."

The Magistrate advanced on me. "Maybe you will if I remove this distraction."

"No!" I screamed and darted forward, but I was too slow to stop him as he levered the anchor block over the edge of the barge. It was only a second before the rope tightened and dragged me into the sea.

I tumbled off the edge of the deck and the water

closed over my head. A roar of fury sounded over the splash of the waves. I flailed for the surface instinctively, but the rope pulled me inexorably downwards.

I saw a dark shape, and felt the pressure of the water as something plunged into the sea. Either Cosimo or the Magistrate had fallen in. Then I realised it was both of them, still fighting. I was fighting my own battle, struggling as the water grew darker while I was pulled deeper, my lungs burning as I tried to tug my hands out of my bonds. Nothing would stop the anchor weight before it reached the seabed. I tried again to free myself as a bubble of air escaped my unwilling lips.

Someone grabbed for me. I couldn't escape. Then I realised it was Cosimo. He swung around me in the water, our legs tangling together as he faced me. We drifted further downwards. Black dots sprinkled my vision and I knew I'd soon have to breathe, even if water was all there was to pull into my lungs. Cosimo's hands tightened around my waist. His chest rose, expanding with air as his gills saved his life. My lungs burned harder in response, desperate to breathe. His hand shifted, his thumb tilting my jaw as he loomed closer.

I jerked with shock as his lips covered mine, then blessed air slid into my mouth from his. My startled gaze collided with his calm blue one. I closed my eyes so I wouldn't have to see him, intimately close.

As the air reached my lungs and my own chest lifted, pressing me harder to him, terror left me. I relaxed, gripping his waistband to keep him close as we completed our journey to the bottom of the sea.

His lips were warm, as were the places where we touched. Elsewhere, the cold water was startling as we slid away from the surface. I opened my eyes, but all I could see was Cosimo's face, closer than any man had ever been to me before. A blush burned my cheeks against the water's chill and I closed my eyes again.

Our fall through the sea seemed to hold us

suspended in time, the water sliding past, our legs tangled together, chests rising and falling in counterpoint as Cosimo breathed for me.

At last, we settled to a stop and my eyes flared open. The water was darker than it had been, but I could just make out grey shapes behind Cosimo. We'd reached the bottom of this part of the sea.

My feet eased further into something soft – sand or drowned soil – and Cosimo reached behind me. Jerking movements pulled at my wrists and I waited for the blessed moment when I'd be free. More tugs followed. Finally, Cosimo moved his head slightly, his eyes steady on mine, trying to communicate. We would have to break apart so he could untie me from the weight. I nodded. He squeezed my hand. I took in the air he breathed out and held it in my lungs, pressing my lips together. Cosimo broke away and the skin around my mouth was immediately chilled.

For the first time, I looked at our surroundings. Over our heads, the sea was cut in half. One side was a pale, almost luminous blue; the other was a smudge of grey where the wastes cut through the water. I wondered how deep we'd come. When I looked in the other direction, I could see what had once been the land, in the Time Before.

I'd thought I would see houses and streets; that I'd be able to envisage what life was like a hundred years ago. It wasn't that easy. Behind me, I could see buildings rising like ghosts, but silt blurred the edges of everything so I couldn't be sure what I was seeing. My respect for the nautilus men who navigated this environment, and found what was of value inside, increased.

My lungs reminded me that I had again stopped breathing regularly. I twisted to see Cosimo tugging at the fastenings around my wrists. The wet rope wouldn't come undone.

A ringing noise started in my head. I needed to breathe more than I needed to be free. I tried to nudge Cosimo. He gave a final tug on the rope and I felt the cool smoothness of water sliding over the places the rope had burned. I was free. I grabbed Cosimo and pulled him to me. Realising how long he'd taken, he turned me towards him and covered my mouth again. I wrapped my arms around his waist and felt the lift of his lungs a moment before the air rushed into my mouth and I could breathe again. His arms wrapped around me, a mirror of my own, and he pushed off, pulling me with him. We both kicked, eager to reach the surface.

I was scared to lose him, that was why I clung to him so tightly. I wondered if that was the reason – the only reason – he was holding me so close.

We kicked together, our legs tangling. It felt like longer to reach the surface than it had been to reach the bottom, but finally air and light exploded around us. Our mouths broke apart long enough for me to suck a huge, grateful gasp of air into my lungs. I expected Cosimo to let me go now we didn't need to share air.

He didn't.

Chapter Twenty-Seven

Cosimo's blue eyes locked on mine, and one hand tightened further around my waist while the other pushed into my still-wet hair, angling my face towards his.

His lips met mine, caressing instead of practical now, and a thrill of emotion surged through me. His tongue slid across my lower lip and I gasped – and our kiss was abruptly over. Cosimo jerked back and reached out to grab the platform beside us. He was breathing heavily, staring at the chunk of the Wastes where the platform connected. From that angle I couldn't see his expression. A blush heated my throat and cheeks. Was he sorry we'd done that?

I shivered. "Um." I tried to say something, but my brain was empty, fried from fear and emotion. "Thank you. For rescuing me," I said when it became evident Cosimo wasn't going to say anything.

He made no reply. I stared up at the sky. "We should get out. It's cold."

Perhaps Cosimo didn't feel the cold. He acted like he'd be happy to stay there all day.

Finally, he cast me a nervous, sidelong glance, as though he expected me to scream at him. I wasn't hypocrite enough to pretend to be appalled by what he had done. "Your father would skin me alive for that," he muttered. "Especially if he had any idea how long Ah've been wanting to do it."

A flush burned my face. A thrill of feeling I couldn't name, but which I liked, rippled through me. He didn't hate me, even though I was a City girl. He couldn't hate me and do that – could he? My heart lurched. I tried to see his face, to judge whether I was mistaken. He still wouldn't look at me. I swallowed. "It's not my father's permission you should be seeking," I told him. I sounded prim, but then I wasn't accustomed to flirting. Not with anyone whose good opinion I cared for.

He looked at me then, a little uncertain. I thought it made him seem endearing, but I would freely acknowledge I wasn't in my usual frame of mind. Since he remained silent, I had to say something. "Besides, I think he always liked you more than … anyone else."

Cosimo looked away. He cleared his throat. He was still staring at the Wastes and I wished he'd look at me. He cleared his throat again and I had a sudden urge to ask if his gills were troubling him, then I wanted to giggle at the ridiculous idea. I knew there was nothing wrong with the devices. Then Cosimo looked straight at me and the mirth died in my throat. Our eyes locked and, by the tides, all I wanted to do was kiss him again.

But instead he said, "We should get out."

I coloured again, at knowing I'd been thinking of kisses while he'd moved on to what we needed to do next. "Of course."

"You first." He helped me clamber out, then boosted out of the water onto the platform. Water poured off my clothes. I glanced at Cosimo but didn't look him in the eye. I didn't know what to say. I looked back at the barges and the sea, which showed no sign of our drama. "What of the Magistrate? Did he drown?" I didn't like to wish for anyone's death, but if he was dead we were safe.

I turned to see Cosimo's face harden. "He met his

own knife." Abruptly, his face crumpled. "Ah didn't mean to kill him. He tried to stop me coming after you. Ah couldn't leave you to drown, could Ah? Ah didn't mean to kill him, but he wouldn't stop."

I took his hand and squeezed, wanting to ease the distress from his face. "You did what you had to do. No one will blame you for it."

He nodded, then looked up. "Do you think it's true? Is he mah father?"

I looked into eyes that were just like his father's, just like his brothers' – half-brothers. I reached into my pocket and pulled out the pendant I'd hidden there. "I found this in his drawer. I don't know, but … I think it might be true, Cosimo."

He nodded, face turned away so I couldn't see how he felt about the matter. He didn't move to take it so I stuffed the pendant back into my pocket.

"We should go back. The machine's nearly done." He looked at me. "And we need some dry clothes."

I nodded. I didn't mean to, but my eyes settled on his lips. Would he kiss me again? Could I ask? Why was I thinking about kissing when we had a balloon ship to finish? I took a step towards the stairs, then stopped when Cosimo didn't come with me, our hands still linked. I didn't want to break the connection.

I turned to face him. His eyes were very blue, his expression more serious than I remembered seeing him before. "Liberty Marchmont." He cleared his throat once more. I didn't have any desire to interrupt this time. He sounded very unlike Cosimo: serious, and utterly, utterly sincere. The thud of my heartbeat sounded louder than the splash of the waves against the platform. "Ah need to ask you something." He took a deep breath. "Ah know … Ah know you might have your pick of any man, and Ah know … Ah know Ah've done nothing to deserve your good opinion. Quite the opposite. But … Ah should like to ask for your permission to court you."

My mouth hung open like the daftest gorm, but my brain was empty of any words, much less the ability to speak them. He hurried on as though my lack of an answer meant no. "When you get to know me, Ah hope you might learn to like me ... a bit."

I was grinning like an idiot and all the formal words had never been further from my brain or mouth. I barely managed, "You want to make a pledge?"

"Is that what you call it on City?" Another flash of white as he smiled. "Yes. Yes, Liberty Marchmont, Ah would like to make a pledge."

My heart bounced against my ribs. My brain wanted to demand, "Why?" but it was fortunately drowned by my heart which was too happy at his declaration to allow me to spoil it by attempting rationality. "I am delighted to accept, Cosimo."

He smiled and I no longer felt cold. "Here. Take this gift to seal our pledge." He let go my hand, but only so he could take the pendant from around his neck. "It was mah mother's." He lifted it over my head.

I shifted my soaking plait out of the way. "Thank you." I reached into my pocket again, turning my hand up to show Cosimo the pendant Melisande had been adamant I take. "It's all I have of value," I told him. "I don't know ..." Could I give him something from the Magistrate?

Cosimo lifted the chain, meeting my eyes. "No, it's *not* all you have of value, Libby." Warmth pinked through my cheeks. "But Ah'm delighted to accept it from you." He slipped it over his neck and pressed the lightest of kisses against my lips.

He took my hand. It might have been a perfect moment, except that I felt a stickiness that had nothing to do with seawater. I turned his hand over, appalled at the dark smear of blood against his lighter skin.

"He struck you," I gasped in horror. Then, practically, "Where?" My eyes dredged over him, seeking the wound. Now it wasn't washed away in the water, I traced the blood up his arm.

"Ah'm fine." He shrugged off my concern.

"You might need stitches."

"It's nothing."

"You'll allow me to be the judge of that. I'm the doctor."

"Ah hope a pledge doesn't give you licence to nag at me non-stop."

His tone was mocking, typically Cosimo, but I was mortified at the truth of it. I swallowed. "I'm sorry. I know I have been – I must have been – insufferable. I shall endeavour to improve." With a surge of feeling as strong as any tide, I wanted to be a better person. I wanted there to be more to me. I wanted to be someone worth loving, worth loving by Cosimo.

"No. You've been nothing of the sort." Cosimo squeezed my hand and a distant part of my mind acknowledged that there could be no muscle or nerve damage to his arm. Most of me simply loved the strength and warmth of his hand around mine. "Ah fell in love with you as you are, Libby: bossy and argumentative, clever and capable, and very beautiful. Don't change when Ah've grown used to all that, for the tides' sake, sweetheart."

I blinked, and waited a moment to catch my breath. There was my *why*, and more than I might ever have hoped for.

He tugged his hand from mine. "Ah'll survive," he said, with nothing to base that assertion on, although he had been through worse, and recently. "Come on, we've a balloon ship to finish."

Chapter Twenty-Eight

Adil and Suri were awake by the time we returned.

"What happened?" Suri asked, watching the pool of water gathering at our feet.

"We went for a swim," Cosimo said.

"You might need stitches," I told him.

"Don't fuss," he replied, but he let me peel back his sleeve to reveal the gash on his forearm.

Adil and Suri trailed after us. "Do you have alcohol?" I was greeted by dumbfounded expressions. "To clean the wound," I explained.

Suri shrugged. "We have water for that."

And high infection rates, I didn't doubt. Still, I'd work with what I could. I checked the wound, which did require stitches. "I'll need a needle and thread, too."

Suri found them for me and I dunked them into a small pan of water boiling over the stove – part of breakfast, I supposed – while I cleaned the wound with fresh water.

"Well?" Suri demanded. "What happened to you two?"

"The Magistrate paid a call," Cosimo said.

Suri looked past us to the door. "Is he still here?"

"No." Cosimo shook his head. I hooked the needle and thread out of the water and started work.

"He's dead," I clarified.

Cosimo winced as I pierced his skin. "I'm sorry.

Three should do it."

Suri sucked in a breath.

Adil sniffed. "Ah can't pretend Ah'm sorry."

Suri nodded. "More news for us to carry when we go."

"Which will be as soon as we like," Adil added.

"Ah'm ready," Suri confirmed.

I fastened the final stitch, and Cosimo pulled off his damaged shirt and hunted for thread the right colour to mend it, throwing me a drying rag from the station's multi-purpose shelves.

"Don't stay on our account," Cosimo told them.

I wrapped the rag around my wet plait and looked at him. "Could you finish your work on New Eden? Josiah needs to know what's happened." The Magistrate's son deserved to know about his father's death before it became common knowledge amongst the reamers.

After a pause, Cosimo nodded. "Ah'll bring what Ah need."

"We'll see you on the dock," Adil said.

They left the shelter. Cosimo mended his sleeve while I packed up the finished stove. Cosimo joined me and piled the half-made one along with several tools into a basket woven from strips of plastic. I folded the blankets we'd used and tidied up so we'd leave the place in a good state for the next people to use it. Five minutes and we were ready.

Back at the dock, Suri and Adil were busy on the barge the Magistrate had used to find us.

"Shall we take the extra boat?" Adil called when we reached the platform.

Cosimo glanced at the barge. "Be mah guest." He looked at me. "We have metal for New Eden. That's gift enough."

I nodded agreement.

A minute later, Adil and Suri called their goodbyes

and began their journey to find any other reamers further along the Wastes.

*

"What are you going to tell Joe?" I broke the silence once we were also underway, heading in the opposite direction to Adil and Suri.

"That his father's dead." He frowned. "Ah thought it might be better coming from you."

I shook my head. "No, I mean – you're brothers. Are you going to tell him that?"

Cosimo stared at me, as though the connection came as a surprise to him. "Brothers …" He shook his head. "Ah need some time first."

I nodded. So many secrets had surfaced in the past few days. It might take us all a while to adjust.

*

The journey to New Eden took all day, and the sky was turning pink as we scraped onto the beach. Like last time, people were waiting to greet us, but unlike last time, they were actually pleased to see us.

Sarah stepped forward with a smile, the waves ripping at her feet as she pulled me into an embrace. "Liberty. And Cosimo. It's a pleasure to see you again." Paul stood at her shoulder, grinning broadly. I spotted Simon in the group who'd come to welcome us. And Josiah.

I hugged Sarah back. "It's a pleasure to be here." I gestured to the boat. "And we've brought metal to pay for our keep this time."

"As though that matters!" Sarah chided. She looked at Cosimo. "Your friends have been busy with the machines. They brought plenty of metal."

I stepped towards the crowd, and Josiah. I turned back to Sarah. "Could we speak to Josiah alone?"

Cosimo nodded. Joe deserved to know what had happened to his father before everyone heard about it.

Sarah looked from one of us to the other. "Of

course." She turned to everyone clustered around us. "Right, you didn't come just to sightsee, time to make yourselves useful. Let's get this cargo unloaded." She led the way to the barge and they started work. We shifted further downwind so no one would overhear.

Josiah's welcoming smile was long gone by the time we were alone. "What's happened?"

"I'm so sorry, Joe. Your father followed us to the Wastes. He attacked us; tried to kill Cosimo and me. I ... I'm sorry, but he's dead."

His expression crumpled. He nodded a tight jerk of his head. "Thank you for telling me." He looked past us to the sea beyond. A minute passed before he spoke, decisions all made. "I need to go back to City. I have to tell Will – and City needs to know it must choose a new Magistrate. I'll collect my things and go now."

"Will you be safe?"

"I know the stars, it's a clear night. I'll be fine." He took two steps towards the path, then looked back. "You will wait for me? Before you go?"

"Of course."

"It'll take us a few days to prepare the machines. Be quick," was Cosimo's response. Joe's action, imprisoning the reamers, hadn't yet been forgiven.

"I won't delay," Josiah promised, hurrying up the cliff path.

I watched him go. I'd be a hypocrite if I claimed to be sorry the Magistrate was dead, but I was sorry for Josiah's pain. "Why is life always such a mess?" I sighed.

"Because it's people living it. People are messy. We can't seem to help it." Cosimo's fingers slipped between mine and I enjoyed the feel of his skin, the warmth of him close to me. I could get used to being pledged. "Come on, your Highness, we've work to do." We followed after Josiah, warm hands linked together.

*

We headed for the barn first, where the reamers were

busy at work in the last of the light.

I gasped when we entered. Where Cosimo had left behind the shell of a balloon ship, the reamers, in the space of two days, had created two more. These had a framework of metal infilled with plastic.

Cosimo stepped forward, exchanging greetings with the reamers and nodding approval of their changes. "We thought lighter would be better," one of the reamers said, walking around the structure with Cosimo. "All we need now are the stoves."

"Ah've brought two with me – one needs more work." He glanced at the balloon ships again. "Will we need three?"

The reamer grinned. "A couple of the New Eden folk want to come, too."

Cosimo nodded. I smiled; more people who wanted to see what was out there.

It had grown gloomy by then, so the reamers packed up. We walked to Emily and Paul's house. That had become the domestic hub for the newcomers, with Emily taking on the caretaking role of providing food for everyone.

"Liberty! Sarah said you were returned!" Emily greeted me with a hug while the others found places around the wide kitchen table. Then she held me at arm's length. "But a short visit only, I understand?"

I nodded. "We'll be off as soon as the balloon ships are ready."

"A trip to the land of sun and roses. I wish you well." Her smile slipped. "Paul wants to go."

And I could see from her expression that she was less enthusiastic about the idea. I remembered her speaking to me before his operation: *he's all I have*. "It's an exciting idea. Aren't you curious to see what's on the other side of the Wastes?"

She waved a hand. "I'm too old to go gallivanting after a dream."

"I don't think you're ever too old to pursue a dream," I countered, softly, to make it an observation not a rebuke.

She turned back to the stove and the stew bubbling fragrantly on its top. "Paul can go on my behalf and discover what's out there. Sit and eat, Liberty."

*

On the evening of the third day, when everything was ready for our flight, Josiah returned. But he didn't come alone.

Chapter Twenty-Nine

"What in the seas ..." I stared at the barge crunching up the sandy beach. Josiah jumped into the shallow waves, rope in his hand, heaving the barge further onto the sand. His passenger stood on deck, smiling like a queen surveying her subjects.

I looked past her, but there was no sign of Will, nor – more surprisingly – of Belle. Why had Hannah come all this way without her fan club of admirers? I glanced at Josiah, wondering if she'd somehow switched allegiance to the elder brother in the space of a day, but her eyes weren't following him, they were looking out at the crowd on the beach.

Other people splashed past me to help the new arrivals and I remembered my manners.

Hannah was helped down by Simon and Josiah so – of course – she didn't get her feet wet, nor even her skirt splashed before she was set onto the firm sand.

"Oh, hello, Doc." She smiled as though surprised to find me here, flicking her hair over her shoulder, half an eye on the people around me. "Joe's been telling me all about the new machines. They sound very exciting."

Since when was Hannah interested in engineering? Or exploration?

"Have you come alone?" I eyed the boat, still expecting someone else to appear.

"No, with Joe."

I pursed my lips. "No, I meant – isn't Will with you?"

"Will's staying on City." As though it were odd of me to ask.

"Didn't you want to stay with him?"

Hannah was looking up at the clifftop now, as though straining to see the wonders of New Eden. "No." She glanced back and laughed when she saw my expression. "Will and I weren't anything serious."

You could have fooled me. At least – you could have fooled me that she'd wanted it to be. Hannah's behaviour made no more sense to me now than it ever had. But the Libby who would have regarded Hannah as an inexplicable natural phenomenon had been washed away by everything I'd experienced since leaving City. I folded my arms. "Why do you want to leave?"

She shrugged and played with her hair again. "Why not?" Her smile grew wider, but there was a brittleness to it.

"What's happened, Hannah?"

She didn't answer, staring at the sea as though she hadn't heard my question.

"You killed Belle, didn't you? And now you've got leave City before someone finds the body."

Hannah turned. Her smile was nearly genuine. "Another joke? What's that, two this year?"

"I've been practising."

"I can tell." She sighed. "My father is now the Magistrate of City."

"I see," I said cautiously, wondering why Hannah spoke as though that was a bad thing.

"No, you don't. He's also getting re-married, so he doesn't need me anymore."

Old Libby would have condemned that as childish – a sulk because she was no longer the centre of attention. Now, I could appreciate that someone who dazzled like Hannah wouldn't let herself be pushed into the shadows if there was an alternative. I smiled. "Well, whatever we find out there, it won't know what's hit it when you arrive."

Hannah grinned and shook her hair back again. "I know, right?"

*

It wasn't until dinnertime that I had the chance to speak to Josiah and catch up on City's news.

"Will has taken over running the recycling plant," Joe told me as we sat down to eat. "He seems determined to show he's capable of industry."

"How did he take the news?"

Joe's expression sobered. "Better than I expected, to be honest."

I wondered about Melisande, but I couldn't think how to frame the question. But Joe might have read my mind. "My mother was equal parts sad and relieved, I think." He looked up. "I'm not an idiot. I know they haven't been happy with each other for years." He fiddled with his cutlery. "An ending also marks a beginning. I hope good things are in store."

The land of sun and roses. My stomach turned liquid when I thought about it. The reamers had tried a flight – perhaps a float would be a better term – that afternoon and professed themselves satisfied. We were ready to go: Me, Joe and Hannah from City, four reamers, and Paul and a girl named Jilly from New Eden.

Hannah's voice caught my attention. She was sitting at the other end of the table, her smile as broad and flawless as ever, her chatter ringing out over the table, demanding everyone become her friend by sheer force of personality. For maybe the first time, I wasn't jealous – or scared – of her. She had her talents and I had mine.

Cosimo's hand covering mine made me jump. "Are you ready for this?"

He had misinterpreted my silence for nerves. I smiled at him, squeezing his fingers. "I can't wait."

*

The next morning, the winds were in the right direction to carry us over the Wastes and far beyond.

After a hurried breakfast, we climbed into the basket of the first balloon ship. This one would convey me, Cosimo and Jilly. Further along the beach stood the other two balloon ships – with two reamers and Paul in one, and the third reamer with Joe and Hannah in the other. The last reamer freed from the recycling plant had decided to stay on New Eden.

Cosimo nudged me to bring my attention back to our own balloon ship. "Come on, your Highness, Ah suppose Ah must show you how to operate this tub else you'll nag me beyond reason to learn."

I wanted to slap him for his cheek. More, I wanted to kiss him. Since the balloon ship was ringed by an attentive audience of New Edeners, I couldn't very well do either. I folded my arms. "If you'd been as willing to teach me how to sail the boat, I wouldn't have needed to nag you at all."

"That's fair truth, Ah suppose." He knelt down. "Everything relies on the stove." He craned to look at me. "Ah suppose you've lit a fire before."

I did swipe him for that. He grinned and ducked back to his job. It only took a minute. The stove radiated heat and the bottles tugged upwards as the hot air reached them. A cheer split the air and I felt the lurch as we left the ground. The balloon strained against the rope keeping it tethered to the sand.

I looked at the people now six feet beneath us, then turned to Cosimo, grinning. "It works."

"Of course it works." His tone was scathing. "Did you think Ah couldn't do it?"

"No ..." I fell silent as possibility ran fully, thrillingly through me. "We can really do this. We can really cross the Wastes."

He grinned. "That's the idea."

I leaned over the edge of the balloon and waved to the figures below, picking out the faces I knew. "It works!" I shrieked at them.

"We can see that!" Sarah yelled back, hands cupped around her mouth.

There was another cheer as the second, and then the third, balloon ship lifted from the ground.

Everyone was smiling and cheering, grinning like maniacs. I glanced back to Cosimo, then couldn't look away from the shine in his eyes as he smiled at me. "We're going to find the land of sun and roses. We're really going to do it." It seemed like a dream. I was going to wake up any moment.

He cleared his throat, his expression suddenly, horribly, serious. "This is your last chance, Libby."

I swallowed. "Last chance for what?"

"There's no turning back once we leave," Cosimo replied. "If you want to stay this side of the Wastes …"

I stared as though he was mad. "I don't want to stay. There's nothing for me here." Nothing I had known, nothing that I valued of my previous life mattered now. All I cared about in the world was right here with me. We were so close I couldn't resist. Ignoring the stove and the wind and the audience for a reckless moment, I leaned forward until our lips met. He tasted warm and sweet. His arms wrapped blissfully around my waist. Everything I needed was right here, right now.

Bonus Material

Want to know what the nine who left found when they crossed the wastes and the seas beyond?
Overleaf you'll find *Across the Empty Seas*, a tie-in short story created exclusively for readers of *Rising Tides*.

Happy reading!

Across the Empty Seas

If the adulthood journey was intended to kill him, surely there were easier deaths than being bitten to death by a million insects.

Ked swatted at the cloud of midges in front of his face. They evaporated, but reformed the moment his hand reached to grab at a branch and pull himself further up the mountainside. The bugs were worse on the lush, uphill slope than they were in the dry valley, but no one had promised that this journey would be easy. Just the opposite.

Ked slapped his neck as another bite made him flinch. Neck to wrist to toe he was carefully covered, but the tiny assassins found a way through his clothes. Every inch of him itched. No, that wasn't true: some ached instead. He forced himself onwards, ignoring the itches and the pain in his hip and lower back. It was hard to believe he'd fought to be allowed to do this.

If he'd wanted not to be bitten to death, he could have kept silent, he reminded himself. He could have let the chance slip by, watched friends undertake the adulthood ceremony while he stayed safe by his family's fire, excused the trial. That's how the elders had seen it. Excused. He'd known he wasn't being excused, but excluded.

Pausing to wipe sweat from his forehead before it could drip, stinging, into his eyes, he swallowed down the taste of disappointment that twisted his tongue, rank and bitter even at the memory. He knew everyone stared at him when they thought he wasn't looking. He knew they saw his leg before they saw him. But the journey into the mountains at sixteen was a rite of passage. It was universal. It was also symbolic. Unless the teenager was exceptionally stupid, there was no real danger. It was the wrong season for floods, and the insects were annoying but not deadly.

There had been failures. That was different. The year Ked was eight there'd been sixteen candidates. They'd set off, together at dawn, as was customary. Four days later, most had returned triumphantly, each clutching a coconut to their chests, or lifting it high to be seen as they'd entered the village, cheered by friends and families. But the slowest three had been too late. The tree had been stripped, all the fruit taken. A single boy might have been cowed by shame, but the three were united in their misfortune. They'd been cheered as loudly as the others, and they'd made the journey again the next year when there were only six other candidates, and they'd brought back their coconuts then.

Ked didn't intend to fail. And he'd been shocked to find that was the only outcome everyone else could see for him. Bem's face was engraved on his memory, her scowl as she'd jumped up and protested, "He can't come with us. He'll slow us down."

It wasn't – officially – a race, but everyone treated it that way. He'd scowled back at her. "I don't expect you to wait for me. You'll be far ahead – won't that make you happy?"

"If you actually make it to the summit, we'll have to carry you back down. You're a liability."

The elders had agreed with her. Ked had argued, but no one had listened. No one listened while you were a child, that was the point of the adulthood ceremony.

So Ked had taken matters into his own hands. The candidates had been due to leave at dawn, so he'd been earlier. He'd slipped out of his bed and started the hike while the moon was still high. Taking the narrow trails, the little-used, overgrown paths, he'd hoped to be overlooked. He'd known the others would overtake him. With his limp and the weakness that meant his right leg grew tired and shaky long before his left, that was inevitable. He didn't care if they were faster, he just didn't want to be caught up and forced to go back.

He wouldn't be the first, that wasn't the point. He just wanted to undertake the journey, return with a coconut, and be acknowledged as an adult, like everyone his age.

Today was day three. The trip usually took four days: two up, two down. The first candidates would be there by now. There were only three candidates this year – and him, creeping out early. If he took another day to reach the tree he'd miss them all, continuing doggedly up while they passed him going down.

Ked paused, bringing his water bottle to his lips. It was close to midday and too hot to walk comfortably, even where the trees provided shade. Even the insects were flagging. There were still some, but they weren't as dense and annoying as they'd been even ten minutes earlier. Ked sat with his back against the wide trunk of an oak tree and tipped his hat down over his face to dissuade the more determined bugs. The drone of insects further away filled his ears, a soporific hum, all the more satisfying for not being accompanied by the prick of a bite and the reflex slap Ked always reacted with. Tugging his sleeves down and checking his water bottle was close by, Ked settled back. There was no hurry. It wasn't a race. No one had ever died during the journey. And everyone had always returned.

As the sun beat down and the insects hummed, Ked wondered why that was. No use in undertaking an adulthood test if there was no one to acknowledge you as an adult afterwards, but he wondered if anyone else had ever been tempted. It was peaceful in the mountains, no pressure. There were plenty of streams and springs for water, roots and berries to eat as well as bugs for protein that he could trap as easily here as back home.

He might stay here forever. The blunt thought stopped Ked's breath. It was an effort to relax his lungs and sigh the impossibility of the idea into the warm air. And yet, it wasn't impossible. He'd proven he could take care of himself. That was the whole point of the adulthood ceremony, after all: prove you were capable of surviving and would be a useful member of the village.

If he escaped, if he stayed in the mountains forever there would be no sidelong looks, no mutterings that went silent when he walked – limped – into a tent. He could keep walking, over this mountain and on to the next. He could keep going until he met the sea. And then he could build himself a boat and head off into the grey horizon. They said there was nothing out there, but if he went, *he'd* be there, wouldn't he?

Ked sighed and shifted against the tree. He wouldn't stay away, tempting as it was. Because if he didn't return, they wouldn't suppose he'd made the decision to stay away. They wouldn't picture him afloat in the broad, empty ocean. They'd suppose he'd been incapable of what the journey demanded. They'd think him fallen into a ravine, his bad leg given way. Future candidates would glance aside, hungry to see his whitened bones. No one would think the best of him, they'd assume the worst. And he was tired of that.

*

Ked awoke shivering. The sun had vanished behind the mountains, leaving this side in shadow. He got up, cursing. Sleep had stiffened his leg to soreness and he tipped his weight on his left leg while he massaged feeling and strength back into his right. It wasted a few, precious minutes, but he knew he'd move faster for it afterwards.

He jerked upright, fingers frozen while he listened. Someone was heading towards him. He glanced around. He wasn't on a main path. But this high, there weren't any main paths, just possible ways through the undergrowth between the trees.

Branches cracked and leaves rustled. Whoever it was, they weren't making much effort to hide their progress. Ked knew what that had to mean: it was the first candidate, returning triumphantly, sacrificing stealth for speed to return to the village quicker.

Whoever it was, he didn't want them to find him here. They could gloat to their family before they gloated to him. Ked slipped through the undergrowth, away from the noise. The thorns on a large bush snagged at him and he sucked in a breath as a sharp prickle sank deep into his thumb. But he continued to push. Once in the middle of the shrub, he was safe. The branches were almost bare of leaves, but still thick and dense enough that he could barely see out. No one would find him here.

The noise increased, then a voice spoke out. Of course: that's why there was so much noise: it wasn't one victor, but two.

The voices came closer, loud enough for Ked to identify them as their owners grew to dark blurs through the branches of his hiding place. Arro and Zim walked side by side, crashing a route through the trees. Arro had a coconut tucked under his arm, while Zim was holding hers in both hands, throwing it into the air and catching it again every couple of steps.

"Wait to see the expression on her face!" Zim crowed as they walked. "Bem was so sure she'd be first."

Arro nodded. "She'll be mad as buckwheat; last after all she said."

"Pride comes before a fall," Zim intoned in a manner worthy of the elders. Then she nudged Arro, nearly making him drop his fruit, and they cackled with laughter.

Their voices faded as they passed Ked, although

their gloating laughter seemed to hang in the air long after they were out of sight.

Ked sighed and fought his way back out of the thorny bush, pausing to rub his various scrapes and scratches while he glanced downhill to check that Zim and Arro were really gone. A burning sensation filled Ked's chest and he took a swig of water, as though that would ease it.

First didn't matter, he reminded himself. He just needed to return with a coconut.

He turned back to face the hill, found a path that wasn't too filled with thorns and vines, nor clouded with too many insects, and started to climb again.

*

Ked walked until it was so dark he couldn't see where to safely put one foot in front of the other. Then he found a sheltered spot, set a fire to keep the insects away, shook out his bed roll and ate some of the dried protein paste from his pack. He didn't have the energy to set up a trap. He was close to the summit now. If he woke with the dawn he could be there by the time the sun rose fully. He'd be the last to arrive, but coming last brought its own advantages. There should be spare fruit. The tree usually bore around twelve, and there were only four candidates. He could crack one open and eat it for his breakfast, a small triumph no one but himself would witness.

Ked was smiling at the idea as he fell asleep.

*

It wasn't the dawn that woke him, but more noise. It was greater than insects or birds would make, and his heart beat faster. Bem, the other candidate. She must have arrived at the summit the night before. Maybe she'd known Arro and Zim had beaten her to it, but maybe not. She'd be burning mad if she knew she'd lost. Ked knew winning meant everything to her.

Ked grabbed his bedroll and pack and ducked

behind a rotten tree stump, but the noise never came close enough for him to see her. She was making enough racket for a dozen candidates. Arro and Zim together had been quieter. Ked craned to see around the trunk as the noise of something heavy being dragged along the path assaulted his ears, but it was too far away to see.

As the noise faded, Ked started his morning routine of massaging the muscles of his right leg in preparation for the day's exertions. He was awake now, so he might as well start walking.

*

The sun had only just topped the mountains by the time he reached the summit. Ignoring the ache of his leg and the trickle of sweat down his spine, he grinned to see the coconut tree, proud and tall in the centre of the clearing. Ked remembered the stories: without sunlight it wouldn't produce fruit, so the ground was kept bare in a wide circle around it.

His leg was heavy, but his heart was light with triumph as he limped close enough to set his hand on the smooth trunk. He tipped his head back, calculating how he might shin twelve metres up the tree to pick a fruit. Easy for Zim and Arro, working together.

Then he frowned. There were no coconuts to be seen. High above his head the tree spanned broad, pinnate leaves in all directions, but where the fruit should have nestled in the joint between tree and leaf there was nothing.

Three candidates had been there before him. Could there only have been three fruit? One year there had only been eight – for eight candidates. But every other year there had been at least a dozen.

Ked stepped back from the tree, checking the ground as though he might trip over a fruit fallen from its place overhead. Nothing.

His heart knocked against his ribs. No coconut meant he couldn't complete the ceremony. He'd have to wait another year. He swallowed. He hadn't been given permission to compete this year. It was insane to think anything would be any different next year – except that they'd be expecting him to sneak out and would prevent him from doing so again. This had been his only chance, and he'd lost it.

Chest hollow, Ked leaned his back against the smooth trunk and slid slowly to the ground. A memory of laughter and the sound of something dragging through the undergrowth returned to him. He stilled, staring at the blue sky. Something heavy being towed over the rough ground. Something perhaps the weight of half a dozen or so coconuts.

No. It couldn't be. His brain protested while his heart accepted the truth. He'd broken the rules to make the journey, and this was his punishment. The other candidates had found a way to stop him. No one would remember who'd won this year. Instead, the tale would be passed down of Ked, the cripple who'd competed against advice and had returned empty-handed. Bem would say it was judgement on his pride in thinking himself equal with his peers, and she wouldn't be the only one.

Ked closed his eyes, the trunk hard against his shoulders. He could stay here. He could disappear into the mountains forever. Hadn't he considered that the day before? Except he wanted to be a part of the village, to be accepted. Now he knew it would never happen he felt in his bones how important it was.

He waited, unable to go forward or back, hoping an idea would come to him. The sun was high when a cloud darkened the sky. Ked blinked, peering around the coconut tree's leaves to see better. It wasn't a cloud. He shaded his eyes to inspect the dark shape. A swarm of insects. He swallowed. The black was absolute. There must be millions of the things. And yet . . . it wasn't behaving as swarms did. The shape didn't change. The edges were as dark as the centre.

Ked watched, head craned to the sun for half an hour as the shape drifted closer. Two other shapes joined it. They weren't swarms.

An idea slipped into his mind, but it was too fanciful to be entertained. People. From beyond the mountains. People who had undertaken the journey he'd imagined for himself.

People were impossible, and yet something was coming towards him, drifting down from the sky like the gods whose stories were even older than those of people.

As Ked watched, all three drifting shapes crashed to the ground, caught in the canopy of trees with a ripping sound as the branches grabbed them and halted their forward motion. Ked assessed the distance as less than a mile away. Then he set off walking.

*

Ked's leg was screaming in protest at the pace he'd set, but when he finally stopped, he didn't care about the pain. "People."

He realised he'd spoken aloud – and loud enough to be heard by the strangers – when they swung to look at him.

"People!" His cry was echoed by a girl about his own age, with dark glossy hair and a face that split into a broad grin at the sight of him. She twisted back to the others. "I told you I saw people! Didn't I tell you?"

"You told us, Hannah," one of the others, a boy, said. He strode towards Ked and held out a hand. "Ah'm Cosimo, and you've no notion how pleased we are to see you." Ked grasped the offered hand as hospitality dictated, although he was hardly these people's host. He couldn't take his eyes off the boy's neck. Something shone at his throat. Metal. Was it helping him breathe? Or speak? The boy was damaged. Ked glanced around. And none of his friends cared – or even seemed to notice.

"Where are we?" the first girl asked.

"The mountains."

"Yeah, but which ones."

"*The* mountains." Ked looked rapidly over the group. Nine of them. "Where are you from?"

"City," the girl replied.

"There are no cities. They were all flooded." Ked spoke automatically, then flushed. Who was he to say where she was from? He'd believed the cities were all flooded, but these people proved that to be a lie.

"City floats in the middle of the sea. We had no idea you were here. We thought we were alone."

"So did we," Ked admitted. He looked past them to the stuff tangled in the trees. "You came in that? Sailing through the sky?"

"Yeah. Balloon ships." The dark-haired one twisted back, grinning. "You're not seeing them at their best."

Ked started towards the remains of the balloon.

"Wait!" He paused as the girl with the plait called out. She hurried towards him. "What's the matter with your leg? Are you injured?"

The dark-haired, smiling one told him, "Libby's a doctor. She's been without a patient for weeks. You'd be doing her a favour if you have a bone that needs setting."

"Shut up, Hannah. I'm just concerned, as anyone would be." Libby turned back to Ked. "Are you all right?"

Ked nodded. "I'm fine. I have limb length discrepancy."

"I see," the plaited doctor, Libby, replied.

"I don't," Hannah protested. "What's limb length discrepancy?"

Ked felt his colour rising. It was years since he'd had to explain. Back at the village, everyone knew. Knew, and judged. He explained, "I was born with one leg shorter than the other. The limp's inevitable." He waited for shock, or perhaps pity.

Hannah simply shrugged. "That must suck."

He found he was smiling. "Something like that." He kept walking, stopping when he was close enough to inspect the pieces of the balloons. Cosimo, the one with metal in his neck, explained it to him. "The important bit is the stove. That warms the air that makes the balloon lift."

"How far did you come?"

They all turned to the tall youth, who rubbed his cheek. "I think we've come around eighteen hundred miles. Maybe two thousand."

Ked breathed out a sigh. Two thousand miles before the craft had fallen back to the Earth. The elders would hardly believe it. "Will you come back with me? To the village? We have to tell everyone."

The newcomers exchanged cautious looks. "Will we be welcome?" A different boy asked that.

"Definitely." Ked retraced his steps. "We thought we were alone. You prove we're not."

They fell into step behind him. Hannah hurried to catch him up, linking her arm easily through his. "Forgive me, but why are you climbing up a mountain if you've got a bad leg?" She looked around. "You don't live this high up, do you?"

"No." He kept walking, finding a way on the overgrown path.

Hannah looked at him, brown eyes shining. She leaned towards him. His heart beat faster. There was no pity, no distaste in her expression. He found he was holding his breath, tensed to feel the warmth emanate from her, the energy that hung in the air around her. "I have to say, if I were you I'd have sent someone else."

"I can't," he said, then amended, "I didn't want to."

The path was too narrow for them to walk side by side. Hannah dropped back. The loss of her made Ked suddenly cold and he was pleased her voice told him she was still close. "Why not?"

"It's part of becoming an adult. Each autumn all sixteen-year-olds come up the mountain alone and return with . . ." His explanation snagged. He didn't want to admit his failure, not even to these strangers who wouldn't understand what it meant. The glossy-haired girl, Hannah, was hanging on his words. He cleared his throat. "We have to return with something valuable to the village."

"I see. So, have you got this valuable thing?"

Ked glanced at her, then beyond her at the group straggling down the mountain, following the route he had set. His heart lifted. This wasn't failure. This was extraordinary success. He could imagine the scene when he returned to the village with a group of people who proved the village wasn't alone. His uneven footsteps cracked twigs underfoot, but in his imagination there was absolute silence as everyone watched the group walk through the ring of tents into the meeting space where all the candidates would be waiting.

Bem's face in the crowd would fall, her net full of coconuts revealed for the petty cruelty it was.

Ked turned to Hannah and smiled. "Oh yes, I'm bringing back something the village will treasure."

Made in the USA
Lexington, KY
26 July 2016